"Who the _____
are you doing in the middle of
Texas?"

Thad barked out.

"I told you. The people of Hope have hired me to be their new teacher," Caroline answered warily.

"You don't look like any schoolteacher I ever knew. You look more like—"

She jerked back, but she was no match for his strength. He drew her down until her lips were mere inches from his.

"You look like a green-eyed angel. Or maybe a devil." His breath was warm against her cheek.

Caroline's fear turned to panic. Her breath caught in her throat as he suddenly pulled her to him, flattening her breasts against his chest. Deep inside she felt a tiny tremor curl along her spine. It was the most purely sensual feeling she'd ever known.

Dear Reader,

Welcome to another great month of Harlequin Historicals. These four selections are guaranteed to add spice to your summer reading list.

Garters and Spurs, from popular author DeLoras Scott, is the tale of Fargo Tanner and his search for the man who killed his brother. But when clues lead him to lovely Sara Carter, Fargo finds himself doubting his intentions.

In the last installment of the TEXAS series, Ruth Langan tells the story of *Texas Hero* Thad Conway, an ex-gunslinger who just wants to run his own ranch—alone. But prim schoolmarm Caroline Adams is determined to change his mind.

When impoverished Sir Giles of Rathborne hatches a scheme to enrich his coffers in *The Cygnet* by Marianne Willman, he turns a young bandit into a missing heiress and falls under her spell.

As a secondary character in *Sweet Seduction,* the first book in the NORTH POINT series, Barbara Johnson was a woman of exceptional courage and depth. Now, in *Sweet Sensations,* author Julie Tetel gives Barbara her own story in which she enters into a bargain with a mysterious drifter in order to keep her family safe.

July also marks the release of our Western short-story collection—*Untamed—Maverick Hearts* with stories by Heather Graham Pozzessere, Joan Johnston and Patricia Potter. Whether you like reading on the beach or by the pool, Harlequin Historicals offers four great books each month to be enjoyed all year round!

Sincerely,

Tracy Farrell
Senior Editor

Texas Hero

RUTH LANGAN

Harlequin Books

TORONTO • NEW YORK • LONDON
AMSTERDAM • PARIS • SYDNEY • HAMBURG
STOCKHOLM • ATHENS • TOKYO • MILAN
MADRID • WARSAW • BUDAPEST • AUCKLAND

Harlequin Historicals first edition July 1993

ISBN 0-373-28780-1

TEXAS HERO

RUTH LANGAN

traces her ancestry to Scotland and Ireland. It is no surprise, then, that she feels a kinship with the characters in her historical novels.

Married to her childhood sweetheart, she has raised five children and lives in Michigan, the state where she was born and raised.

To Bret Charles Shrader
Our newest treasure

And to his big sister, Caitlin Bea
And their parents, Mary and Dennis

And, as always, to Tom,
Who hung the moon.

Prologue

Texas, 1863

"Drink this, Mama."

The girl held the broth to her mother's lips and watched in frustration as, after only three sips, the cup was pushed weakly aside.

"You have to drink it if you're ever going to get stronger, Mama."

The woman's eyelids fluttered, then closed, as if even that small movement were too great an effort. For long minutes she lay, her chest rising and falling with each labored breath.

The newborn baby lying in the wooden cradle began a pitiful bleating. The woman's eyes opened and focused on the girl beside the bed.

"You're like him, you know."

"Pa?"

The frail head nodded once. "You're tough, Jessie. Like Jack. And that one..." She nodded toward the baby, whose wailing had grown louder. "He's going to be the toughest of all."

"How do you know, Mama?"

"Listen to him." She closed her eyes a moment, too weak to go on. When the feeling passed, she opened her eyes and continued as though there had been no interruption. "He'll be a handful for you, Jessie. It's going to be hard raising a baby brother all alone."

"Hush now, Mama. Don't talk like that." The girl's brow furrowed. Whenever her mother started talking about death, Jessie felt a knot in the pit of her stomach. "You'll be here to help."

"I wish I could, Jessie. But it's never been like this before. I just know that something's gone all wrong."

"Danny's reading the doctor book, Mama. He'll find something that'll help you get your strength back."

Across the room, seven-year-old Danny squinted at the pages of the book in the flickering light of the fire. A few minutes later he closed the book and crossed the room. He exchanged a quick look with his sister before giving a sad shake of his head. Squeezing his mother's hand, he felt the thin, shallow pulse.

"Pa will be back soon, Mama," the girl said. "He'll get you strong again."

The woman's voice was barely more than a whisper. "I know you believe that your pa can do anything, Jessie. But there are some things even Big Jack Conway can't do."

"Stop it, Mama." In her grief the girl's tone became angry. "You've got to stop talking about death and start fighting back."

"That's what you'd do, isn't it, Jessie? No matter what, you'd fight back." She closed her eyes, and the two children could see the blue veins through the fine pale skin.

Olivia Barton Conway had endured her husband's dreams of conquering this wild frontier and had allowed herself to be led far from everything she knew and loved. Her family farm; her brothers and sisters, who had settled in the rolling gentle countryside around Maryland; even her church, which had brought her such comfort through the years. The harsh weather, the inhospitable land and the loneliness here in the little sod shack fifty miles from her nearest neighbor had taken their toll. Her delicate health had become more fragile during the long and difficult third pregnancy. In the three weeks since the birth of her second son, she had not once left her bed.

"You're a scrapper, you are, Jessie," she said, slurring the words. "And so's the baby. He should have died. Everything about his birth was wrong, and still he fought for life." She gave a weak smile. "Thaddeus Francis Conway. The first of the Conways to be born in Texas. He carries my father's name, and my grandfather's. See that he does them proud."

Her eyes closed again and her son and daughter knelt beside the bed, their hands pressed to hers as though willing her their strength.

"Don't go, Mama," the little boy whispered.

His older sister said nothing. But when their mother's eyes suddenly opened and stared, unseeing, at the infant in the cradle, Jessie felt a cold shiver along her spine.

Picking up the squalling baby, she held him close to her heart and watched as her mother took a final breath, then went very still.

"Come on, Danny," she said. "You know how it always soothed Mama to hear you read. Sit here by the fire and read, and let Mama rest awhile."

The boy hunkered down beside the fireplace and began to read aloud. As she had since the baby's birth, his sister filled a glove with cow's milk and placed one of the fingers in the infant's mouth. The crying stopped abruptly as the baby sucked greedily.

She looked over at the still form in the bed and thought how right it was that Mama should finally get the rest she deserved. Her life had never been easy. Loving a man like Big Jack Conway probably hadn't been the smartest thing Mama had ever done. But, as she was fond of saying, at least she'd always known that she was loved.

Tears threatened, but Jessie blinked them away. At almost eleven, she was too old to cry. Besides, hadn't Mama said she was just like Pa? Too tough to cry. Or maybe just too ornery. And now that all the work had fallen to Jessie, there wasn't time to grieve. At least that was something Mama would have understood.

As if comprehending the solemnity of the occasion, the baby burped contentedly and drifted back to sleep. Jessie placed him in the cradle and recalled what her mother had said.

"I'm going to see that you grow big enough and strong enough so that this land will never do to you what it did to Mama," she whispered. "You'll see, Thad. You're going to be the toughest Conway of all."

Chapter One

Mexico, 1885

Thad Conway heard the creak of the outer door of the jail. Out of habit his hand went to his hip, where a gun usually rested. This time he had no weapon with which to defend himself.

In the darkness he heard the unmistakable click of a pistol being cocked. It was a sound like no other. A sound he knew well. He braced himself for what was to come.

A glance at the slit in the upper wall revealed the glint of stars in a darkened sky. Midnight, he figured. Not a time for proper callers. Even in a Mexican jail.

Rusty hinges protested as the inner door was swung wide. The light cast by a lantern momentarily blinded him before he made out two figures. The man holding the lantern was also holding a gun. The other man inserted a key into the lock and opened the cell door.

"You will forgive the delay, Señor Conway," said the raspy voice, heavily accented in Spanish. "It took our rider two days to reach Don Esteban's land and two days to return with the news we sought."

Thad spoke not a word as he waited.

In the awkward silence that followed, the jailer cleared his throat and continued. "Don Esteban confirmed that the mare in your possession was not stolen. It is as you said—you purchased the mare from him."

Thad's only reaction was a slight narrowing of his eyes.

As if feeling the heat of his anger, the man took a step back. "I hope you will understand our mistake. A man like you..." The jailer's voice trailed off for a moment before he shrugged and added, "We have all heard of your reputation with a gun. It was a natural conclusion to assume that The Texan had stolen Don Esteban's prize mare."

Quelled by the look Thad had levelled on him, he turned to the man behind him, who handed over the pistol and a leather holster.

"Your weapon, *señor.*"

Without a word Thad strapped on the holster and slipped the gun into place. When he was finished he picked up his hat from the bunk beside him. For the first time he broke his self-imposed silence. "My horses?"

The words were not so much a question as a challenge.

The jailer stared at the floor, afraid to meet his cold expression. "They are outside."

Thad strode past him, past the man with the lantern and out into the cool night air. With infinite patience he examined the mare, assuring himself that she had been well taken care of in his absence. Then he turned to examine the stallion before checking his saddlebags. Tightening the cinch, he pulled himself into the saddle and caught up the reins of the mare.

Without a backward glance at the jail that had confined him for the last four days, he headed for the border.

Behind him, the two men gave a sigh of relief that the fate of the infamous man known as The Texan was now out of their hands.

Texas

"Better brace yourself, ma'am. The road's about to get pretty rough." The stage driver's voice strained to be heard above the din of creaking harness and thundering hooves.

Caroline Adams gripped the edge of the seat and swallowed back her fear. A rough road was nothing new to her. From the moment of her birth, nothing had been smooth or easy. But this was a far cry from the teeming streets of the city where she'd been born. There, at least, she'd taught herself the skills necessary to survive. But here in this untamed frontier, everything was new. And frightening.

Struggling for composure, she reminded herself of the lesson for the day from her book of instructions. A lady must endure all of life's discomforts with grace and charm; that was precisely how she would endure the jostling of the stage. Grace and charm. She choked down the muttered oath that escaped her lips as the wheels flew over ruts and rocks in the road and dust swirled into her nose and mouth, causing her to gag.

She was grateful that the other passengers had disembarked at an earlier destination. At least now she was alone, with no one to see her if she made a mistake. She lifted her spectacles and rubbed the tender spot on the bridge of her nose. She wasn't yet accustomed to wearing the things. Even though the round wire frames were fitted with plain glass, the spectacles restricted her vi-

sion. But the inconvenience was a small price to pay if she
was able to enhance her prim, bookish appearance.

She glanced down at the plain, mud brown gown and
matching jacket she'd chosen. As instructed, the seam-
stress had made the garments a size larger than necessary so that they wouldn't cling to any part of Caroline's
anatomy. In her valise was another gown in drab gray,
with simple white collar and cuffs; it, too, was intention-
ally ill-fitting. The high-top boots she wore were plain
and serviceable. Though her mass of thick black hair
could never be tamed, it had been brushed into a neat
knot at the back of her head. The few tendrils that
worked free of the pins were covered by an ugly, unin-
spired brown hat. Though she hated the frumpish gown
and hat, she wore them with pride; they were her ticket
to respectability.

Despite the wild swaying of the stage, Caroline picked
up the book she'd been reading and turned to a new
chapter. By the time she reached Hope, Texas, she intended to know by heart every word of *Dr. Harvey Hattinger's Rules for Headmistresses.* She would be the best
teacher the town of Hope had ever seen.

Over the rumble of wheels she heard another sound.
Gunshots. Unmistakably gunshots.

The stage lurched wildly, tossing her to the floor. By
the time she'd managed to pull herself upright and peer
out the window, she saw four horsemen riding toward the
stage, their guns aimed at the driver. When she glanced
out the other window she saw a body hurtle past her line
of vision and realized that the armed guard who rode
along on the stage had been shot. Shot. And she carried
no weapon with which to defend herself. Her heart
thundered inside her chest.

She counted three more gunmen riding toward them on the opposite side, all aiming their rifles at the driver. Seven men in all—against a single driver.

"Pull up," one of them shouted, "or you'll join your partner in the dust!"

In response, there was a muttered curse and the sound of a gun's report.

Caroline was tossed around like a rag doll as the stage suddenly shifted direction and hurtled out of control.

Thad Conway ran a hand over his beard, then lifted his hat to wipe the sweat from his forehead. He had just spent the last six weeks in the saddle, all the way to Mexico and back for Don Esteban's finest mare, who trotted smartly on a lead rope behind his stallion. He was hot, tired and out of sorts, especially after those four nights in jail. What he needed was a bath and supper. And a bottle of whiskey at Lilah's to wash away the dust of the trail.

He looked up sharply at the sound of gunshots. With a sigh he moved out at a fast pace. So much for the pleasant ending he'd been planning.

Caroline clawed at the edge of the seat, trying to pull herself upright. At that moment the wheel of the coach hit a half-submerged boulder, causing the vehicle to become airborne. For long seconds, she was certain they were tipping over. But at the last moment the stage remained upright and continued on, pulled by the frantic team.

Dragging herself to the open window, she managed to peer out. What she saw caused her heart to stop. There was no driver. The crazed team raced across the flat stretch of ground at breakneck speed.

Caroline had no idea what lay ahead. She knew only that she had to attempt to leap from the stage or risk being carried to her death.

A sudden anger flared inside her. She had come so far, endured so much; she would not see it all snatched from her now, when a new life was within her reach. With the stage rocking and swaying wildly, she struggled to wrap her fingers around the handle of the door. Each time she got close, the horses would shift direction, throwing her to the floor. And each time she dragged her way back until, with a last desperate attempt, she managed to grasp the handle. Twisting it, the door flew open and Caroline was propelled through the air. She sailed across prickly cacti and the sharp edges of rock, landing with a terrible thud against hard-packed earth. She lay, unable to move, struggling for breath.

The thunder of hoofbeats seemed to surround her, and she heard a man's voice.

"Look at this, Luke!" the voice hooted. "It's female."

The gunmen studied her with the hunger of a pack of wolves, then looked up suddenly as a lone man on horseback charged down the hill, guns blazing. In some distant part of her mind, Caroline found herself wondering how a single rider could stand a chance against seven armed men.

The man called Luke swore savagely. "It's The Texan."

At his words, there was a collective gasp from the others. Their frightened reaction caused a shiver along Caroline's spine. Who must this stranger be, if even armed gunmen trembled in fear of him?

She watched in amazement as two men fell and the others scattered for cover. But still the rider charged ahead, returning their gunfire without flinching.

As the stranger managed to bring down two more gunmen, Caroline saw blood spurt from his shoulder. His gun dropped to the ground and his arm fell uselessly to his side. In that instant, three men surrounded him and dragged him off his horse.

When one of the gunmen lifted his pistol to the stranger's temple, Luke growled, "No. I want him awake to watch. Tie him up. Then, when we're finished with the woman, we can all have the pleasure of killing him."

Hearing that, Caroline struggled to get to her feet. She had no doubt of what these villains intended to do to her. She had to escape. But the leap from the moving stage had taken its toll. Her body would not respond to her commands. Her attempts to sit up were stiff and awkward.

She looked up to see the stranger's eyes narrowed in fury. And then her view of him was blocked as the three gunmen formed a circle around her. One of the three, with a cruel, twisted grin, had tucked the guard's pistol into the waistband of his pants. He was already wearing the stage driver's boots.

"You the only passenger?" Luke demanded.

Caroline watched them without responding. Her mind worked feverishly. She had to escape these madmen. But how?

"I'll bet she's been knocked senseless." The other gunman took a step closer. With the toe of his boot he boldly lifted her skirt and kicked at her ankle. "Can you talk, woman?"

Caroline watched with a feeling of revulsion as he leered down at her.

"Fox, check her hands for rings," Luke ordered.

The gunman grabbed her hands and, seeing nothing, turned them palms up to make certain she wasn't hiding anything.

"She's not wearing any rings, Luke."

"See if she's wearing a locket or some other jewelry."

"With pleasure." Laughing, the gunman caught the front of her dress in his hands and ripped it open, revealing a delicately embroidered chemise beneath. Caroline gasped, then fought back the cry that rose to her throat.

Though the gunman could see that she wore no chain around her neck, he was obviously enjoying the task given him. "I'd better check this out more carefully, Luke. I'm going to have to strip her."

The other two gunmen joined in his laughter as he bent closer. Without warning he let out a shriek of pain as she raked her fingernails across his cheek.

"Looks like you got a wildcat by the tail," Luke taunted.

Touching a hand to his face, Fox stared at the blood a moment, then slapped her so hard her head snapped to one side.

Biting her lip against the pain, she made not a sound.

"You little witch," he cried. "Now you're going to pay for that."

"Go ahead, Fox. It's the least she should do for you, in fact, for all of us, if she isn't going to have anything else of value. After all, we don't rob stages for the fun of it."

"Maybe you don't. But this ought to prove to be more fun than I've had in years."

While the other two laughed, the gunman dug his fingers into her hair and yanked her head back until the pain brought tears to her eyes.

"You know," he said, tossing her hat aside and pulling the spectacles from her face, "if it weren't for those ugly clothes and the fact that you don't know how to treat a man, you might not be half-bad."

He started to press his lips to hers but she twisted away and gave him a vicious kick with the heel of her boot as she scrambled free.

The two men hooted with laughter as Fox groaned and doubled up with pain. But when she got to her feet and started running, the laughter died on their lips.

Luke fired into the air and she spun around to face him. With the bodice of her gown gaping open and her hair spilling around her face and shoulders in wild tangles, she no longer resembled the prim female they'd seen lying on the ground only minutes ago.

"This woman has spirit," Luke said, eyeing her with new appreciation. He took several steps toward her, an evil smile splitting his lips. "I think she's going to be more rewarding than the gold we got paid for this."

"You'll have to kill me first." Caroline's words were spoken through gritted teeth.

"So, the woman has a voice after all." Luke threw back his head and gave a cruel laugh. "Honey, that's what they all say. But they don't mean it. Nobody ever wants to die."

He was too busy talking to see the fire in her eyes. But The Texan had seen it. And he could hear the ice in her tone as she warned, "Then you don't know me very well. I'll die before I'll submit."

With that she turned and began to run. Though her movements were hampered by the clumsy skirt and petticoat, she was surprisingly swift. Luke soon overtook her. Flinging her roughly over his shoulder, he carried her back to where the others stood laughing and jeering.

He tossed her to the ground and she had to bite her lip to keep from crying out. As she lay there, her breath coming in painful gasps, the three men circled her.

"Now," Luke said with a grin, "we're going to introduce you to pleasure, Texas-style."

He leaned down and ran the tip of his knife between her breasts, cutting open her chemise. Seeing the way she cringed, he said to the others, "You don't suppose she's never done anything like this before, do you, boys? A virgin. Now wouldn't that be better'n gold?"

The other two laughed in agreement.

They were so busy, none of them took any notice of the man who had been working feverishly at his ropes. Now, as the strands began to unravel, he lifted his hands to his teeth and tore at the last of the bindings.

As Luke grabbed a fistful of the woman's hair, he felt the cold steel of a revolver pressed to his temple and heard a savage voice directly behind him.

"Unless you let go of her right now, there won't be enough left of you to pleasure a woman ever again."

In one quick motion Luke dragged Caroline in front of him, holding her like a shield, and pressed his knife to her throat.

With a nervous laugh he cried, "You wouldn't want to risk hurting an innocent woman, would you, Texan?"

Caroline's eyes widened as the stranger calmly leveled his revolver. She could see, by the steely look in those eyes, that he had every intention of doing just that. She had no time to react as, with calm deliberation, he pulled the trigger. The sound of the gunshot echoed through her ears as the man behind her slumped against her, pressing her to the ground. For one terrible moment she didn't know whether or not she'd been hit. She felt the sticky warmth of blood seeping through her gown. Hers? she wondered. Or his?

While she recoiled in horror, there were several more blasts of gunfire. By the time she managed to crawl out from beneath the dead gunman, his two partners had disappeared over a ridge.

Disgusted at their escape, the stranger holstered his gun.

Rendered speechless, Caroline could do nothing more than stare at the man who, alone and without a single flicker of emotion, had calmly shot down five vicious killers and sent two more retreating. He had to be every bit as vicious as the men he'd shot. And she was now at his mercy.

Everything about this stranger bespoke danger. He was tall and rangy, with a gun belt slung low on his hips. Black pants and tall boots were caked with dust. His hair was bleached the color of bronze by the sun, and his skin, beneath several days' growth of golden beard, was tawny. Pale blue eyes narrowed as he took in the gaping bodice, the wild spill of hair. There was a hardness to his features that had her throat going dry. If those gunmen had been afraid of him, she had even more reason to be.

His voice, when he spoke, was low and deep, his tone abrupt, as though he resented having to stay with her when he could be chasing the two who got away. "Woman, what's your name?"

She swallowed and prayed her voice wouldn't betray her terror. "Caroline Adams."

Caroline. His eyes narrowed perceptibly. Caroline was cool, correct, proper, like the woman he had first seen. Right now, the name didn't suit her. Not when she was

lying here, half-undressed, with her hair tumbling around
her shoulders and her eyes still wide with fear. And her
voice. There was a breathless quality to it, unlike anything he'd heard before.

He dropped to one knee beside her and she cringed
from his touch.

"Are you badly hurt?"

"Just a few bruises." Seeing the direction of his gaze,
she nervously drew the remnants of her bodice together.

At the first sight of her, Thad's throat went dry.
Though she tried to hide it, he'd already glimpsed the
lush body hidden beneath the drab, shapeless clothes. It
wasn't often in this hot Texas wilderness that he was
privileged to see unblemished skin that had never been
touched by the sun. He pulled his gaze upward past a
pale, creamy throat to a face so beautiful it made his
breath hitch. Thick masses of dark hair swirled around
her face and shoulders. Little corkscrew curls kissed her
cheeks. Her eyes could have been green or gold. In the
sunlight they danced with glints of amber. Her nose was
small and tilted up as though in disdain. Her mouth was
perfectly formed, with a full lower lip that for some
strange reason made him think about the taste of cool
whiskey on a sultry night.

If he hadn't seen her with his own eyes, he would have
sworn this couldn't be the same female he'd first
glimpsed, wearing spectacles and a silly hat on hair
wrapped as tight as a pig's...

His frown deepened. The transformation from spin-
ster to seductress electrified him. This woman whose
cheeks flamed beneath his gaze was more tempting than
any of the girls at Lilah's could ever hope to be.

"Where did you come from?" Thad tried to keep his gaze averted, to give the woman time to compose herself and rearrange her clothing.

"I was on the stage." Caroline sat up, clutching her bodice, unaware of the fact that her skirt had twisted, displaying a shapely leg. "They shot the driver and guard."

"And you were thrown clear?"

"I jumped."

She could read the surprise in his eyes. "You jumped? From a runaway stage?"

"I didn't see that I had any choice."

He studied the small, slender figure. There was a strength there that wasn't visible at first glance. "Can you stand?"

Again she backed away as he made a move to touch her. Ignoring her protest, he helped her to her feet. Though she winced slightly and he heard her sharp intake of breath, she remained standing and disengaged herself from his grasp.

So the lady didn't want his help. Well, he was in no mood to give it. But it looked like they were stuck with each other for the moment.

"Where are you headed?"

"A town called Hope."

He experienced another shock. Glancing at the darkening sky, he hoped his sudden brisk tone masked his surprise. "You won't be able to make it before this storm rolls in."

Taking up the reins, he led his horses beneath an outcropping of rock and began to unsaddle his mount.

As she watched, Caroline's eyes widened in disbelief. "You mean you intend to spend the night here?"

"May as well. It looks like the best shelter from the storm."

"But..." She searched her mind frantically. She couldn't just spend the night here, alone with this dangerous stranger. "What about the stage? And the horses?" She thought about her clothes and her precious store of books. She had spent every last dollar to buy those books. "My trunks were aboard the stage."

He shrugged. "You can keep an eye out for the team tomorrow, when we head for town. If we don't find the stage in pieces along the trail, it will mean they made it to town, and your things along with them."

He slipped the saddle from his horse and nearly dropped it as pain shot through him.

Caroline saw the way he gingerly touched a hand to his shoulder and felt a sudden wave of shame. This man had just saved her life, and she had completely overlooked the fact that he'd been shot. "Let me help you. You're wounded."

"It's nothing. Just a bullet."

Just a bullet? She studied the crimson stain that smeared his sleeve and chest. "Have you ever been shot before?"

"Enough times to know I won't die."

"Maybe, but the pain must be terrible. I'll bind it for you." Turning away, she tore a strip from her petticoat and swiveled to face him. "Give me your arm."

Reluctantly he stuck his arm out at a stiff angle and watched as she wrapped the white cloth around his wound. While she bent to her task he studied the top of her head. It barely reached his shoulder. When she rolled back his sleeve and tied the ends of the cloth, her fingers brushed his skin. Soft. Her touch was so soft. He felt his stomach muscles contract and he pulled away more roughly than he'd intended.

"That'll do it," he said gruffly. "I'll have Doc dig out the bullet when we get to town."

He set about making a fire. When that was done he untied a bedroll from behind his saddle and tossed her a blanket. Using his saddle for a pillow, he lay down and pulled his hat low over his face.

"What are you doing?"

He glanced up. "Going to sleep."

"But what...?" She heard the rumble of thunder and shivered.

"Look," he said patiently, "I can see that you don't like the idea of sleeping with a stranger. You can sleep out there if you want." He pointed to a stand of cacti a hundred yards away, then closed his eyes and pulled his hat lower. "But I'd advise you to take shelter in here with me and the horses. It doesn't rain often in this part of Texas. But when it does, it pours."

Fuming, Caroline wrapped the blanket around her shoulders and watched as he calmly rolled to his side. Within minutes he was sound asleep.

Chapter Two

The first drops of rain splashed Caroline's face.

Snatching up a thick club for protection, she scrambled under the outcropping of rock where The Texan slept. She stood uncertainly, staring morosely into the night, and wondered for the hundredth time how far she was from town.

If she started walking... Somewhere in the distance a coyote howled and the hair on the back of her neck rose. She changed her mind. Her only hope was to wait out the night. She wouldn't stand a chance alone in this wilderness.

She glanced at the sleeping figure. Even at rest he looked dangerous. The rifle lay in the dirt beside his left hand. His right hand rested atop his pistol.

He had chosen his shelter carefully. He and the horses were protected from the rain. Even the fire was untouched by the storm.

Taking care to choose the farthest corner of the shelter, she sat down with her back against the rock and drew the blanket firmly around her. Her hand, hidden beneath the blanket, gripped the club. She had no intention of relaxing her guard. Though she was weary beyond belief, she would keep watch until morning.

The rain came down harder, pelting the dry earth and creating little rivers. Dry gulleys soon filled until they were engorged and spilled over their banks. And still the rain fell.

Welcome to Texas, Caroline thought miserably. Shivering, she hunched deeper into the blanket and struggled to keep her eyes open. The patter of the rain on the rock had a hypnotic effect. Soon she was lulled into sleep.

Thad knew the exact moment when the woman gave in and sought shelter. With his eyes closed he listened as she crouched in the far corner. He heard the whisper of cloth as she drew the blanket around her and tried to find a comfortable position on the hard ground. He listened to the unsteady sound of her breathing and heard the slight change in rhythm as she drifted into sleep.

His arm throbbed. He knew from past experience that the wound was beginning to fester. He'd hoped to ignore the bullet in his flesh until he got to town, but now he decided that, with the pain deepening, he'd better deal with it.

Taking a knife from his belt, he thrust it into the hot coals. From his saddlebag he withdrew a bottle of whiskey and took a healthy swallow to steel himself for what was to come. Clenching his teeth, he pulled the knife from the fire and cut away his sleeve and the bit of cloth that Caroline had tied around his arm. Then, without giving himself time to change his mind, he sliced into his flesh and began to probe for the bullet.

Pain ripped through him and he caught his breath. It took every ounce of willpower to focus his attention on the task at hand. Through the river of blood that soaked his shirt, through the tissue and muscle that resisted the point of his knife, he probed until at last he felt the scrape of metal. Sweat trickled down his brow, nearly blinding him as he gently withdrew the bullet. His fingers trembled as he poured the whiskey on the open wound. Swearing, he leaned back against the rock and struggled to absorb the pain. Taking a swallow of whiskey, he gritted his teeth and poured another liberal amount on the raw flesh.

A sound disturbed Caroline's sleep. As she struggled awake, she heard it again. A catch of breath. A hiss of pain. Someone in distress.

As her eyes slowly adjusted, she couldn't believe what she was seeing. Blood streamed down the stranger's arm, smearing the front of his shirt. In his hand was a bloodied knife. When she realized what he'd done, she tossed off the blanket and crossed the distance between them.

"I thought you were going to wait until you reached a doctor in town."

He looked up at her through eyes glazed with pain. "Infection started. The bullet had to come out."

"Did you get it?"

He nodded and reached for the bloody cloth that had been cut away.

When she saw what he intended, she snatched it from him and tossed it aside. "You need a clean binding." Lifting her skirts, she tore another strip from her petticoat.

As she caught his hand he lifted the bottle and poured more whiskey on the wound. The sudden sharp pain caused him to suck in his breath and let it out on a long, slow curse. His strong fingers curled around hers, nearly crushing them. Before she could cry out he realized what he'd done and released his death grip on her.

As Caroline began to wrap his arm with the strip of cloth, he took a long pull on the bottle, then closed his eyes and leaned his head back.

She looked down at him and felt a wave of compassion. Sweat beaded his brow and upper lip. Pain was evident in the taut lines of his face.

What sort of man was this that he could calmly, purposefully inflict that sort of pain upon himself when necessary? She gave an involuntary shiver. Worse, what sort of land was this that it bred such harsh creatures?

She had come to Texas seeking escape. Now she wondered if she'd bargained with the devil.

"Tell me if this binding is too tight."

He nodded. Even Thad's pain couldn't dull the impact when her fingers brushed his flesh. He absorbed the first jolt and lay very still, awash in strange, troubling feelings. At least, for the moment, her touch was able to take his mind off the pain. For that he was grateful.

"Why didn't you ask for my help?" Though her question was sharp, her touch was surprisingly gentle.

"Out here, if you ask for help, it's a sign of weakness." He watched her from beneath lowered lids. Her head was bent, her hair spilling forward to brush his cheek as she worked. He inhaled the woman scent of her and felt a sudden flicker of excitement. His drawl held the warmth of laughter. "Besides, you were sleeping. I figured if I woke you I'd have to answer to that club you were hiding."

So much for the element of surprise. Caroline felt her cheeks grow hot and thought of a few curses herself. Curses that would curl his hair. Then she remembered *Dr. Harvey Hattinger's Rules for Headmistresses.* Rule number five admonished that a lady never display her temper. She bit back the response that sprang to her lips and forced her tone to remain level.

"A woman alone can't be too careful."

He hadn't missed the way her eyes had widened in surprise; for a moment he'd read the anger that blazed there. Then, just as quickly, she'd blinked and the look was gone, replaced by a cool, penetrating stare. He would give Caroline Adams one thing—she kept her feelings under careful control.

Caroline felt rather than saw the way he watched her as she worked. It disturbed her more than she cared to admit. "You'd better get some sleep now."

"Not just yet."

As she started to get up his hand curled around her wrist, stopping her.

Caroline had never felt such strength. It frightened her. In fact, everything about this stranger frightened her.

As she struggled to break free, his grasp tightened.

To cover her fear she allowed her anger to surface. "Let go of me."

Though her voice was even, he could read the fear in her eyes. "In a minute." His voice lowered. "You intrigue me, Teacher."

His thumb moved in lazy circles across her wrist and she knew he could feel the way her pulse raced.

"Who the hell are you? And what are you doing in the middle of Texas?"

"I told you." She swallowed and fought to keep the panic from her tone. "The people of Hope have hired me to be their new teacher."

"You don't look like any schoolteacher I ever knew. You look more like—"

She jerked back, but she was no match for his strength. With no effort he drew her down until her lips were mere inches from his.

"You look like a green-eyed angel. Or maybe a devil." His breath was warm against her cheek as he whispered, "I've never seen eyes that shade before."

Caroline's fear turned to panic. Her breath caught in her throat as he suddenly pulled her against him, flattening her breasts against his chest.

"And I've never seen skin that pale. I'm going to have to touch your skin, Teacher, to make certain it's real." He traced a work-roughened finger lightly along her throat and felt her pulse flutter beneath his touch.

Caroline struggled to show no emotion. But deep inside she felt a tiny tremor curl along her spine. It was the most purely sensual feeling she'd ever known.

His tone deepened. "Looks like I'll have to taste those lips, too, and see if they're as soft as they look."

Before she could protest he covered her mouth with his. His lips were warm and firm as they moved over hers with a thoroughness that left her breathless.

Heat. Thad hadn't expected such heat. In fact, he'd only meant to taunt her while he gave himself a little pleasure. The sort of pleasure he always found in a woman. But this woman wasn't like any he'd ever met before. She appeared prim and proper. But the lips that yielded beneath his tasted dark and sultry, and the body beneath the nondescript gown was lush and ripe.

He had an almost overpowering need to savage her mouth and shake loose her cool control.

"Teacher." He gripped her roughly by the shoulders and held her a fraction away.

His touch caused the strangest sensation.

He saw the confusion in her eyes as her lids fluttered. "When I kiss a woman, I expect her to kiss me back."

Her eyes widened, then narrowed as she opened her mouth to hurl a response. "Go to..."

His lips cut off her words. It gave him a perverted sense of pleasure to catch her unawares. Though he'd intended merely to taste her lips, he suddenly took the kiss deeper. He could hear his own heartbeat pounding in his chest as his tongue explored her mouth.

Shock sliced through Caroline. She hadn't been prepared for this assault. But even as she recoiled from his touch, she felt herself responding in a primitive way that left her stunned. The touch of his lips on hers electrified her. And for one fleeting moment, she experienced something she'd never believed possible. For one brief moment she felt a thrill of pure pleasure.

The body beneath hers was lean and hard, his hands rough. But his lips were soft. Softer than a man's should be. He smelled faintly of horses and leather, alien scents to her. Everything about this man was alien. And dangerous. She knew nothing about him except that his very presence brought fear to hardened gunmen. This handsome, dangerous stranger could take her here, now, and she would be powerless to stop him.

That thought was like a sudden splash of cold water. In the blink of an eye, she forgot everything except her anger at his boldness.

"You have no right." She pushed free of his lips, though he still held her imprisoned in his arms.

She dragged breath into her lungs while he watched her with that same calm, deliberate look. There was a stillness about him, a watchfulness that reminded her of a hunter.

"Earlier today you almost killed me."

He arched a brow in surprise.

"When you aimed that gun at the man holding me, you didn't care whether or not the bullet hit me first."

"Woman, if I'd wanted you dead, you'd be lying out there with the others. When I aim a gun, I know who's going to be hit by my bullet."

When he released her she stumbled to the far corner of the cave.

He nodded toward the club, which now lay exposed beside her blanket. His tone was low, dangerous. "Stay in your safe corner, Teacher." A slow smile touched the edges of his mouth. "And make certain you keep that club handy."

Caroline watched as he took another long drink of whiskey before shoving the cork in the bottle. Using his saddle for a pillow, he pulled his hat over his face.

She knew that she was too agitated to be able to sleep now. The thought of that sudden, shocking kiss had her pulse still racing, her blood still heating.

She glanced over at the sleeping figure and felt a hot, simmering anger. It infuriated her that the kiss meant so little to the man those outlaws had called The Texan that he was already sleeping as peacefully as an infant.

Across from her, the man she watched was struggling with powerful new reactions of his own. The woman's fear was genuine. As was her determination to resist. But hidden beneath those obvious emotions was another, more subtle, more controlled. Though she tried to hide it, he sensed a simmering sensuality in the very proper Caroline Adams.

He'd never met anyone who intrigued him as much as the mysterious new schoolteacher. She wasn't at all what she pretended to be.

* * *

It wasn't the rain that woke Thad; it was the absence of sound. No birds chirped. Even the insects had gone strangely quiet.

Something—or someone—was close at hand.

His first thought was for the woman. But there was no time to shield her. His fingers wrapped around the rifle. In one smooth motion he came to his knees and lifted the gun to his shoulder.

He saw the man reach for Caroline. As the man's hand snaked out, Thad's finger released the trigger and the sound of gunfire shattered the stillness. He heard Caroline cry out as the body dropped to the ground beside her.

As Thad started toward her, a voice behind him commanded, "Drop the gun, Texan, or I'll drop you where you stand."

Without turning, Thad tossed the rifle into the dirt.

"Now the gun belt," came the voice.

With one hand Thad unfastened the gun belt and it dropped to the ground at his feet.

"That's better."

Thad turned to face the gunman called Fox, whose lips twisted into a grim smile. "You don't look so tough to me, Texan." He glanced toward Caroline, who had scrambled to her feet and stood with the blanket around her. "Getting acquainted with the woman, are you?"

Thad said nothing as he gauged the distance between himself and the gunman. He'd have only a few seconds to disarm the man. Not enough time to dodge a bullet. But if he was lucky, the first hit wouldn't be fatal. He'd have to see that Fox didn't get a second chance to fire.

As if reading his mind, the gunman kept his gaze leveled on Thad as he addressed Caroline. "I still haven't showed you a proper Texas welcome, but I'm going to remedy that as soon as I take care of our hero.''

Caroline's first waking thought had been that she was caught up in a nightmare. Now she realized it was even worse. The man holding the rifle was part of the vicious gang that had killed the driver and guard. He had come back to finish what he'd started. But why? Why would an outlaw risk the wrath of a gunman like The Texan?

She swallowed back the panic that threatened to choke her. There was no time for fear. She needed a clear mind and an iron will if she were to survive.

Keeping the blanket around her, Caroline took a step closer to the gunman. Her throat was so dry she feared for a moment that she wouldn't be able to speak. Haltingly she said, "It's Fox, isn't it?"

He was genuinely pleased that she remembered his name. And when the blanket slipped a little, revealing Caroline's creamy throat, his pleasure became even more evident.

"It isn't fair that you know my name and I don't know yours."

"Caroline." Her voice lowered seductively. "Caroline Adams."

As she sauntered closer the blanket slipped a little more, tugging her dress from her shoulder. Feigning innocence, she glanced at her naked flesh, then drew the blanket tight.

Fox, having seen an expanse of bare skin, was suddenly distracted as he studied her through narrowed eyes.

From his position Thad was impressed. It was just about the best acting he'd ever witnessed. The schoolteacher didn't even appear frightened. But he'd caught the first glimpse of fear in her eyes before she'd composed herself. And he could see the way her hand trembled.

"Guess we won't be needing you around anymore, Texan," Fox called smugly.

As he aimed his gun, Caroline lifted the edge of her blanket and brought the club down as hard as she could on Fox's arm.

That was all the time Thad needed. With one leap he landed on Fox and brought him to the ground, where the two men wrestled for the pistol.

Caroline heard the gun's report and saw Thad jerk backward as the bullet ripped through his shoulder, opening the already raw wound. With a growl of pain he reached for the gunman, but his movements were slowed and Fox easily dodged his grasp.

As the gunman got to his feet, he lifted the pistol and took aim at Thad's chest.

"No." Caroline brought the club crashing over Fox's head and watched as he went down on his knees.

But the blow wasn't enough to stop him. With a savage oath he turned and aimed the gun at her.

Her chest heaving from the exertion, Caroline whispered a prayer for courage and slowly squeezed her eyes shut. Her puny club was no match against his weapon. But at least, she thought with a flash of pride, she had given The Texan a brief reprieve.

She heard the gunfire and waited for the pain. Her eyes flickered open and she gave a gasp of surprise. The Texan and Fox were once more struggling over the gun. Plunging into the fray, she lifted her club and brought it down on Fox's head. This time he dropped to the dirt and stayed there.

"Nice going." Thad rolled aside and lay struggling for breath. Between gasps he muttered, "You pack a mean punch with that club, ma'am."

She flushed with pleasure at his unexpected compliment. "Is he ... ?"

Thad felt for a pulse and looked up. "No such luck. Would you mind bringing me the rope from my saddle?"

When Caroline returned with his lasso, he tied the unconscious man's hands and feet and, with great effort, tossed him over the mare's back.

Caroline watched as Thad slowly saddled his stallion. She could see the effort it cost him as blood seeped through his binding and streamed down his arm.

"We have to get that bullet out."

"Later." He grimaced in pain. "Right now I'd just like to deliver you and our gunman to town."

"But—"

He held up a hand. "Sorry, Teacher. I think I've had all the excitement I can handle for a while."

Chapter Three

Caroline bent and retrieved her hat and spectacles from the rock shelter.

Thad's pain was momentarily forgotten as his gaze centered on her rounded bottom. Did she do these things to entice him, or was she really unaware of what she was doing? He watched as she carefully twisted her hair into a knot and adjusted her hat. Then she affixed her glasses to her nose and modestly held the remnants of her bodice together.

In the blink of an eye she was transformed into the plain, homely creature he had first seen.

Without a word he helped her into the saddle, then, with great effort, pulled himself onto the horse's back behind her. She felt the sudden, shocking jolt as his arms encircled her waist and grasped the reins. She was reminded once again of the kiss they'd shared during the night. She hoped and prayed with all her might that this stranger had forgotten. And though she knew she'd never forget the feelings that kiss had aroused, she vowed to put it out of her mind forever.

Thad nudged his stallion into a trot and the mare, despite the dead weight of Fox, danced alongside them. Caroline was pressed against the length of his torso.

Keeping her spine rigid, her head high, she held herself stiffly as they started toward town.

How could she possibly endure being held like this all the way to Hope? It would be a test of her determination, she decided. If she truly desired a new life, she would endure anything. Even the heat that danced along her spine at this man's touch.

Thad breathed in the fragrance of rose-scented water that clung to her hair. It stirred long-forgotten memories. Of a mother whose face he had never seen, and whose memory was kept alive only in stories told him by his family. Of an older sister who'd been both mother and father to him. Their mother's jar of rose water had been as precious as gold, evoking remnants of the life left behind. Even now, all these years later, Thad could still see in his mind their sod shack and the stretch of land along the Rio Grande they called home. Life here in Texas had been hard. And austere, compared with most. But the memories still brought him pleasure. It was a life that suited him. He could imagine no other.

He watched the wind play with the little tendrils of dark hair that pried loose from Caroline's neat knot. He knew nothing about Eastern fashion. But the dress she was wearing was just about the ugliest he'd ever seen. Not to mention that ridiculous bonnet perched atop her head and the simple round glasses.

He was clearly puzzled. Most of the women he knew would do anything to make themselves look pretty. Why would any woman, so young and obviously beautiful, try to make herself appear plain?

He pulled his hat low on his head to shade the sun from his eyes. What the hell did he care? Caroline Adams was none of his concern. And as soon as he deposited her in town, he'd go about his business.

Still, he was curious.

"Where are you from?"

She gave the slightest pause before she replied, "Boston."

"How'd you find out Hope needed a schoolteacher?"

"There was a letter from the mayor posted in our church."

"And you just volunteered to travel thousands of miles to fill a need?"

Caroline nodded.

He waited. But when she offered nothing more, he muttered, "Did you know the town was in the middle of nowhere?"

"It sounded like—" she almost said heaven, but caught herself in time "—the kind of challenge I was looking for."

"Challenge?"

She heard the smile in his voice and found herself bristling. "Do you think cowboys and gunmen are the only ones who thrive on adventure?"

"No, ma'am." His tone was still warm with laughter. "It appears to me that you've already had enough adventure for a year or two. A whole herd of gunmen, a dead driver and guard, a runaway stage."

"Not to mention a crude cowboy with the manners of a mule."

He threw back his head and roared. "Now, ma'am, I'd say more like a stallion. But I'll admit, it was a fine adventure."

"Don't flatter yourself."

He swallowed back his laughter. Pressing his mouth to her ear, he muttered, "Would you care to kiss me again, Schoolmarm? This time we'll see who backs off first."

His voice, low and teasing, caused her pulse to accelerate. With every mile, she had become more and more aware of the muscled body pressed to hers, of the work-roughened hands guiding the reins.

As the sun rose high in the sky, Caroline began to question her wisdom in trusting this man. How did she know if he was really taking her to Hope? She had seen how efficiently he'd disposed of those gunmen. She could be facing an even worse fate at his hands. He could be taking her to a cabin miles from the nearest outpost.

She glanced at the rifle resting in the boot of the saddle. If she were to move her hand slowly, she might be able to make it look as if she were merely flexing her fingers. Then, if he made any sudden moves, she would be able to defend herself.

Thad felt the slight tensing of her muscles as she moved her hand. A faint smile touched the corner of his lips as her fingers curled around the barrel of the rifle.

"I think that hat pin of yours might be a better weapon."

At the sound of his deep voice so close to her ear, she stifled a gasp. "I don't know what you mean." Composing herself, she turned slightly, and though her tone was haughty, he could see the betraying blush on her cheeks.

"Don't ever play poker, Teacher."

She bristled at the laughter that colored his words. "How can I be sure you're taking me to Hope?"

"You can't." His tone sent a shiver of fear along her spine. "You'll just have to trust me."

"Trust you? I'd rather..." She bit her lip. It wouldn't do to reveal anything more to this stranger. After all, as her etiquette book advised, a lady always kept her thoughts to herself. "How much farther?"

"Just beyond that ridge."

Caroline scanned the area for any sign of the team. Wouldn't the horses have left a trail if they'd passed this way? What if her trunks were lost along the way and never recovered? The thought of losing the warm shawl she'd knitted and the prim gray dress she'd planned to wear in the classroom was bad enough. But the thought of losing her precious supply of books was almost more than she could bear. She had no money left with which to replace them.

"There's the town."

As the horses crested the ridge, Caroline looked down on the dusty little town of Hope. A wide dirt trail ran through the center of a row of wooden buildings.

The stallion, sensing food and shelter, began to strain against the bit. Thad gave him his head and he broke into a run. The mare sailed behind, keeping pace.

As they drew closer Caroline could make out the buildings. At the beginning of town was the blacksmith's shop, and beside it a barn and stables. Across the road was a general store, a dry goods store and a sheriff's office and jail. Further on was a saloon and rooming house. At the very end of town she could see a church. Dotted here and there on distant hillsides were solid-looking houses and barns.

As they started down the wide, dusty trail through the center of town, Caroline saw heads turn as people caught sight of their horse.

She hoped that they would go first to the jail with the now conscious Fox, who muttered obscenities with every movement of the mare. She prayed she could quietly slip into the sheriff's office before anyone took notice of her state of undress.

Behind their hands women whispered as they passed, and children ran ahead, shouting about a gunman. Caroline assumed that they were talking about Fox.

She noted that the street soon filled with people, all taking in the unusual scene. Her hand gripped her torn bodice. She was acutely uncomfortable at the sight of so many cold, staring faces.

Thad Conway looked neither left nor right. It was as if the townspeople weren't even there.

As they approached the jail, one man separated himself from the others and made his way toward Thad's horse. His hair had gone white, and a drooping white mustache contrasted sharply with skin the color and texture of aged leather. Though he was no taller than the others in the crowd, there was a solidness about him. When he spoke, his voice rang with authority.

"Texan. What brings you to town? The only time we ever see you is when we need you or you need us. And you haven't needed us in all the years I've been here."

When Thad said nothing, the sheriff cleared his throat. "Got a present for me?"

"Yeah, Sheriff Horn. His name's Fox. Riding with Luke Cochran's gang. Don't know why they attacked the stage. They're usually more interested in strongboxes than passengers." He shrugged, deciding to keep the rest of his thoughts to himself. "They killed the driver and guard. The rest of the gang are dead."

The sheriff glanced toward the man who was tossed over the mare's back and spoke sharply to a deputy before looking up at the woman seated in front of Thad. "I'm glad you brought me a gunman. But I'm more interested in the woman."

"Oh." Thad grinned. "This is Caroline Adams. Your new schoolmarm."

He slid from the back of the horse and helped her from the saddle.

"Miss Adams." The sheriff offered his hand and she self-consciously wiped her hand along her skirt before extending hers.

"I'm sure glad you're here, Miss Adams. We were worried. The team hauled the stage into town last night, but there was no one aboard. We were afraid you'd all been . . ."

"I would have been, if it hadn't been for this man."

"The Texan always seems to find trouble," the sheriff said dryly. "Are you alright, ma'am? You weren't wounded by those gunmen?"

"I'm fine. But my things . . ." Caroline said eagerly, turning to the sheriff. "Were they still aboard?"

"Yes, ma'am. They're in my office. I was just getting up a posse to start searching for you." Caroline felt a wave of relief that her baggage hadn't been lost.

"The attack took place by Circle Rock. You'll find the bodies of the driver and guard," Thad said, "and the rest of the outlaws. I'd go with you, but I want Doc to take a look at my shoulder."

"Took another bullet, did you?" Sheriff Horn glanced at the blood that soaked the front of Thad's shirt.

Touching his hand to his hat, Thad turned to Caroline. "I'll leave you with Sheriff Horn." As he sauntered away, the crowd hurriedly stepped aside to clear a path. He took no notice of them.

"Miss Adams," the sheriff said, "we sure are glad to welcome you to Hope."

As a crowd gathered around her, Caroline glanced down at her torn clothing. This was certainly not how she'd planned to present herself to the people of Hope.

But once again, it seemed, her destiny had been taken out of her hands. It was the story of her life.

As she watched the stranger enter a small building beside the jail, she lifted her head in an unconscious gesture of defiance. No more would she be a victim of her past. From now on, her life was an unwritten book. And today was a brand-new page.

Thad crossed the dusty road and opened the door of a neat wooden building. Inside, a man looked up from the small child who lay on the examining table. Standing beside him, a handsome Comanche boy of about ten watched his every move.

"Thad." The doctor's wide smile faded when he saw the blood that soaked Thad's shirt. "Bullet?"

Thad nodded and slumped wearily into a chair.

"I'll be with you in a minute." The doctor completed his examination and handed the child to his young mother, who hovered nearby.

After a few softly spoken commands, he watched them leave, then turned to Thad.

For a few seconds the two men merely stared at each other, then, with a wide smile, the doctor said, "Jessie and Morning Light were worried about you." With a grin, he added, "Hell, so was I. What kept you?"

"It's a long story." Thad tousled the Comanche boy's hair. "Runs With The Wind, I think you've grown a foot since I left."

The boy gave him a look of adoration.

As Thad removed his shirt and lay on the table, the doctor plunged his hands into a bucket of water and began scrubbing.

Examining the wound, he shook his head. "Been doing my job again?"

Thad's laugh was cut short by a sharp pain. Sucking in his breath he said, "The bullet was festering so I dug it out. But now there's a second one."

"What is it about you?" Dan Conway asked as he began to probe. "Can't you ever keep your gun in your holster? Or do you just like pain?"

"Yeah, it's the pain. I just can't seem to stay away from it. I guess it all started at the age of four when that mustang stepped on my foot and I discovered I liked pain."

Across the table, Runs With The Wind laughed heartily at Thad's joke.

As the doctor probed further, his face revealed his concern. "I'd better give you some chloroform. This one is going to hurt."

"I don't want to be knocked out. I need to get to the ranch."

"Not tonight. You can stay with us. Morning Light complains that you haven't spent enough time with your niece and nephews."

"How are little Danny and Kate?"

"Fat and sassy. You can see them for yourself tonight."

"I'll come by in a day or two. I promise. But tonight I have to get to my ranch. I've been away so long, Manuel and Rosita will think I'm not coming back."

"You're not. At least not tonight." The doctor reached for a brown-tinted bottle on his shelf, but Thad stopped him.

"I mean it, Dan. No fancy drugs. Just dig out the bullet and let me get on my way."

"All right." The doctor handed Thad a piece of rawhide. "Better bite down on this. Hard."

With the boy at his side, Dan Conway worked quickly. He cut open a flap of flesh and began to probe for the bullet. While he worked, he described in detail every step of the operation to Runs With The Wind. The boy listened intently.

"In time you'll be able to tell the difference between bone and muscle and the feel of a bullet embedded in flesh."

The boy nodded.

"You have to work quickly, especially when you're dealing with a patient so thickheaded he won't allow you to use modern medicine."

Despite the somberness of the occasion, the boy chuckled.

Neither of them was aware of the door opening or of the figure that paused just inside the room.

As soon as the crowd dispersed, Caroline had a compelling need to see that the man who had saved her was getting the attention he deserved at the medical dispensary. It was not that she wanted to see him again, she told herself firmly, but she had not properly thanked him. A lady should always thank a gentleman for coming to her rescue. Besides, she didn't even know his name.

While she watched, Thad spit the rawhide from his mouth and muttered, "Get on with it, dammit. It hurts like hell."

The front of the doctor's shirt was smeared with fresh blood. Leaning close he stuck the rawhide back into Thad's mouth and continued probing.

"One more thing, Runs With The Wind. If a patient starts swearing at the doctor, the doctor has the right to gag him. If that doesn't work, a well-placed blow to the jaw usually does the trick."

Caroline couldn't believe what she was hearing. How could this man call himself a doctor? What sort of primitive practice was this, that a man could be subjected to such pain without even being given chloroform or laudanum?

Inching closer, she stared down at the stranger, lying on the table. Sweat beaded his brow. Pain was etched in his eyes.

A piece of leather? Is this what was offered a man who risked his life to save another? Worse, while he was forced to lie there, racked with pain, must he be tormented with cruel taunts? Her gaze swung from Runs With The Wind to the doctor. A couple of savages. What sort of place was this? she thought miserably.

"If you'll take a seat, ma'am," the doctor said without looking up, "I'll be with you when I've finished here."

"I—came to see the man they call The Texan."

Thad turned his head. Through a mist of pain he made out the familiar figure. Again he spat out the rawhide. "Forget something, Teacher?"

"I . . . never properly thanked you," she said.

At the questioning looks on the faces of the others, Thad explained quickly, "This is Caroline Adams. She survived the attack on the stage. Miss Adams, this is Dr. Dan Conway."

Dan studied the woman in the torn, muddy gown and nodded stiffly before stuffing the rawhide into Thad's mouth and bending to his work. "The whole town was worried about the empty stage."

He fell silent when the tip of his knife scraped metal. Unceremoniously dropping the bullet to the floor, he began to mop the blood that now flowed like a river from Thad's shoulder.

At a choking sound from Thad he paused. Again Thad spat the rawhide. In a voice rough with pain he swore savagely. "The damned cure is worse than the ill. The bullet never hurt as much going in as it just did coming out."

"Remember that the next time you find yourself facing a gun. You don't have to jump into every fight." Dan poured a liberal amount of disinfectant on the raw wound, then began neatly suturing it.

"Make certain your stitches are fine and even, boy," he instructed in level tones. "And when you're through, disinfect the wound again. In an emergency, whiskey will do."

When the doctor had finished sponging the blood, he turned to Runs With The Wind. "It looks like you're finally going to have a real teacher. Miss Adams, this is Runs With The Wind. He'll be one of your students."

Caroline nodded toward the boy, trying to hide her revulsion at the bloody surgery she'd just witnessed. "It would seem that you've already been learning some important lessons."

"I want to be a healer for my people."

"It's nice of the doctor to let you watch."

"He's more than a doctor," the boy said proudly. "Since the death of my father, he has become my father."

Caroline saw the look of pride on the boy's face. And when she glanced at the doctor, she could see a similar look in his eyes. Her earlier hostility toward him began to dissipate. Despite his tough-talking manner toward his patient, he was willing to share his knowledge. Like another she had once known.

Thad grimaced with pain. With his good hand he wiped the sweat from his forehead. "Is there something else, Teacher?"

"I'm just happy to see that you're being taken care of. And to thank you again for saving my life."

"How much danger were you in, Miss Adams?" Dan asked.

"Our stage was attacked by seven gunmen."

"Only seven?" Dan soaked a linen cloth and began scrubbing his hands. "You have to figure that one of these times a gunman is going to get in a lucky shot and you're going to find yourself dead."

At his softly spoken words, Caroline looked up sharply. "Are you suggesting that he shouldn't have come to my aid, Doctor?"

"No. I'm suggesting what everyone in Texas knows—Thad Conway rushes in where even angels fear to tread."

"Thad Conway?"

Thad grinned. "Sorry. I guess I forgot to introduce myself."

Seeing the angry look she shot the doctor, Thad said quietly, "Don't mind Dan. He just can't stop worrying about my hide."

"I should be grateful," the doctor said. "At least I get a lot of practice whenever Thad's around. He's suffered more gunshots than any man I know."

Caroline swallowed, thinking about how quickly the man whose name she now knew to be Thad Conway had drawn his gun. "If he's that good with a gun, maybe you shouldn't say anything that might make him angry."

"You don't understand," Thad said with a laugh. "Dan can say whatever he wants. He's my brother."

"Your big brother," Dan put in. "And don't you forget it."

Chapter Four

His brother! The town doctor? For a moment Caroline almost relaxed. This cowboy had a brother. And a nephew. Somehow, Thad Conway seemed less forbidding now that she was armed with such facts. A moment later, however, she took one glance at him and felt again the tingle of apprehension. Family or no, Thad Conway was a dangerous man.

Dr. Dan Conway smiled, and Caroline could see the resemblance between the two men in the shape of their lips and the way their eyes crinkled in sun-bronzed faces.

"I don't usually work under such primitive conditions, Miss Adams," Dan said softly. "But Thad was adamant about not getting any chloroform. He claims he still has work to do."

"I do." Shakily Thad sat up and swung his legs to the floor. For a moment the room spun in dizzying circles and he waited until his vision cleared. "While I was in Mexico I was able to coax Don Esteban into selling me his prize mare. She has perfect bloodlines."

"You can't breed her tonight," Dan said reasonably.

"No. But we've been on the trail too long. I want her in a corral where she can grow sleek and fat until her time comes."

"The mare will keep. That shoulder, on the other hand..."

"I'm fine." Thad slipped from the table and reached for his shirt.

Caroline had a quick impression of a muscled torso and heavily corded arms as he pulled on his shirt. Though he winced in pain, he managed the buttons before he slapped a wide-brimmed hat on his head.

Feeling vaguely uncomfortable, Caroline extended her hand to the doctor. "It was nice meeting you, Dr. Conway. And you, Runs With The Wind." She smiled at the boy. "I look forward to seeing you in school."

The boy nodded shyly.

Turning to Thad, she said, "I'd better get back to the sheriff's office. He was kind enough to give me a horse and rig. He said it goes with my position as schoolteacher. By now he's probably loaded my trunk aboard."

When she was gone, Thad turned toward his brother and extended his hand. "Thanks again, Dan. Tell Morning Light I'll see her later in the week."

As he clasped his brother's hand, Dan said with a chuckle, "You'd better plan on supper tomorrow or she'll have your hide."

"Tomorrow, then." Thad tousled his nephew's hair before heading out the door.

Outside, the tinny sounds of a piano filtered from the saloon. Carried on the breeze was the sound of feminine laughter.

Squinting into the sunlight, Thad glanced toward the swinging doors and paused. It was tempting to think about a bottle of whiskey, a hot bath and a woman to scrub his back. Then, remembering the work that would be waiting at the ranch, he strode resolutely down the street until he reached his horses. Pulling himself into the saddle, he caught up the mare's lead rope and headed out of town.

Caroline held the reins between sweating palms. When the sheriff had told her that the schoolhouse was a mile or more from town, she'd had to struggle to keep from allowing her fear to surface.

Now, as she crested a hill and stared down at the rough cabin nestled among a stand of trees, she felt a fresh rush of panic.

What did she know about this strange land? How would she withstand the elements? She'd heard that the heat was intense, and that a cold northern wind could drop the temperature to below freezing within hours. And what about the people? Would they be friendly like the doctor, the sheriff, the mayor? Or would they be savages like the outlaws that had attacked the stage?

What would she eat? The sheriff had told her that he'd tucked sacks of flour and sugar into the back of her rig. But she couldn't possibly get by on that alone. She halted the rig beside the cabin and swallowed back her apprehension. She would survive. Hadn't she always managed somehow?

At the sound of horses' hooves pounding the earth she whirled, then released a sigh as she recognized Thad Conway.

As he drew close he caught the fear in her eyes and saw the way she tensed before stepping down from the rig.

"Looks like we just keep crossing each other's paths." He'd had no intention of stopping. He was eager to get home. But, he told himself, there was no harm in helping her. Just this once.

He slid from the saddle and tied his two horses to a rail that ran the length of the cabin. "Need a hand with your things?"

"Thank you." Caroline lifted a scuffed traveling bag from the back of the rig and strode toward the door. Untying the latch, she shoved the door open and peered inside. Wild creatures had left their tracks in the thick dust that covered the rough floor. A dank, musty smell pervaded the air. Lifting her skirt, she stepped inside.

The cabin consisted of a schoolroom on one side, living quarters on the other, divided by a wall and door. In one corner of the living quarters was a bed made of rough logs and a lumpy mattress stuffed with corn husks, many of which had tumbled to the floor. Standing in front of the small window was a scarred table and two chairs. Along the far wall was a blackened fireplace.

Setting down her bag, she crossed the room and opened the door that led to the schoolroom. Inside was another blackened fireplace, along with a table and chair and a row of rough-hewn chairs in various sizes to accommodate the children.

Thad paused just inside the door and watched as she moved slowly around the room. She touched each chair, then ran a hand almost reverently over the table that would serve as her desk.

"Where would you like this?"

Caroline looked up, and for a moment he could read her confusion as she studied him, the huge sack of flour balanced on his good shoulder as effortlessly as if it weighed nothing at all.

"Anywhere." She walked toward him, wrinkling her nose at the dust that swirled with every step. "How long has it been since the town has had a teacher?"

"Two or three years, I guess." He set the sack in a corner, and Caroline watched as he made a second trip to the rig for the sugar, and then a third trip for her trunk. When he returned he found her struggling to remove the mattress from the bed.

"Here," he said, "let me help you."

Together they hauled it outside and dropped it. Instantly several mice darted away into the tall grass. Seeing them, Caroline shuddered. "I believe I'll burn the corn husks."

"Good idea." With the blade of his knife Thad slit open the muslin and began shaking it until it was empty. Stepping over the pile of dried husks, he hung the cloth on a tree branch and followed her inside.

Caroline had found a broom and was busy sweeping. For a moment he watched her from the doorway, unexpectedly enjoying the way she looked, the silly hat still perched atop her head and her spectacles slipping down her nose. Then his practical nature took over.

"What are you planning to fix for supper?"

She stopped her sweeping but avoided his eyes. The same question had occurred to her. Her stomach was already growling. "I don't know. Something simple, I expect."

"Did you buy any salt pork in town?"

She shook her head, too proud to admit that she couldn't afford such luxuries.

He glanced toward the sacks of flour and sugar. "That's all you have?"

She nodded, feeling her cheeks begin to flush. When he saw her reaction, he turned away. "I'll see what I can do."

Caroline watched as he walked to his horse and removed the rifle. A short time later, while she struggled with an armload of logs for the fireplace, she heard the sound of gunshots. By the time she had coaxed a fire and filled several empty buckets with water from a nearby stream, Thad had returned with a deer slung over his saddle.

He was pleased to note that Caroline had a batch of biscuits on the fire. Oblivious to his presence, she was on her knees in the corner of the room, scrubbing at the layers of dirt and grime. He watched her for several minutes, amazed that she could continue at such a pace.

From his saddlebags Thad produced coffee and a blackened pot. Soon the wonderful aroma of coffee, freshly baked biscuits and sizzling meat filled the air.

While they waited for dinner to be ready, Caroline took her broom outside and swatted the length of muslin that hung from the tree, filling the air with dust. When she had finished, she stuffed the muslin sack with dried grasses and sprigs of evergreen.

Thad helped her carry it inside, where they placed the fresh mattress over the bed frame. The fragrance of evergreen mingled with the scents of food.

From her trunk Caroline removed a thin blanket and down pillow. The pillowcase was embroidered with tiny pink morning glories. Unfolding the blanket, she shook it gently over the bed and tucked it in at the edges.

Then she walked to the fireplace and added another log. Kneeling, she wiped her hands along her dirty skirt and stared at the flames. The thought of how far she had come and how many twists and turns her life had taken had her smiling dreamily.

She was finally here, in Hope, Texas, where she would be known as Miss Caroline Adams, schoolteacher. A proper lady. She closed her eyes and enjoyed the heat of the fire on her cheeks.

This cabin was hers. Hers, she thought fiercely. For as long as the townspeople wanted her.

Her head nodded and she leaned back against the pile of logs she had stacked beside the fireplace. The people of Hope would like her, she vowed. They would approve of her. And she would never, never do anything to earn their disapproval.

Thad leaned a hip against the doorway and rolled a cigarette. Crossing to the fireplace, he lifted a flaming stick to the tip and inhaled deeply.

Turning, he studied Caroline while she slept. Her glasses had dropped to her lap. A wayward strand of dark hair dipped seductively over one eye. The flickering flames of the fire cast her face in light and shadow. Her lips were pursed in a little pout and he found himself tempted once again to taste them.

Dropping to one knee, he leaned his hands on his thigh and chanced a closer look. She was stunning, with flawless skin and perfect, even features.

Who are you, Caroline Adams? he asked silently. And what the hell are you doing out here?

He suddenly stood and walked to the open door, absently rubbing his aching shoulder. Why was he lingering here when there was so much to be done? He'd been so impatient to be on his way. He still had a long ride before he reached his ranch. But there was something about this woman. Though she hadn't asked for his help, he had some inexplicable need to give it.

He heaved a sigh of disgust. He would wait only long enough to finish his cigarette. Then, he vowed, he'd be on his way.

* * *

Caroline awoke with a start. For a moment she was completely disoriented, then, as she made out the tall figure leaning against the doorway, she gave a little gasp.

Thad drew smoke into his lungs and tossed the cigarette away. He seemed momentarily caught off guard before he composed his features.

"I'm glad you're awake. I was just leaving."

"But the dinner..." She scrambled to her feet and looked down when she heard her glasses drop to the floor. Bending to retrieve them, she put them on before walking toward him.

"Sorry. But I have to get to my ranch."

"Is it far from here?"

He thought about pulling that silly hat from her head. And those spectacles. Instead he clenched his hands at his sides. "The start of my land lies just beyond that ridge." He pointed and she followed his direction. "But the ranch house is at least an hour's ride."

"An hour." She shivered, though from the cold or the thought of being so far from her nearest neighbor, she wasn't sure. "You must be hungry. You've been on the trail all day. At least you could take the time to eat."

He was so hungry his ribs were nearly stuck together. But the thought of staying on, with the darkness hovering just beyond, was a little too tempting. Besides, it wasn't food he was hungry for.

He prided himself on being smart enough to know when to advance and when to retreat. "I unhitched your horse and turned him into the enclosure out back. Saw to his food and water, too. He'll be fine until morning."

"Thank you."

He noticed that she kept a proper distance between them. That only made her all the more tempting. He itched to reach out and drag her into his arms, and found himself wondering what her reaction would be.

"Well then." He touched a hand to his hat. "I'll say good-night."

"Good night."

As he strode toward his horses, he saw her outlined in the doorway. Though she smiled bravely, he saw the way she kept her hands folded together.

"Be sure and latch the door," he called. "In case some critters want to warm themselves at your fire."

She nodded.

When the men in Hope got a look at the new schoolmarm, there'd be more than just critters looking to break down her door.

He caught up the lead rope for the mare and flicked the reins of his mount. Both horses started up at a fast pace.

Turning in the saddle, Thad saw her still standing in the doorway, her figure clearly etched by the firelight behind her.

As he crested the ridge he turned again. She was still standing where he'd left her.

She looked so alone, so vulnerable. She was afraid. Though she tried to put on a brave face, he could sense her fear even from so great a distance.

With a savage oath he urged the horses into a run. Damn the woman. There was something about her that tugged at his heart. And though he was a man who preferred his life uncomplicated, he knew he'd have to find out more about this mysterious Caroline Adams.

Chapter Five

Caroline opened her trunk and removed the linen towels wrapped around several chipped cups and plates. For a moment her eyes filled with tears at the delicate morning glories that rimmed the fragile china. Mama's china. The only thing of value she'd had to give her daughter.

Mama had been so proud. "It was your grandmother's. Real china," she had said to ten-year-old Caroline. "It's what proper ladies use."

"I'll treasure it," Caroline had whispered.

"No, darlin'. Keep it if you can. But sell it if you have to. Do whatever is necessary to become a fine lady."

Caroline hadn't sold it. She'd come close many times. But she always managed to get by without selling Mama's china.

Filling a plate with venison and lifting a hot roll from the pan, Caroline placed the food on the scarred table, then filled a cup with steaming coffee. Alone at her table she ate her supper and watched the darkness steal across the land.

Sipping coffee, she listened to the sounds of the night. At first she was aware of only the terrible, empty silence. Then, as she began to truly listen, she heard the buzz and chirp of insects. A night bird cried as it soared high overhead. Somewhere in the distance a coyote howled.

She'd never heard such strange, peaceful sounds before. All her life, on the teeming streets of a big city, she'd been assaulted by the harsh strains of men's voices, cursing, shouting, the gentler tones of women laughing, weeping, the cries of children fighting and the ceaseless creaking of wagon wheels. Even late into the night, the sounds of saloon brawls had assailed her.

And if it wasn't the noises, it was the smell. Of garbage rotting, of sewage spilling along the sides of the streets.

She drained her cup and sat back, her ears attuned to the new and different voices of a Texas night. Then she looked around at the sparse, dusty cabin. Her cabin. All hers. For as long as the people of Hope wanted her here.

With a little laugh of delight she ladled water from a bucket hanging over the fire and washed her dishes. Then, stripping off her filthy gown, she washed herself and then her clothes. When she had draped the dripping garments over the two chairs, she pulled on a shapeless cotton shift.

Carefully banking the fire, she crawled beneath the blanket. Within minutes she was fast asleep, a smile of contentment on her lips.

At the rumble of wagon wheels, Caroline looked up from the clothesline she was stringing between two trees. She was grateful that she'd taken the time to pull her hair back into a prim, tidy knot. Quickly withdrawing the spectacles from her apron pocket, she put them on.

No sooner had the first wagon pulled up when a second and then a third followed, sending clouds of dust billowing across the open expanse of yard around the cabin.

A small blond woman climbed down from the first wagon, followed by three giggling children.

"Hello. I'm Jessie Matthews. And these are my children, Jack, Lisbeth and Frank."

There was something familiar about this open, friendly woman, but Caroline couldn't quite place it. "It's nice to meet you. I'm Caroline Adams."

As the two women clasped hands, Jessie nodded toward the wagon and said to her children, "Fetch those dishes. But be careful. Some of them are heavy."

A beautiful, dark-haired woman climbed from a carriage and moved toward them, followed by a boy and girl. The woman's walk was so graceful she seemed almost to float. She wore a pale, doeskin dress with a fringed hem. A beautifully beaded belt encircled her slim waist.

As Caroline watched, the two women embraced, then separated.

"Miss Adams, this is my sister-in-law, Morning Light, and her son, Danny, and daughter, Kate," Jessie said.

Caroline smiled at the children before turning to their mother. "Morning Light. Are you also the mother of Runs With The Wind?"

At the mention of the boy, the Indian woman beamed. "He told me he met you. He was my brother's son. I am the wife of Dr. Conway."

At the woman's bright smile, Caroline turned to Jessie. "But how is it she's your sister-in-law?"

"I'm Dr. Conway's sister."

Caroline was suddenly able to place the smile. "Then you must also be Thad Conway's sister."

Jessie nodded. "I understand you've already met Thad."

"Yes. He rescued me from a band of gunmen."

The children, having returned with linen-wrapped dishes still steaming from the oven, overheard and began to giggle. The oldest, Jack, said with a trace of pride, "If there are gunmen around, my Uncle Thad will find them."

Caroline arched a brow. "And why is that?"

"My pa says it's because Uncle Thad was just born to fight. He says Uncle Thad must have come into this world scrapping, because he's been scrapping ever since."

The other children giggled their agreement.

"Hush now," Jessie said sharply. Nodding toward the items in their hands, she explained, "There's a bit of stew and a loaf of bread. And a jug of milk." She grinned. "I figured you wouldn't have a cow yet."

"I brought eggs and several plucked chickens," Morning Light added in her formal tone. "I knew you would not yet have a flock of chickens."

"I'm obliged." Caroline led the way to the cabin and held the door as the others entered ahead of her. "That's very kind of you."

"Not at all." Jessie smiled and waved at three women who were climbing down from a third wagon. "I'm sorry we weren't here to greet you last night. Our ranch is too far from town to hear much news. But when my husband told me that you'd arrived, I hurried over to help you clean the schoolroom. I know it hasn't been used in a couple of years." Jessie helped the children set the dishes on the table, then glanced around the clean cabin. "I see we're too late."

"I'm grateful for your thoughtfulness. It's true I did a bit of cleaning last night and again this morning,"

Caroline admitted, "but I didn't have the energy to clean the schoolroom, as well."

Jessie groaned. "I'm amazed you could do anything after a journey all the way from Boston."

At the mention of Boston, Caroline's smile faded.

Jessie missed the look that crossed Caroline's face, but it wasn't lost on Morning Light, who was too polite to acknowledge what she had seen.

"You must have been exhausted," Jessie said. "Especially since, from what Cole told me, your trip was far from uneventful."

"It was frightening," Caroline admitted, "facing seven gunmen and a runaway stage. I thought the work would help me forget my fears."

Jessie opened the door for the three women approaching, their arms laden with more gifts. "Miss Adams, this is Cora Meadows, Sara Waverly and Belva Spears."

The three women could not have looked more different. Cora, who was as plump as she was tall, wore her brown hair in braids that she twisted around the top of her head like a crown. The style gave her plump face an even rounder appearance. Sara Waverly would have been pretty, with a trim figure and small, even features set in a heart-shaped face framed by brown curls, but her face wore the pinched, tight expression of someone who expected the worst from life. Belva Spears, whose heavy black gown couldn't conceal a tall, angular body and the thinnest arms Caroline had ever seen, had lively blue eyes in a suntanned face sprinkled liberally with freckles that had turned to age spots.

Caroline greeted them warmly and accepted their gifts of fruit cobbler and preserves. Cora had brought a bolt of sheer white fabric, which she laid carefully on the bed.

"I remembered that there were no curtains on these windows." With a grin she added, "Our last teacher was Mr. Canby, who insisted on keeping the windows open summer and winter so the children could fill their lungs with fresh air. He detested curtains or any other frills in his schoolhouse."

Belva Spears nodded. "He was very stern, and very frugal."

At the mention of the town's former teacher, Sara Waverly suddenly brightened. "I thought he was just what the children of Hope needed. He kept a willow switch beside him on his desk and used it frequently on children whose minds wandered from their lessons."

"He called it his friend," young Jack said matter-of-factly. "And said we'd all get to know his friend well." He ran a hand over the seat of his pants. "Mr. Canby was right."

"I certainly hope," Sara said sternly, "that you will continue Mr. Canby's policy of strict discipline."

Caroline tried to hide her feelings of revulsion as she turned away. But she made a vow to herself that there would be no switches in her classroom.

"So," Cora Meadows went on in a happier tone, "I thought I'd stitch some curtains while I was here."

"And I've made a rag rug for the floor." Belva unrolled a richly colored rug and set it in front of the fireplace.

"Oh, how beautiful. I never expected such generosity."

Sara's tone grew frosty. "I suppose, after a life in Boston, you are accustomed to such luxuries, Miss Adams. But I do hope you won't allow such frivolous things in the schoolroom."

Caroline glanced at the table groaning with food and thought that she was indeed enjoying luxuries beyond her imagination. Choosing her words carefully, she said, "You must all stay for lunch."

With a laugh, Jessie admitted, "We'd already planned to invite ourselves."

The women and children set about scrubbing down the walls, the windows, even the chairs in the schoolroom. And while they worked they laughed and chatted amiably.

Caroline heard about the dozen or so children who would be attending the school. And about Cora's young son, who had been paralyzed after having been thrown from a horse.

"Ben still loves horses," she said with a trace of weariness. "He lies in his bed all day and watches the horses running across the meadow. It breaks my heart that he'll never ride again." She turned away to hide her quivering lip. As she gave the walls a vigorous scrubbing, the smile was soon back on her lips.

A while later Caroline heard about the loss of Belva's husband a year ago, when a gunman had taken his horse, his gun and his boots and left him lying in his own blood in a field just beyond town.

"Has anyone ever caught the gunman?"

Belva shook her head. "Ezra was known as a man of peace. The gunman had to know that he wouldn't fight back. There was no reason to kill him." She wiped away the tears that sprang to her eyes, surprised that, even now, the mere thought of the good man she'd lost could make her weep. "But if I ever get his killer in the sight of my gun, I'll make him pay for what he did."

"What a wicked thing to say," Sara Waverly snapped. "You must learn to accept what life hands you, Belva, just as I've learned to accept the loss of my husband. It does no good to speak of revenge."

"How did your husband die, Sara?" Caroline asked.

"His heart just gave out one day while he was plowing the fields," she responded.

"He probably died from lack of affection," Jessie whispered as she scrubbed a wall with more vigor than necessary.

Caroline gently changed the subject and soon heard about the babies born and the youngsters who were already beginning courtship. And twice Cora bluntly mentioned the names of the town's most eligible bachelors.

"An educated woman is considered quite a prize out here." Sara allowed her gaze to roam the young teacher, noting the drab, shapeless gown and plain, round spectacles. "Even if she isn't the prettiest woman in the territory."

Across the room Jessie was surprised to see the young schoolteacher cover up a smile. It occurred to her that most young women would be extremely unhappy upon hearing such a statement. But Caroline Adams seemed genuinely pleased.

"There's the banker's son, Emory Blake, who cuts a fine figure."

"Too cold," Jessie sniffed. "Besides, he's gone to Fort Worth."

"What about the new preacher, Reverend Symes?" Belva asked. "He strikes me as a fine, upright young man."

"He won't last long," Sara said curtly.

"And why is that?" Jessie swatted six-year-old Frank's hand as he tried to help himself to a taste of fruit cobbler.

"He preaches a false religion," Sara said smugly. "Why, last week he actually suggested that there was nothing that couldn't be forgiven. Nothing." She gave a snort of derision. "Can you imagine such nonsense?"

"We were talking about eligible young men." Belva could hardly contain her impatience with Sara.

"What about Uncle Thad?" eight-year-old Lisbeth asked with the wisdom of her gender. "If I was all grown-up, that's who I'd set my cap for."

"Your Uncle Thad," Sara said sternly, "would make a terrible husband."

For a change, everyone seemed to agree with her. The other women, including his own sister, nodded in agreement.

"He'd be off every night at the saloon or getting himself shot up," Cora said with a shake of her dark bonnet.

"Pity the poor woman married to him." Belva stopped her scrubbing. "At least I had ten good years with Ezra. Why, Thad Conway's wife would never know whether or not he'd be coming back for supper. She'd be lucky to have a year with a man like that before he'd wind up dead from some silly saloon brawl."

"I worry about Thad," Jessie admitted. "I guess some of it was my fault. But I did my best for him, without a ma or pa to guide me. Thad grew up wild, and he's still wild. And I don't think anything or anyone will ever tame him."

"I don't care," Lisbeth said fiercely. "Uncle Thad's still the best-looking man in town." She glanced at the new schoolteacher for support. "Isn't that right, Miss Adams? You said you met him."

"Well, I have but..." Caroline bit her lip. "I'm afraid I didn't really pay much attention. There were gunmen and..." She shrugged. "I think it's time to eat."

She hoped none of them noticed how uncomfortable she'd become at the discussion of eligible men. It wouldn't matter to her how wealthy or polite or handsome they were. She had no intention of marrying. Not now. Not ever.

They enjoyed a picnic lunch outside in the late afternoon sun. Through the open doors, the schoolroom sparkled.

Within the hour the women and children climbed into their wagons in preparation for the return to their homes.

"Will we see you at Sunday services tomorrow?" Belva asked.

"Yes. Of course." Caroline thought how pleasant it would be to attend church in town and have a chance to meet all the people. "I don't know what I would have done without your help," she called.

"It was the least we could do." Jessie waved from her wagon and her children waved and shouted to their cousins.

Morning Light offered her hand. "I was eager to meet the woman who would be teaching my children."

Caroline glanced at the well-mannered boy and girl who followed their mother to their carriage. "You have beautiful children, Morning Light."

"Thank you." The young woman's eyes softened. "Like all the People, they have been reared to respect knowledge. They are eager to learn all you can teach them, for they know that they have a special responsibility."

"And what is that?" Caroline asked.

"You will hear soon enough from the others in the town." She glanced meaningfully at Sara Waverly's retreating back. "I am the sister of a Comanche chief, Two Moons. And my husband is the one who carries healing to all who need it. Our children are the bridge between his culture and mine."

Caroline was touched by the young woman's words. "Do they find it difficult?"

"At times." Morning Light's tone became grave. "There are some people who fear anyone who is different. And fear can make people react in strange and often cruel ways."

As the wagons and carriage pulled away in a cloud of dust, the young Comanche woman's words remained with Caroline. She knew, firsthand, the cruelty of people who stood in judgment of others. She felt a twinge of fear, then quickly shrugged it off. She refused to dwell on such thoughts on a beautiful day like this. Instead, she would read another chapter of *Dr. Harvey Hattinger's Rules for Headmistresses*. That always buoyed her spirits.

With Manuel by his side, Thad checked the herd of mustangs on the north ridge.

"Damned fences," he muttered, glaring at the miles of wire that crisscrossed the land.

"Why do you hate it so?" Manuel asked.

"When I was a boy, all this land was free and wild. Look at it now. Towns everywhere. And people, all complaining about the herds of cattle and mustangs destroying their land. Their land," he spat. "As if all these Easterners have the right to come and destroy a way of life forever." He glanced at the man beside him and swore savagely. "I hate fences."

Manuel grinned. It was the same thing he heard every time he rode with Thad Conway. At least the man was consistent.

"Which stallion are we after?"

"That one," Thad called. "The chestnut."

The dark-haired man nodded and lifted a coil of rope from his saddle.

"I'll circle around to his other side." Thad nudged his mount into action until he was positioned. Then, lifting his lasso, he signaled for Manuel to do the same.

Though the mustang was agile, he was unable to avoid two ropes. Within minutes Thad and Manuel's mounts trotted smartly toward the buildings in the distance with the stallion held fast between the men.

When he was turned loose in the corral, the two men leaned against the rail and watched as the animal pranced back and forth, his head high, his nostrils flaring. "I think, my friend," Manuel said softly, "you have made a good choice."

"I hope so. I made Don Alvarez a very rich man because of his mare. I'd hate to waste all that horseflesh on the wrong stallion."

"Now you sound more like a proud father than a horse breeder." Manuel glanced toward the ranch house. "That was the way Rosita's father spoke about me when I asked for her hand."

Thad threw back his head and laughed. "I'll bet he's not saying that now."

The handsome man shrugged. "He thinks I should tend to my own ranch now, instead of working for you. He keeps reminding me that if I would return to Mexico, I could work on his vast holdings and Rosita could live like her mother, with servants to attend to her every need instead of working like one herself."

Thad glanced at him. "Maybe you ought to consider his offer."

Manuel shook his head. "Rosita knows that the land would never be mine. Here in Texas I am a man. On her father's land I would be little more than a hired hand. And when her father dies, her older brother will inherit everything. He is an even harsher taskmaster than his father." He met Thad's gaze. "I prefer things the way they are. So far I am able to manage my own small ranch and still keep working for you. The pay is fair. Someday soon, Rosita and I will have enough to enlarge the herds and the ranch house."

"Why would you want to enlarge the house?" Thad asked.

Manuel grinned. "Rosita wants a baby." He glanced at Thad. "With such a fine house, I should think you would want to find a woman to share it, and children to fill it with laughter."

"I feel about marriage the same way I feel about fences," Thad said vehemently. "Both close a man in and take away his freedom."

Manuel coughed discreetly. "I hope you will be good enough to refrain from repeating such things in the presence of my wife."

"You know I will."

Manuel nodded. Thad Conway was very good at keeping his thoughts to himself.

Both men looked up at the clang of the dinner bell. With a last glance at the stallion, Thad led Manuel to the house.

Over a dinner of tortillas and spicy venison, Thad listened to the musical voices of Manuel and Rosita as they brought each other up-to-date on the events of the day.

Later, while Rosita cleaned up the kitchen, Manuel sat by the back door mending a harness.

"We will say good-night," Manuel called.

Thad nodded. Lighting a lantern, he bent over the columns of figures and wondered again if he'd been a fool to invest so much money in one mare. He leaned back. She was one fine piece of horseflesh. If she gave him the foals he was hoping for, she'd be worth any price.

As the shadows lengthened, Thad found his thoughts veering from the ranch and turning instead to the new teacher. Caroline Adams. Her name played through his mind. As did the memory of the way she'd looked when she'd fought against her captors. There had been something wild, something primitive about her. She had stirred feelings in him. Feelings he couldn't quite fathom.

He had a sudden urge to see if she was all right. Taking up his rifle, he strode out the door. Just one last visit, he assured himself, to make certain that she was comfortably settled in. And then he'd be able to put her out of his mind.

Caroline added another log to the fire and turned around to admire the cabin. The colorful rag rug in front of the fire softened the dark wooden planks of the floor. The fresh white curtains at the windows made the rough dwelling look like home.

With the door to the schoolroom open, she could appreciate the gleam of wood, the perfect symmetry of the students' chairs arranged in neat rows with her table at the front of the room.

Her muscles were beginning to protest the hours of scrubbing and cleaning. But though she was tired, it was a pleasant sort of feeling. She had accomplished so much this day. She had met the women and children of the town; she had made friends. And though she tried to deny it, it had been especially interesting to meet Thad Conway's family. Some of the things revealed had only reinforced her original impressions of him as a dark and dangerous gunman.

Knowing that, why was she so fascinated by him?

She shook her head as if to put aside any more foolish thoughts. She would not waste her time thinking about a local gunman. Tomorrow, at Sunday services, she would have a second chance to present herself to the people of Hope. This time she intended to make a better impression.

Tonight she needed more than a quick wash in a bucket of water. The thought of the clean, sparkling river that ran behind her cabin had her smiling.

She carefully set her spectacles on the table beside her bed and let down her hair. Catching up her simple white nightshift, she closed the door to the cabin and made her way to the river.

Quickly shedding her clothes, she scrubbed them and hung them on low branches to dry. Then, picking up the gob of sticky, homemade soap, she waded into the water.

Thad brought his horse to a halt at the top of the ridge and stared down at the little cabin. Smoke wafted from the chimney, and the light of the fire could be seen through the curtained windows.

Though he knew it was a flimsy excuse, he'd brought along the last of Rosita's spicy tortillas for Caroline's supper.

As he spurred his horse forward, he heard a sound and turned toward the river. At the sight of a shadowy figure, his hand went to his gun and he slipped silently from the saddle. With his horse trailing, he made his way on foot through the underbrush.

When he drew close enough to make out the figure he realized his mistake. It was Caroline. As he'd never imagined he'd see her.

He knew he ought to leave. But just as quickly as the thought came, he discarded it. There was no way he could walk away from this scene. Leaning a hip against the trunk of a tree, he watched through narrowed gaze.

After the heat of the day and the exertion of cleaning the cabin, the cool water felt heavenly against Caroline's naked flesh. Sitting in the shallows, she began to rub the soap across the bottoms of her feet, smiling at the simple pleasure. Lifting first one leg, then the other, she soaped them, then kicked them in the water, watching the suds float away. She ran the soap across the flat planes of her stomach, then across her breasts and upward over her throat. Rubbing her hands together until they were soapy, she washed her face, then splashed water upward until the soap was rinsed away.

With a little laugh she got to her feet and began wading into the water. Her rounded bottom swayed slowly as she took careful, tentative steps. The gentle waves surged against her with every move she made. Gradually the water reached her waist, then her shoulders. Lathering her hair, she ducked under the waves and rubbed her scalp until all the soap had disappeared. She came up sputtering, then began to swim in slow, lazy circles. Every so often she would dip below the water, then come up for air. Each time a deep, throaty chuckle would break from her lips.

Even in her childhood she'd never felt so carefree. It was the most glorious feeling in the world.

* * *

When Thad had first come upon Caroline in the water, he'd thought only to enjoy the view. But the longer he stayed, the more aroused he became.

This wasn't the prim, proper schoolteacher she wanted everyone to believe she was. Nor was she the tough, shrewd woman who had caught her attackers unaware and had fought them with astonishing skill.

At this moment, believing she was alone, she was as graceful as a colt, as frisky as a kitten. And she was more beautiful than any woman he had ever known.

He had an unreasonable desire to stride through the water and carry her to shore, where he would make her his own. Instead, he clenched his hands into fists at his sides and continued to stand as motionless as a statue.

As she started walking from the water he allowed himself one final glimpse. He had already concluded that there was no graceful way to let her know of his presence. The wise choice would be to remain hidden from view until she was safely back in her cabin. Then he would return home without bothering to let her know he'd come calling.

The scheme might have worked. But, just as she reached the shallows, his horse whinneyed.

Caroline froze in her tracks. As the reality of her situation dawned, her clothes were forgotten, as was her modesty. All she could think of was making it to the safety of her cabin.

As she raced past the thicket, a man's figure separated itself from the shadows. A scream of pure terror escaped her lips. And Caroline found herself face-to-face with The Texan.

Chapter Six

For Caroline, time was suspended. She rocked back on her heels. Then fear gave way to rage. A rage that exploded through her with all the fury of a thunderstorm.

"You evil, wicked man! Knowing that I am alone and unprotected, you dared to invade my privacy?" With a cry she advanced on him, her fists raised as if to strike. Then she suddenly realized that she was completely naked. With a shriek she turned back and snatched up her nightshift, holding it in front of her like a shield.

Cursing his bad luck, Thad crossed his arms over his chest and leaned against the tree. The best way to handle this, he figured, was with humor.

"I think you'd better put that on, ma'am, before you catch your death in this night air."

Caroline wanted to strangle him. Using her most commanding voice she hissed, "You will turn away and give me some privacy."

Thad choked back a laugh as he complied. "I think it's a bit late for that, ma'am."

She glowered at his back, daring him to turn around.

As she struggled to fit her wet arms through the sleeves of the gown, she nearly turned the air blue with rich, ripe curses. The kind of curses Thad only heard in saloons.

Stunned, he swiveled to face her. She was just smoothing the fabric over her damp hips. As the hem of her gown drifted to her ankles, he caught his breath. With her dark hair cascading over one shoulder and a sheer white gown plastered to her skin, revealing every line and curve of her lush body, she looked like an angel who had just fallen to earth. But when she opened her mouth and swore again, he quickly changed his mind. The vision before him was no angel.

"I wonder if the good people of Hope would like to hear such words coming out of the mouth of their new schoolmarm."

For a moment she was speechless. Then she attacked again. "And I suppose you'd be just the one to tell them, wouldn't you?" In a huff she scooped up her damp clothes and held them in front of her. "Will you also tell them how you hid yourself in the bushes and watched me while I bathed? Will you admit to everyone that you are no better than a low-life, slimy slug, crawling through the brush on your belly like a snake to take advantage of a helpless woman?"

Wherever had she learned such words? "The whole town already knows I'm all those things you just called me. But you? Helpless?" He laughed and took a step closer.

In the moonlight she could see the glint in his eyes. Was he still laughing at her? she wondered. Or had she now goaded him to anger? He stood, feet apart, gun belt low on his hips, reminding her once more of his fierce reputation.

"Woman, you're about as helpless as an enraged she-bear. On second thought," he added, his voice dripping sarcasm, "a bear would have been more exciting to watch." He saw her eyes narrow and realized that he'd touched a nerve. "At least bears catch fish while they splash around in the river. All you're going to catch is a chill."

"And whose fault is that?" She refused to back down or to back up a single step. She would not allow him to get the better of her. "If it weren't for you, I would already be back inside my warm cabin, preparing for bed."

Her words caused strange things to happen to his insides. The thought of her preparing for bed created an image in his mind that had him growing warmer by the minute. He kept his words deliberately curt. "Don't let me stop you."

In the heat of anger she jabbed a finger into his chest. "A gentleman would step aside for a lady."

"I never pretended to be a gentleman." His fingers closed around her wrist. "And from that display of temper, Miss Caroline Adams, you have no right to call yourself a lady."

Those words were the ultimate insult. But when his hand closed over hers, her heart skipped a beat. Panic clogged her throat. She'd forgotten how strong he was.

She began to berate herself. Once again she'd allowed her temper to get the better of her. The litany of Harvey Hattinger's rules swam through her mind, taunting her.

"I—" she swallowed "—was taken by surprise." She licked her dry lips and saw the way he watched her. Her uneasiness grew. "I don't know what came over me. I don't usually react in such a manner."

Thad was clearly puzzled. Was this docile creature the same one who, only moments ago, had used language that would make a horse soldier blush? Now what game was she playing?

His voice lowered dangerously. "What's going on here? Who are you, Caroline Adams? You sure as hell don't belong in a town like Hope."

She stared pointedly at his fingers, which were locked around her wrist. "Let me go."

"When I get some answers."

"I've already told you all I intend to. Now let me..."

Lifting a hand to her shoulder, he drew her fractionally closer. Drops of water still clung to her dark lashes and he had an almost overpowering urge to touch his lips to them. Instead he muttered, "Woman, there's something about you that just seems to bring out an ornery streak in me."

She held herself stiffly, fighting the feelings that rippled through her at his touch. They were standing so close she could feel the heat of his body through her thin gown. It warmed her even while it frightened her.

In the moonlight her dark, waist-length hair was a counterpoint to skin as pale as the sun-bleached rocks of the desert. The opaque gown did nothing to hide the lush body beneath. The little pulse that throbbed at her temple enticed him. Without thinking he pressed his lips to the spot.

A kick by a mule would have been less shocking. The moment his lips touched her skin, his hands closed over her shoulders, dragging her roughly against him.

He moved his lips from her temple to her cheek, and then to her ear. Soft. He would never forget how soft her skin was. Once before he'd dared to touch it; she was even softer than he'd remembered.

Caroline stood perfectly still, struggling to hide the conflicting feelings that raged through her. She hadn't wanted this. But now that he was holding her, kissing her, she couldn't deny the pure pleasure of it.

His lips traced her jaw, then moved slowly upward until they found her mouth. But even then he held back, outlining her lips with his tongue.

She forgot to breathe. Her heart forgot to beat as his tongue made a slow journey around her full lower lip.

For the space of a heartbeat he paused, and she thought she would die waiting, waiting for his mouth to cover hers. The kiss, when it came, was the merest brushing of lips against lips.

Without realizing it, Caroline curled her hands into his rough shirt, drawing him closer. He heard her little sigh of pleasure. And then, unable to deny himself any longer, he took the kiss deeper. His mouth covered hers in a savage kiss and his hands left her shoulders to roam her back, pulling her firmly against the length of him.

A hint of evergreen fragrance clung to her shift. Her hair was scented with bayberry soap. As his mouth moved over hers he savored the fresh, clean taste of her.

The moon hid behind a bank of clouds, leaving them in shadow. As he changed the angle of the kiss, Caroline's lids flickered open and she caught sight of him. Dark as night. Mysterious. He was not a man to be trusted. And then, as his mouth worked its magic on her, she forgot everything except the pleasure.

The kiss was rough. As rough as the man. And almost bruising in its intensity. His work-roughened fingers were strong and sure as they moved along her back, igniting fires wherever they touched. His mouth was tempting, his kiss practiced. He tasted as dark and mysterious as he looked.

She was a fool to allow this to happen. But the truth was, she was helpless to stop it. All she could do was endure. But a nagging little thought came unbidden to her mind. She was not enduring; she was enjoying. His touch, his kiss, brought pleasure beyond belief. Pleasure she had studiously avoided until this man had stormed into her life.

This wasn't what Thad had planned. In fact, he'd intended to keep his distance, to make absolutely certain that he didn't touch her. But now that he had, there was no turning back.

He didn't know how to be gentle. He was all rough edges and tough talking. Now that she was in his arms, he found himself wanting to be soft and easy with her. But his needs had taken over. Needs that had him holding her even tighter, and kissing her harder, until he ached to take her here, now.

She shivered and he was instantly aware of the fact that she was wet and cold. And he was going to be responsible for her death if he didn't get her back to her warm cabin immediately.

What the hell had he been thinking of? The fact was, he hadn't thought at all. He'd merely reacted to this damnably enticing female.

He lifted his head and took a step back, breaking contact.

Caroline trembled and opened her eyes.

"You'd better get back."

At his abrupt words she nodded, but her mind was still befuddled. She stood very still, staring at him. The touch of him lingered on her flesh; the taste of him on her lips.

He saw her shiver again and mistook it for cold.

"Go on home now." His words were gruff.

He stepped aside and she began to walk toward the cabin, praying her legs wouldn't fail her. When she reached the door she turned. He was leading his horse and following at a much slower pace.

When he reached the cabin he removed the linen-wrapped food from his saddlebag. "I thought you might need something for supper."

He thrust the dish into her hands and turned away. Before she could say a word he pulled himself into the saddle.

As his horse started away he called over his shoulder, "Be sure you lock your door, schoolteacher. And from now on, take your bath in the privacy of your cabin."

His hands, holding the reins, were shaking. He swore savagely, then urged his horse into a run.

The day was glorious. The sun was a bright yellow globe in a cloudless sky. Mile after mile of tall grass, dotted here and there with acres of bluebells, waved in the balmy breeze.

As the horse-drawn rig rolled along toward town, Caroline caught glimpses of houses and outbuildings on distant bluffs. Where she came from, the houses had been built so close together they were practically touching. Only the very wealthy had lived in big houses with yards and fences and outbuildings to store their carriages.

Flicking the reins, she turned the horse and rig down the single dusty road through town. She passed swarms of families, all dressed in their finest and all heading toward the church at the end of town.

As she approached the church, she recognized Jessie Matthews and her three children in their wagon.

Jessie waved, and Caroline pulled up alongside them.

"Good morning, Caroline. I'd like you to meet my husband, Cole. Cole, this is the new schoolteacher, Caroline Adams."

Caroline nodded to the darkly handsome man seated beside Jessie.

He touched a hand to his hat and called a greeting before stepping down from the wagon and helping Jessie and little Lisbeth to the ground. Then he came around and offered a hand to Caroline.

"Thank you." She stepped down and waited as he hitched her horse beside his.

She heard the children call out loudly and turned in time to see Dan Conway assisting Morning Light from their carriage. Behind her followed the children, Runs With The Wind, Danny and Kate.

"Well, Miss Adams, I'm glad to see you stayed around to give our town another chance," Dan said, tipping his hat respectfully. "After the sort of welcome you received when you first arrived, I was afraid you might take the first stage out of here."

"It will take more than a few gunmen and a runaway stage to send me packing, Dr. Conway."

"That's very good news for Hope, ma'am."

As they started up the steps of the church, Jessie said, "I'm afraid there are so many of us, we fill an entire pew. But if you'd like to join us, Caroline, I'm sure there's room for one more."

"Why, thank you. That's very kind." Trailing behind them, Caroline noticed the heads turning to catch a glimpse of the new teacher. When Dan and Morning Light and their children filed into the pew, she joined them, and was followed by Jessie and Cole and their children.

During the services, Caroline realized just how kind these people were to include her. It would have been awkward to sit alone, knowing that everyone was watching her. Enveloped in the bosom of this big, comfortable family, she felt completely at ease.

The preacher had a rich, resonant voice, which he used to his advantage as he spoke about the healing power of love. In a softer voice he denounced those things that led good people astray. He spoke about the saloon, where many a drunken cowboy found himself at the wrong end of a gun after too much to drink. And he spoke of the evils of games of chance, where even respectable ranchers lost more than they could afford to repay. And in a tone that sounded more like a loving father than a preacher burning with righteous indignation, he urged everyone to look into their hearts and admit their own weaknesses so that they could return once more to the healing power of love.

The children sighed and shifted on the hard benches. Men coughed. Women fanned themselves with their handkerchiefs, many of them nodding vigorously with each pronouncement from the pulpit.

Caroline slid her spectacles back up to the bridge of her nose and stared straight ahead. Her hands were folded primly in her lap. She decided she liked this preacher and his message of love. He reminded her of another kind man, who had taken a lonely, frightened little girl and turned her life around.

She glanced down, smoothing her skirts. She was glad she'd chosen the dove gray gown that buttoned clear to her throat, with a crisp white collar and white cuffs on the long, slim sleeves. She had coiled her hair into a severe knot until not even a single strand could slip free. Over that she had pinned an ugly gray bonnet with no ornamentation except a crisp white ribbon.

Her feet, encased in sturdy, serviceable boots, were hot and sticky. She thought about how wonderful the cool water of the river had felt the night before, and suddenly her cheeks turned bright pink as she was reminded again of the scene with Thad Conway. Knowing she was blushing only made it worse. She could feel the heat burn her face as she struggled to put his image out of her mind.

Last night, after he'd left her so abruptly, sleep had been impossible. Instead she'd tossed and turned, fighting the feelings that still heated her blood and caused her pulse to leap.

Suddenly the congregation was standing and opening their songbooks. Caroline was grateful to hide behind the pages as the voices around her swelled in song.

When they filed from the church, Caroline saw Cora Meadows standing beside the young preacher. With a sinking heart Caroline realized what the woman had in mind.

"There you are!" Cora called. "Caroline Adams, meet Reverend Symes. Reverend, this is the new schoolteacher I've been telling you about."

Caroline's hand was encased in a warm, firm handshake. Reverend Symes was thin, almost frail, with a high, narrow forehead and sad, hound dog eyes. But when he smiled, she caught a glimpse of the warmth and humor that lurked inside the man.

"Miss Adams." His glance took in the prim gown and bonnet. "I read your qualifications and was pleased that you would travel all this way to impart your considerable knowledge to the children of Hope."

Caroline flushed, avoiding his eyes. When she glanced at Cora, she saw the woman smile in triumph. Her matchmaking chores completed for the moment, Cora caught up with Belva Spears, who was walking alone.

"When will your duties begin?" the preacher asked.

"Tomorrow."

"So soon?" He glanced around, speaking to those who crowded around. "This is certainly our good fortune, to have a teacher who is actually eager to begin."

They chatted politely among themselves, and several of the families approached, waiting patiently as the preacher introduced each of them to Caroline. It was obvious as she smiled at the children and went out of her way to put them at ease that she thoroughly enjoyed their company.

After the crowd thinned and Reverend Symes went back inside the church, Caroline made her way to her rig. As she approached it, Jessie called, "Caroline, how would you like to come out to our ranch this afternoon and join us for Sunday supper?"

"Thank you. I'd like that very much."

"Fine. Cole and the children will come by for you later in the wagon."

"I don't want you to go to so much trouble. Just give me directions and I'll bring myself."

As Jessie began explaining where their ranch was, she suddenly paused. "Will you look at that."

Following the direction of her gaze, Caroline saw Thad stepping out of the mercantile. On his shoulder was a heavy sack, which he deposited into the back of a wagon.

"In town on a Sunday morning and can't even come to services," Jessie complained.

At her call he looked up. A slow smile spread across his face. At his sister's beckoning, he strolled lazily toward their wagons. He kissed Jessie's cheek, then tipped his hat to Caroline.

"'Morning, Miss Adams." His eyes danced with teasing laughter. "Seen any slimy, slithery creatures lately?"

Caroline felt her cheeks grow hot and forced a thin smile to her lips.

"You should have been at Sunday services, Uncle Thad," Lisbeth scolded him.

"Well, you see, Little Bit," he said teasingly, "I couldn't stand to see anything bad happen to you."

"I don't understand."

He tugged one of her long ringlets. "I knew if I went inside that church, a bolt of lightning would fall from the sky and the building would cave in on all of you. So you see, I saved your life by skipping the service."

She giggled despite her mother's frown.

"You're setting a fine example for my children," Jessie said tartly. Suddenly, Jessie's frowning lips curved into a bright smile as a new thought struck. "You never come to Sunday supper, Thad. Why don't you come today?"

"Sunday supper?" He began to shake his head. "You know I don't have time for—"

"But you promised to take me hunting someday, and someday never comes," young Jack said accusingly. "Why can't you do it today?"

Thad grinned at his oldest nephew. "You're right, Jack. Why not today?"

"That's wonderful." Jessie shot him a triumphant smile. "Since you live the closest to the schoolhouse, why don't you pick up Miss Adams?"

Caroline realized she was trapped. As was Thad.

Her eyes widened as she turned to him, praying that he would excuse himself from that chore. Surely a man as glib with words as Thad Conway could come up with a plausible excuse.

Instead, after seeing her stricken look, he gave her an infuriating grin and said, "Why, I'd be happy to pick up our schoolmarm." Catching her around the waist, he swung her up to the seat of her rig, allowing his hands to linger a moment before saying, "I'll be by in a couple of hours, ma'am.'' He handed her the reins, then sauntered away.

Amid much calling and waving, Jessie and Cole and their children rode away in their wagon.

Minutes later, as Caroline passed the mercantile, Thad stepped through the doorway with another heavy sack on his shoulder. With a wicked grin he gave an exaggerated tip of his hat before depositing the sack in the back of his wagon.

Caroline tossed her head and drove by without a word.

Chapter Seven

Thad reined in his stallion at the top of a rise and stared down at Caroline's small cabin. Smoke plumed from the chimney. Gauzy white curtains billowed at the windows. The fragrance of freshly baked biscuits wafted on the breeze.

From the corner of his eye he caught the flutter of movement and turned his head. Caroline was walking across the meadow, gathering wildflowers. Her arms were overflowing with them, and still she stopped, admired and picked more.

Knowing she hadn't yet spotted him, he remained where he was, enjoying the view.

She still had on the shapeless gown she had worn to church that morning. The skirt billowed and flattened with each gust of wind, clearly outlining her hips and legs as she walked. She stooped, picking a handful of bluebells, before moving on.

He waited, unaware that a smile of pure appreciation touched his lips.

Suddenly she caught sight of him and stopped in her tracks. He nudged the horse into a walk until he was beside her. Up close he caught his breath at the sight of her. Little strands of dark hair had pried loose from the prim knot and danced around her cheeks. Cheeks as pink as some of the flowers in her arms. Her eyes, reflecting the sun, seemed more amber than green. Her lips were pursed in a little moue of surprise.

"For the schoolroom?" he asked.

She glanced at the flowers, then back at him. "For your sister. I couldn't accept her hospitality empty-handed."

"Let me help you." He surprised himself by sliding from the saddle and holding out his arms.

After a moment's hesitation, she handed him the flowers that were overflowing her grasp. As their fingers brushed she felt the heat. If he felt it, as well, he kept his reaction carefully hidden.

Thad walked down the hill beside her, one hand balancing the delicate bouquet, the other holding the reins of his mount. When they reached the cabin she stopped, then burst into peals of laughter.

"What brought that on?"

She laughed harder. Catching her breath she said, "You. I wonder what the townspeople would say if they could see their dangerous Texan with an armload of flowers."

"Let's just keep this our little secret then," he said with a smile.

He followed her inside, then stopped to glance around admiringly. In two short days she had made this rough cabin into a home.

She set her flowers on the table, then turned and took the rest from him.

"I suppose I could keep it a secret. As long as you don't repeat the awful words you heard me say last night."

His smile grew. "Ma'am, I wouldn't dare repeat them. Who'd ever believe that the proper Miss Adams would even know such words, let alone say them? Why, they'd probably run me out of town for spreading ugly rumors."

He watched the way she turned away, busying herself bundling the flowers. But he caught the flush of color on her cheeks.

"Something smells mighty fine." He tactfully changed the subject.

"I baked sour-milk biscuits." He saw the color deepen on her cheeks as she turned to face him. "Actually, I hadn't planned on it, but the jug of milk that Jessie brought me turned sour overnight, so I had to put it to use."

"Isn't there a root cellar under the cabin?"

Caroline seemed puzzled. "I don't know. I never checked."

Following Thad outside, she watched as he began to walk the perimeter of the cabin. Halfway around he stopped and kicked at the dirt. A minute later he lifted a half-buried wooden door and led her down three steps into a cool, dark cellar beneath the cabin.

She breathed in the rich, dank smell of moist earth.

"You can store milk and smoked meats down here, as well as summer fruits and vegetables. But you'll need a lantern," he cautioned. "And I'll fix a latch for that door so it won't blow shut while you're down here."

She shuddered at the thought of being trapped beneath her cabin, then quickly shrugged away the fear at the realization that this cellar would add to her independence. In no time she could have it stocked with food. Enough food to sustain her during lean times. In her life there had been too many lean times.

He wiped his hands on his pants before helping her up the few steps of the cellar. Though each of them felt the jolt at his simple touch, they both turned away quickly.

While Thad replaced the door, he called over his shoulder, "Ready to go to Jessie's?"

"I'll just get my things."

"I'll leave my horse here at the cabin and hitch yours to the rig."

She hurried inside, where she wrapped her biscuits in a linen towel and picked up the bouquet of flowers. When she stepped outside, Thad drove the horse and rig around to the door and helped her up beside him.

About a mile from her cabin he pointed to a cluster of buildings in the distance. "There's my ranch. The bigger buildings are the barns and horse stalls. The smallest building is the ranch house."

Caroline noted the hills dotted here and there with horses. All of them had the look of care about them, their coats lustrous and shiny and their coloring rich.

"Do you raise any cattle?"

He shook his head. "Horses. Someday I'll have the best bloodline in the state."

She heard the note of pride in his voice and had no doubt that one day he'd have what he wanted. If he wasn't shot down in a gunfight first.

"Looks like a good day to go hunting," he remarked as they rolled across the meadow.

"What will you and Jack hunt?"

"Deer maybe. Or turkeys or pigs. The boy's good with a rifle," he added proudly.

"And that makes you happy?" She tried to keep the edge of anger from her tone, but it crept in. "Do you want him to grow up to be like you, with a reputation for a fast gun?"

"There are worse things." He squinted into the sun.

"Like what?"

"Like being dead at the end of someone else's gun. Or how about being a fool, a coward or a liar?"

At his words she flinched and looked away. In a trembling voice she said, "Wouldn't you rather be known as a man of peace, a man of honor?"

"A man of peace." He bit off the words with venom. "Ezra Spears was a man of peace. Look what it got him. An early grave."

She turned to face him. "But..."

"And as for a man of honor..." He turned a level gaze on her and she could feel his struggle to contain his anger. "I live by my own code. But I tell you this—my word is my bond. As long as the people of this town don't bother me or mine, I'll do the same."

"And you think that's enough?" Her own temper flared. "Why should the good people of Hope ignore a gunman in their midst?"

His tone was low, his words precise. "One day you'll learn that there's a big difference between a gunman and a man who's good with a gun."

"And which are you?"

He shrugged. "I guess you'll have to figure that out for yourself, Teacher."

They rode for several miles in strained silence. Then, as the rig rolled across lush green fields, Thad pointed to a sprawling house and a series of sturdy outbuildings in the distance. "There's Jessie's ranch."

Caroline lifted a hand to shield the sun from her eyes. "It's so big."

"Cole's one of the most successful ranchers in these parts."

They passed a series of fenced pastures, where sleek cattle grazed, and continued on until they pulled up in front of the house. A low, wide veranda ran the length of the front of the house. On the veranda were several well-worn rockers, plumped with colorful cushions.

Thad handed the reins to a grinning youth who shouted a welcome.

"Learned how to toss that lasso yet, Illinois?"

The boy shook his head. "I'm still practicing."

"Better master it before roundup time." Thad jumped down, then offered his hand to Caroline. "Illinois, this is the new teacher, Miss Caroline Adams. Caroline, this is Tommy Wilkins."

"Miss Adams." The boy touched a hand to a wide hat that sheltered his freckled nose from the sun.

"Will you be coming to school, Tommy?"

He seemed startled by her question. "No, ma'am. I'm too old for school."

"How old are you?"

"Fifteen," he said proudly. "Been earning my own keep since I was twelve."

She felt a sudden kinship with the youth. "Can you read and write and do sums?"

"Yes, ma'am. My ma taught me before she passed on."

"That's fine, Tommy. It was nice meeting you. I hope I'll see you again."

At her smile the boy blushed clear to his toes before taking the reins and leading the horse and rig to the barn.

"Why do you call him Illinois?" Caroline asked, following Thad up the broad steps to the veranda.

Thad shrugged. "It seems like everybody who comes to Texas these days is from someplace else."

Caroline turned to him with a sudden smile. "You mean that's why they call you The Texan? Because you were born here?"

"One of the few." He gave her his famous smile, and she found herself wondering how many women had fallen under the spell of that smile. "Come on, Boston, let's see what Jessie's planning for supper."

The house was as warm and inviting as the welcoming veranda had suggested. The rooms were big and airy, with high ceilings supported by thick wooden beams. The rooms seemed to flow one into the other, with a large front parlor for company, a rear family parlor and a huge kitchen and dining room.

Pulling off her apron and smoothing her skirts, Jessie hurried forward to greet her brother and Caroline.

"Flowers? Oh, Caroline, how nice." Jessie lifted the bouquet to her face to inhale the perfume, then sent Lisbeth and her cousin Kate scurrying away to find vases.

"And sour-milk biscuits," Caroline added, feeling suddenly shy.

"I'll set them on the stove so they stay hot." Jessie took them from her guest's hands. "Morning Light and I are just finishing up in the kitchen if you'd like to join us."

"Where's Cole?" Thad asked.

"Out in the barn with the boys. He figured he'd manage to get a lot of work out of Jack today before you got here."

As Thad swung through the door, Jessie added in a low voice, "Jack would do a hundred chores today just for the chance to go hunting with his idol."

"Aren't you concerned that he might learn to like guns a little too much?"

Jessie gave her a gentle smile. "Yes, that worries me. But don't believe all the things you hear about my brother, Caroline. There are so many rumors about him, it's hard to tell fact from fiction."

Though the words were spoken softly, Caroline had the distinct impression that she had just been quietly rebuked.

Morning Light looked up from the table where she was rolling out a thin layer of pastry. Sprinkling it with honey and chopped pecans, she sealed the edges and placed it in the oven to bake. Soon the kitchen was filled with the wonderful aroma of sweets.

"What can I do to help?" Caroline asked.

"There's china in a cabinet in the dining room. The girls can help you set the table."

Followed by a giggling Lisbeth and Kate, Caroline made her way to the dining room, where a table big enough to hold at least twenty people dominated the room. Against one wall was a huge cabinet and hutch. As she unloaded the china, Caroline ran her hand along the smooth wood of the cabinet. Though it had been handcrafted, it was a beautiful piece of furniture.

"Did your father make this?" she asked Lisbeth.

"No, ma'am. My Uncle Thad."

Seeing Caroline's look of surprise, she said proudly, "Uncle Thad made the table, too, and all the chairs. He told Mama it was the least he could do for her after all she'd done for him through the years."

"And what did she do?" Caroline moved around the table, setting down plates and cups. They were a perfect set, she noted. And not one of them chipped.

"Mama raised Uncle Thad after their mama died."

"How old was he when that happened?"

"Three weeks" came Jessie's voice from the doorway. She wiped her hands on a towel. "Ma never rallied after giving birth."

Caroline was thunderstruck. A three-week-old baby. No wonder Jessie was so defensive of Thad's reputation. She was as much mother as sister to him. Caroline ducked her head and continued setting the table.

"These are beautiful dishes," she remarked.

"They belonged to Cole's mother. When he brought me here to his ranch, I thought I'd just died and gone to heaven. My brothers and I had grown up in a little sod shack smaller than the henhouse out back."

"Your brothers must have loved it, too." Caroline lifted fine silver from a wooden chest and parceled it out to the two little girls, who eagerly began placing knives, forks and spoons beside each plate.

"Dan never got a chance to spend much time here. He headed east that same summer to begin his studies. And as for Thad, he spent nearly all his time down at the barns with the horses. Or chasing across the fields after mustangs. From the time he was born, he seemed a whole lot more comfortable with animals than with people. He's a loner like my father," Jessie said softly. "I guess that's why he keeps his distance from the folks in town. He doesn't dislike them. He's just more comfortable with his own company."

When the table was set, Caroline followed Jessie to the kitchen, where Morning Light had just arranged several glasses of buttermilk on a tray.

"It will be another hour or two before the food is ready and the men return from their hunt." Jessie took the tray from her sister-in-law's hands and led the way to the front veranda. "Let's just sit a spell and enjoy the quiet."

Morning Light laughed softly as they settled themselves in the rockers. "When our men return, there won't be another minute of peace."

"Tell me, Caroline," Jessie asked conversationally, "did you find it difficult leaving a big city for a small town like Hope?"

"Not at all." Caroline glanced out at the vast expanse of rolling hills, empty except for an occasional knot of cattle. "I was eager to come here."

"Did your family not try to persuade you to stay with them?" Morning Light studied the young woman, who seemed uncomfortable discussing herself.

Caroline's hand tightened perceptibly on the glass and she took a moment to drink. "I have no family. My mother . . . my folks are dead."

"Have you no brothers or sisters?" Jessie asked with concern.

"No. There was only me."

"It must have been difficult, severing all ties with the past, disposing of all your belongings before beginning a journey of such a great distance."

Caroline merely nodded her head, then sipped again.

Morning Light, with her gift of sensitivity, studied the young woman a moment before tactfully changing the subject. "Are you comfortable in the schoolhouse?"

"Oh, yes." Caroline's smile returned to light her eyes. "It's a lovely little cabin. I already feel as if I've come home."

"But it's so small," Jessie countered. "And so far from everyone."

"Maybe that's why I like it." The moment the words were out of her mouth, Caroline regretted them. To cover up, she said quickly, "In a big city, you never have any privacy."

"Did I hear someone mention a big city?" Cole Matthews poked his head around the corner, followed by six-year-old Frank and Dan Conway and his son, Danny.

Jessie looked up, surprised, then hurried across the room to press a kiss to her husband's cheek. "I thought you went hunting with Thad and Jack."

"We've been out in the barn," Dan explained. "Runs With The Wind was the only one who wanted to go along for the hunt. They've been gone a couple of hours now. They should be back soon. Jack said even a chance for a ten-point buck wouldn't cause him to miss one of his mama's special Sunday suppers."

At the sound of horses' hooves thundering toward the house, they all looked up expectantly, then gathered at the top of the steps. Young Jack led the horsemen. Over his saddle hung the carcass of a deer. The ear-to-ear grin told the story.

Before anyone could ask a single question, he slid from the saddle and rushed up the steps, followed by Runs With The Wind. Both boys began talking so fast, half the words were lost. But everyone understood that Jack had brought down the buck with a single shot.

Caroline noted that Thad stayed in the saddle, allowing the boys their moment of glory.

"Runs With The Wind spotted him," Jack said. "But he told me it should be my kill. Uncle Thad gave me his rifle and let me shoot first. And I brought him down, Pa. With one shot."

Cole clamped a hand on his son's shoulder. "Good job, Jack. Why don't you let Illinois take him to the barn. When supper's over, you and your uncle can skin him and portion out the meat."

The boy turned to where Thad still sat quietly on his mount. "Will you help me skin it, Uncle Thad?"

"Sure will." Thad gave him a slow smile. "And after this first time, you won't be needing my help anymore."

A short time later, their hands and faces washed, their hair slicked back, the men and boys trooped to the table, where the women and girls were waiting.

The meal was a festive affair, with everyone laughing and talking.

"Next Sunday," Cole announced solemnly as he carved a whole roasted pig, "it'll be smoked venison, supplied by Jack."

The boy beamed and gazed adoringly at the uncle who had given him such a special gift this day.

Caroline glanced around at the happy, noisy band of dissimilar people who had somehow forged a bond of love. Family. She felt her throat constrict painfully.

Dan turned his attention to the new schoolteacher. "You and I have something in common, Miss Adams."

"Oh?" She paused in the act of lifting the cup of coffee to her lips. "What is that?" she asked eagerly.

"Sheriff Horn told me that you studied at Miss Tully's School for Ladies in Boston."

For a moment her eyes went wide before she slowly nodded her head.

"I took my medical studies in Boston at Harvard." Dan's voice lowered. "I must admit that I never quite fit into the big city, though I did meet a lot of good people. We may have some mutual friends."

Caroline's hand jerked violently. She felt the coffee spill over the rim and set the cup down with a clatter. "Oh dear," she moaned, "now look what I've done."

"No harm. Leave it," Jessie said absently. "Wouldn't it be nice if you and Dan discover that you know the same people? You'll have to get together later and compare names."

"Yes. That . . . would be nice." Caroline made a great show of dabbing at the spilled coffee with her napkin.

Across the table, Thad noted the stricken look in her eyes. The color had drained from her cheeks. His eyes narrowed in thought. Something had caused the schoolmarm to become extremely uncomfortable.

Secrets. The mysterious Caroline Adams was brimming with them. And he had a sudden urge to uncover them. All of them.

The day had suddenly taken on an even greater glow. There was nothing Thad Conway enjoyed more than a challenge.

Chapter Eight

Caroline moved the food around her plate and struggled to swallow. The lovely afternoon had suddenly lost its festive feeling. The wonderful food tasted like ashes in her mouth. She was a fraud and a liar. And sooner or later, through some foolish mistake on her part, she would be unmasked.

What had Thad said on the ride here? He'd rather be called a gunman than a fool or a liar. She was both. But there was nothing to be done about it. She had no choices left now. She must live with the lie.

The dinner seemed to drag on forever. She should have been enjoying herself. The children were polite, even though it was obvious that they were eager to be excused so they could admire Jack's trophy hanging in the barn.

The men were relaxed, having eaten their fill. The women, having been duly praised for their efforts, began to gather up the dishes.

Caroline was grateful for the chance to help. She sprang to her feet and moved around the table, stacking plates.

The conversation was easy, pleasant. Young Jack, in a burst of exuberance, said, "Ma, I found out why Uncle Thad took so long to get home from Mexico. He said he had to spend a couple of nights in jail.''

At the ripple of shock that seemed to pulse around the table, the boy added defensively, ''But he didn't do anything wrong. It wasn't his fault.''

''It never is.'' Jessie shot her brother a look but said nothing more.

Thad was aware of Caroline standing just beside his chair, about to reach for his plate. He felt her hesitate; sensed her accusing stare.

Instead of defending himself, Thad merely scraped back his chair and said with a grin, ''Let's get at that deer, partner. I'd like to be on my way before dark.''

He pushed past her without a word.

Caroline watched as the others followed suit, leaving the three women to clear the table.

Silence hung over the room for a few minutes as Jessie removed a kettle of water from the fireplace. Striding to the kitchen, she filled a pan with hot water and began to wash the dishes. While Morning Light returned to clear the table, Caroline picked up a linen towel and began to dry.

''Poor Jack,'' Jessie said with a sigh. ''He's in such a hurry to grow to manhood and experience all the adventures he's dreaming of. And the man he most admires is my brother.''

''Jack seems like a son you can be proud of.''

''I am proud of him.'' Jessie handed her a wet plate and reached for another stack of dirty dishes. ''But he's impatient with childhood. Like Thad,'' she said, more to herself than to Caroline. Then, looking up, she added, ''I guess that was my fault. Thad never had time to be a little boy. He was only seven when I took him and Dan clear across Texas to Abilene, Kansas.''

"But that's—" Caroline mentally calculated the map she had memorized "—hundreds of miles from here. Did you travel by stagecoach?"

"Horseback," Jessie said softly. "All the way there and back."

"With a seven-year-old? You must have had an awfully good reason for taking on something that tough."

Jessie's eyes took on a faraway look. "The best reason in the world." She suddenly cleared her throat. "That's where I met Cole."

"In Abilene?"

"Along the trail." Jessie laughed, and whatever lingering sadness she'd felt was brushed aside. "He sure had his hands full with me and two little brothers. We gave him all kinds of trouble."

"From the looks of the two of you, I'd say it was worth it."

"Oh, it was worth it."

Jessie dried her hands on her apron and walked to the back door, where she tossed the contents of the dishpan on a single, scraggly rosebush. For a moment she examined the stem, noting the beginnings of leaves and branches. Satisfied, she returned to the kitchen and removed her apron.

Beckoning to her sister-in-law, who had just entered carrying the soiled tablecloth and napkins, Jessie called, "Come on, Morning Light. Let's take Caroline to the barn and see what our men are up to."

The three women crossed a wide expanse of ground where chickens squawked and vied for the grain that had been freshly scattered.

The barn was a huge cavern, rich with the scent of hay and dung and earth. In one corner the men and children stood in a semicircle, blocking the view of the boy and his

deer. The deerskin had been tossed over the top rail of a
stall.

As she drew closer, Caroline could make out two figures hunched over. Thad and Jack had removed their
shirts. Each of them wielded a knife with precision. Their
chests were smeared with blood, as were their hands and
arms and even their faces. But from the happy smile that
split young Jack's lips, it was clear that he was enjoying
this new responsibility.

Jack looked up as the women approached. "Pa says
the buck had to weigh a couple of hundred pounds.
When the hide's tanned, Uncle Thad will show me how
to make it into a winter coat. There's enough meat here
to feed us for a month."

Jessie looked properly impressed.

"There's enough for you, too, Miss Adams."

"That's very generous of you, Jack."

He grinned, and she could see traces of Thad's smile
in the boy's lips. "It was my Uncle Thad's suggestion.
You being new to town and all, he said you wouldn't have
much food in your root cellar."

"Then I'm grateful to your uncle, as well."

She glanced at Thad and found him studying her. Heat
touched her cheeks and she knew he could see that she
was blushing.

"Will you help me take the meat to the smokehouse,
Uncle Thad?"

"Sure will, Jack."

Caroline found her gaze riveted on Thad's muscular
torso as he bent to his task. The wound in his shoulder
had left a fresh scar, which, though jagged and puckered, showed no sign of infection. She was fascinated by
the corded muscles of his arms and back as he folded a
large square of leather around the chunks of meat. When

he lifted the burden into a cart, his muscles bunched and tensed, then relaxed when he straightened.

Plunging his hands into a bucket of water, he washed the blood from his skin, then stood and pulled on his shirt. He was tucking in the ends of the shirt when he turned and caught Caroline staring at him.

"Ready to go home now, Teacher?"

She swallowed and found herself blushing even more. Dragging her gaze from him, she managed to nod her head.

"I'll just haul this to the smokehouse, and then I'll bring the rig around to the house."

While he and Jack leaned their weight against the cart, the others made their way to the house.

A short time later the creak of wheels signaled the arrival of the horse and rig.

Stepping out onto the veranda, Caroline extended her hand to Jessie and Cole. "Thank you for a wonderful afternoon. It's been a long time since I've enjoyed such a fine meal."

"I hope we can do it often," Jessie said. "And you can tell us how our children are doing in school."

Caroline then shook hands with Dan and Morning Light.

"Maybe next time we'll get to talk about Boston," Dan said, accepting her handshake.

She kept her smile in place. "That would be nice."

To the children she called, "I'll see you in the morning."

Amid the squeals of excitement she saw the dubious look that came into young Jack's eyes and reminded herself that not all of the children were looking forward to their first day of school. It would be hard to compete with the kinds of things Thad Conway could teach the boy. But, she promised herself, she would find a way to capture Jack's interest in books and learning.

She accepted Thad's hand and was helped into the rig. Turning, she waved as they pulled away. And then, as they sped into the evening shadows, she draped her shawl around her shoulders. It wasn't the night air that had suddenly chilled her. It was the thought of being alone with Thad Conway.

"You're awfully quiet, Teacher."

She felt his gaze on her and kept her own averted. "It's been a full day. I'm just tired, I guess. But pleasantly so. Your family is lovely."

"Yeah. They're pretty special."

"Your sister told me that she dragged you across Texas to Abilene when you were only seven."

He gave a short laugh. "Dragged isn't quite the word. She left us behind, so Dan and I followed her. When she found out, she had no choice but to take us along or give up the journey."

Caroline found herself wondering again at the land that bred such independent people. "How old was Dan?"

"Fourteen, and already doctoring everyone in need of it. That's how he first met Morning Light. We found her along the trail. Badly wounded but still ready to carve up anyone who tried to touch her."

Caroline was intrigued. "Was it love at first sight?"

"That'd be my guess." Thad flicked the reins as they crested a hill. "They never saw each other again for a dozen years or more, but when they met again, the spark was still there between them."

"And Jessie and Cole?"

Thad gave a low chuckle. "I don't think all their scrapping at first was exactly love. Cole's mission was as desperate as ours. He was the toughest gunslinger I'd ever met."

"A gunslinger? Cole Matthews?" She thought about the successful rancher she'd met. He didn't exactly fit the description of a hardened gunman.

"I guess you'd call him a gunslinger with a badge. Cole was a federal marshal on the trail of his father's killer. Lord, I wanted to be like him. He was tough." He laughed again, low and deep in his throat. "Only Jessie was tougher."

"You make that sound like a compliment."

"Out here it is." He flicked a glance over her. "If you show a weak side to this land, Teacher, it'll bury you."

"Is that a warning?"

"I guess it is." He paused for the space of a heartbeat before saying, "Do doctors make you uncomfortable?"

The question surprised her. "Of course not. Why should they?"

He shrugged. "Then I guess it's just Dan that makes you nervous."

He felt Caroline stiffen beside him. "I don't know what you mean." In the gathering darkness, her voice sounded strained.

"Oh, I think you do, Teacher."

The rig rolled across a flat meadow, while its occupants remained tensely silent. When they pulled up to the tiny cabin, Thad leaped to the ground and offered his hand to help her down. When she alighted, he glanced at their hands, still joined.

Without thinking, he lifted his other hand to her cheek to brush aside a strand of hair. It was nearly his undoing. He felt the softness of her cheek, the silkiness of her hair, and he abruptly lowered his hand to his side, where he curled it into a fist.

"I'll say good-night now, Teacher."

She swallowed, and it sounded loud in her ears. "Good night, Thad."

He took a step back. "I'll unhitch your horse and saddle mine."

She nodded, grateful that he would soon be gone. Maybe then she could relax and let go of some of the tension that held her in its grip. Tension that always surfaced when he was near.

He climbed to the rig and flicked the reins. A moment later she stepped inside the cabin. From the window she watched as he unhitched her horse and turned it into the small enclosure. When he lifted his saddle from the railing and walked toward his stallion, she turned away and busied herself in the room.

Nighttime had settled across the hills, leaving the cabin in darkness. She fumbled with a lantern, then turned toward the fireplace, determined to chase the chill from the room.

Minutes later, when Thad led his horse out of the enclosure, he could see the first puffs of smoke from Caroline's chimney. Standing outside, he could see her clearly illuminated by the light of the fire.

Dangerous, he thought. If he could see her this clearly, so could anyone else who happened to pass this way in the night.

He didn't knock. Instead he tried the door, hoping she'd had the sense to latch it securely.

The door swung inward and Caroline looked up sharply. She lifted a hand to her throat in alarm.

He'd intended merely to teach her a lesson about using caution. But the vision that greeted him had him stopping in his tracks.

She'd been caught in the act of undressing. She had removed her spectacles and taken the pins from her hair. It tumbled in a riot of coal black curls down her back. Her feet were bare. The neat row of buttons on her gown was unfastened to the waist. Underneath she wore a creamy white chemise that displayed more than it covered.

He felt his breath catch in his throat. He hadn't felt this awkward since he was fourteen and discovered that girls and even grown women watched him whenever he rode through town.

Now that he'd blundered in, he had to explain himself. "I think you should keep a gun in the cabin."

She clutched the gaping edges of her bodice in one hand and tossed her head angrily. "I think it's obvious how I feel about guns."

His tone hardened. "They can make the difference between living and dying."

"And you would know about that, wouldn't you?"

Suddenly angry, he took a menacing step closer. "Yes. I'd know about that."

"How many men have you buried?"

"So many I've lost count, Teacher. The first was my father, when I was seven."

He saw the shock on her face. His voice lowered. "Didn't Jessie tell you why we went to Abilene?"

She shook her head.

"My father didn't come back from a cattle drive. We found him in jail, awaiting hanging for a crime he didn't commit."

Caroline's hand went to her mouth. "Did they...hang him?"

"We broke him out of jail."

"You mean . . . you and Jessie and Dan?"

He nodded. "But one of the deputies managed to wound Pa during the escape. He hung on long enough to make it to Texas. We buried him beside the Red River."

"I'm sorry." She could think of nothing else to say.

"Don't be. Big Jack Conway lived the way he wanted to. And before he died he gave us a sense of who we were and what we wanted to be. More than that, he gave us each other. I may have been only seven years old, but I already knew I'd be willing to die for Jessie or Dan." His tone hardened. "Or kill for them."

Something in the way he said it made her go very still.

He didn't know why in hell he was unburdening his soul to this woman. But there was something about her. Though he was a man of few words, she made the talking easy.

He touched a hand to the gun at his waist. "Cole taught me how to use a gun while we were on the trail to Abilene. When we got back to Texas and thought we were safe, a crazy gunman threatened to...violate Jessie. I may have been only seven, but I knew what I had to do. And I did it."

He saw the stricken look on Caroline's face before she struggled to compose herself. She thought about what Jessie had said earlier that day, about her little brothers never having had the time for childhood. For some strange reason, she felt tears sting her eyes. "But you were only a little boy."

He saw the tears and was moved by them. Stepping closer, he whispered, "Don't cry for me, Caroline. I was never a little boy. There wasn't time for such things when Texas was a wilderness.''

He knew he shouldn't touch her. But the softness of her skin was such a temptation.

Tossing aside the need for caution, he lifted a hand and wiped the corner of her eye. Soft. Even softer than he remembered. And now that he had touched her, he wanted more. So much more.

"It's terrible to be afraid, to have no one. . . ." She realized she was weeping for another child who'd been afraid and alone, and had been forced to do tough things to survive.

Thad opened his arms and she moved into them, allowing the tears to dampen the front of his shirt. Tenderness. It was something he wasn't good at. But with her it seemed natural. Beneath the ladylike pose, beneath the defenses that surfaced when she was threatened, there was something...something wounded and vulnerable that made him want to comfort her, protect her.

"I don't like knowing you're alone out here," he murmured against her hair. "You're far from town, far from the nearest ranch. Anything could happen to you and no one would know."

"I can take care of myself." She lifted her head to face him.

He could see the dampness of tears still on her lashes. "Yes, you certainly can." He lifted both hands to her eyes and wiped the tears with his thumbs. It seemed the most natural thing in the world to frame her face with his hands and lower his lips to hers.

He felt the first flicker of flame, low and deep inside. He could feel the heat building, and still he kept the kiss easy.

Caroline stood very still, absorbing the shock.

As if in slow motion his hands tangled in her hair, drawing her head back until he took the kiss deeper.

With a little moan she clutched at him, her arms encircling his waist.

He pulled her firmly against him and his mouth savaged hers. A sudden, wrenching need, more powerful than anything he'd ever experienced, nearly swamped him. He wanted her. More than he'd ever wanted his freedom or his independence. There was no denying it. He felt need war against reason.

What was happening to him? This wasn't the kind of woman a man could take and then walk away from. She was the kind that made a man think about making promises and setting down roots. And building fences to keep away all harm.

Her kisses were as fervent as his. The fire that raged through him was blazing in her veins, too. And her hands were soft, seductive, drawing him even closer. Whatever passion he felt, whatever needs, she felt them, too, however much she might try to deny it.

Her scent filled him, clouding his mind. Her sighs were like whispered promises. He was being caught in some silken web and soon he'd be so tangled he'd never be free.

He had to remind himself of the freedoms he'd always cherished.

With all the control he could muster he pushed himself free of her embrace.

When he stepped back a pace, she held herself very straight, struggling for breath.

"I still say you need a gun, Teacher."

"Maybe you're right." She was surprised at how difficult it was to speak. "At least then I'd have some protection against you if you forced your way in here again."

His voice was calmer now. "I didn't force. The door was unlatched. And you didn't send me away."

"You didn't knock," she said accusingly.

"Neither will someone bent on harming you. From now on, Teacher, keep your door latched." He gave her a smoldering glance that said more than words.

Even now he felt a rush of heat at the sight of her. Dark hair tumbled over her shoulders, drawing his gaze to the open bodice and the cleft between her breasts. He still ached to have her.

"Though I doubt a latch, or even a gun, would stop anyone who really wanted to get to you."

He stalked outside and pulled himself into the saddle.

Caroline crossed the room and stood framed in the doorway.

"Why did you spend time in a Mexican jail?" she asked.

Even from this distance she could see the whiteness of his teeth as he smiled. "It was a case of mistaken identity. Like my pa, somebody mistook me for a horse thief."

He nudged his horse into a trot. Caroline latched the door. Leaning against it, she listened to the sound of hoofbeats until they disappeared.

Hours later she still lay wide-awake, alert to the sounds of the night. Thad Conway was a strange and complex man. Something happened to her whenever he got near. Something that terrified her. Something that could destroy all she'd worked for.

Chapter Nine

In the late morning the children began arriving for their first day of school. Carts, wagons and small rigs littered the school yard. In the enclosure with Caroline's horse were half a dozen other horses and ponies.

Two large dogs that had accompanied their young masters dozed in the doorway of the school. A gray-and-white cat wandered in and leaped to a window ledge, where it promptly curled up and went to sleep.

Caroline met parents and grandparents, aunts and uncles who accompanied the children to their first day of school. She learned the names of practically everyone in the town. And she even met youngsters who were too young to attend school. They watched their older siblings with envy as they entered the sparkling school-room.

"We've waited for this day for more than two years." Sara Waverly introduced her eight-year-old son, Ethan, and ten-year-old daughter, Emma.

Ethan was small and frail like his mother. Emma was taller than her mother by several inches, and broader in the shoulders than most of the boys. Sara watched with approval as both children quietly took their seats without talking or laughing with the other children.

"I've let them know that if you have to scold them, they'll face more discipline at home. I expect a report on their behavior."

Caroline nodded, feeling a wave of sympathy for the two nervous children, who seemed isolated from all the others around them.

A young mother caught Caroline's hands in both of hers. "I can read some, so I've managed to teach my son, Winton, the words, but I was never very good with figures." Bright dots of color highlighted her cheeks as she admitted, "I couldn't teach him what I didn't understand. But now you'll teach my son all the things he'll need to know to get by, Miss Adams."

"I hope so," Caroline said with a smile.

As she studied the eager, expectant faces of the children, she fervently hoped so.

Most of the morning was taken up with learning the names of her students. After a break for lunch and a chance for all of them to run outside and exercise limbs and lungs, the afternoon session was dedicated to determining which groups the students would be in.

Caroline asked each student to read and to do sums on a small slate. Then she broke the classroom down into several groups according to skill and several more according to age.

From her precious store of books she chose one for each reading level. The children, many of whom had never seen a real book, were delighted. The books, which would be treated like treasures, were to be kept on a shelf in the classroom and read only during school hours.

Toward the end of the school day, when she noted that the children were growing restless, Caroline offered to read aloud from a novel of adventure. Passing a slate among them, she encouraged them to jot down any words that were unfamiliar to them. If they couldn't write them, they were told to raise their hands.

The story immediately caught their fancy, and the children listened raptly to her voice. At the end of the chapter, they discussed the words and sought the meanings.

Reluctantly Caroline put down the book. "I'm afraid that's all the time we have today."

Jack and several of the older boys looked up hopefully, and she knew they were eager to return home and finish their chores. Several of the younger students, however, seemed actually sorry to see the day end.

Caroline accompanied them to their horses, carts and wagons and waved as they rolled from the school yard and followed the many trails home. Then she returned to the classroom and tidied up. As she straightened chairs and pulled the door shut, she looked around the empty room and felt tears mist her eyes. Her first day as a teacher. Hugging her arms around herself, she sank into her chair. She had loved it. Loved every minute of it.

Miss Caroline Adams, teacher. Respectable member of the town of Hope, Texas.

Lady.

Lowering her face to her hands, she gave in to the desire to weep. Then, chiding herself for her weakness, she got to work.

Caroline opened the door between the schoolroom and her cabin. She had spent the past hour preparing for the following day's lessons, and her mind was filled with words, sums and challenges for young minds.

Now, however, it was time to think about what she would fix for her supper.

As she closed the door, she paused. Something was amiss, though she couldn't quite put her finger on it.

She sniffed the air. The unmistakable hint of sweet pipe tobacco lingered. It was a scent she would never forget. Suddenly, she felt the hair on the back of her neck begin to rise.

Through eyes wide with fear she peered around. The table and chairs were exactly as she'd left them. A vase of wildflowers was resting in the middle of the table. A few petals had scattered, as though disturbed by a gust of wind. But the door had been closed. Had she latched it before going into the schoolroom? She couldn't recall. She'd been so eager, so excited about the first day of school.

Would she have heard someone come in during the day? She thought about the sounds of children's voices and laughter. It would have been an easy matter for someone to enter this side of the cabin without being heard in the schoolroom.

She crossed to the fireplace. The ashes, now cool since the morning's fire, dusted the hearth. They, too, had been scattered by a sudden breeze.

Circling the room, she ran a hand over the small table beside her bed where she kept a pitcher of water and a basin. Pausing beside the bed, she noticed a wrinkle in the quilt. She touched a finger to the spot and felt something hard under the covers.

Her throat went very dry. For a moment she couldn't move. Then, pulling back the bed covers, she stared at the small, deadly weapon and jumped back, frozen with fear.

Tentatively she moved closer and forced herself to pick up the knife. The hilt was still warm; the blade icy cold.

The first time she'd seen it, it had been pressed to her mother's throat.

She had no doubt the knife had been left here for a reason. Someone wanted to send her a message. A message that left her no doubt as to its meaning. She hadn't escaped her past, after all. It had followed her all the way to Texas.

She dropped the knife and raced across the room to latch the door.

"I think this is the best group of mustangs yet," Thad said, leaning on the top rail of the corral.

"They are twelve beauties," Manuel agreed.

Thad secured the gate and paused to admire the day's roundup.

The horses milled about, sending up a cloud of dust. But when Thad and Manuel forked hay over the rail and filled a trough with water, the mustangs settled down to eat.

"That reminds me," Thad said, glancing at Manuel, "have we eaten today?"

"Not since early morning. I thought about it many times, but you were always too busy chasing just one more mustang."

"Yeah, there always seems to be just one more mustang," Thad remarked with a laugh.

The two men led their horses toward the barn. A few minutes later they headed to the house. Inside, while Rosita finished cooking supper, they washed, then took their places at the table.

At the sound of a horse and wagon approaching, Thad looked up from his meal and scraped back his chair. Minutes later, when Caroline rode up, he was standing on the porch, a rifle in his hand.

Her cheeks, he noted, were brighter than usual. "Is this a social call, Teacher, or did you come to give me a lesson?"

"I—need to ask a favor." She stepped down from the wagon.

He watched the sway of her hips as she came toward him and his mind was flooded with thoughts and images that, if revealed, would make her blush. He reminded himself that that kind of thinking always seemed to lead to trouble between them. "Well, favor or no, it's neighborly of you to come calling. You're just in time for supper."

With his hand beneath her elbow he escorted her to the door.

"No. You don't understand. I have no time..." She caught sight of the beautiful young woman lifting a piece of crockery from the fireplace and words failed her. "I didn't know...I mean, I didn't realize..." Embarrassed and awkward, she looked from the young woman to Thad, then back to the woman.

"Rosita, this is the new schoolteacher, Caroline Adams. Caroline, this is Rosita Alvarez."

Caroline nodded stiffly at the smiling woman.

"And this is her husband, Manuel."

For the first time Caroline turned her head and noted the handsome young man seated at the table. At his warm smile she visibly relaxed. "It's nice to meet you." Turning to Thad, she said softly, "I need to talk to you."

"All right. We'll talk over supper."

"I mean alone."

He guided her across the room and held a chair. "As soon as we've eaten."

When she started to refuse he said curtly, "Manuel and I haven't eaten since breakfast. And let me warn you, after the work we've done today, we could eat a mule without bothering to skin it first."

"I'm sorry." Taking the chair he indicated, Caroline watched as the men tucked into their meal. At Rosita's insistence, Caroline spooned some of the meat mixture from the crock and tasted it. It was hot, spicy and delicious.

She'd forgotten how hungry she was. Now, while the others enjoyed their meal, she decided to do the same, since Thad was obviously not going to give her a minute of his time until he'd satisfied his own hunger.

"Rosita, this is wonderful. I've never tasted anything like it," Caroline said after several more bites.

"Thank you." The young woman flushed with pleasure.

"You are familiar with our food?" Manuel asked.

Caroline shook her head while Thad explained, "Miss Adam's from the East. Boston. They probably haven't even heard of half the spices Rosita uses." To Caroline he said with a smile, "You may want to go easy." He filled her glass with water and continued eating.

The bread, Caroline noted, was soft like a pancake. The others ate it wrapped around a mixture of finely chopped meat and peppers, seasoned with an assortment of spices. There were more peppers on a platter. Some were fresh, some dried. The coffee was hot and very strong. For dessert there were thin, crisp pastries baked over the fire in narrow strips and brushed with egg white, honey and chopped nut meats.

"You outdid yourself, Rosita." Thad leaned back, sipping steaming coffee.

"I knew you two would be gone all day when you said you were hunting the mustangs," she said with a smile. "And I knew you would not take the time to eat."

"Next time I will make him stop," Manuel vowed, "even if it means passing up a mustang or two." To Thad he said, "I know what you are like when you set your mind on something. You are like a plow horse with blinders. You see neither left nor right, but only the furrow you are digging."

"Did you say horse?" Caroline asked teasingly. "Or did you say mule?"

They all laughed while Thad merely arched a brow at her joke.

"Manuel says that Señor Conway can see a hundred mustangs and choose the one that will fetch the best price or sire the finest foal," Rosita said with a glance at her husband.

Manuel nodded. "It is true. I have never seen a better judge of horses."

"I wish I was as good with people," Thad said.

"You are a very good judge of people," Manuel said softly. "They do not fool you."

"Don't like me much, either."

"Those who do not like you are those who do not know you."

"Or those who've been on the wrong end of my gun."

"I have never known you to draw on a man who did not deserve it," Manual said.

While Caroline finished her meal, she thought about the high regard these people had for Thad Conway. It seemed in direct contrast to what she had expected.

But what had she expected? she asked herself as she glanced around. Certainly not this civilized house with a cozy fire and warm, friendly faces around a dinner table. Not the desk in the corner, with open ledgers and a shelf of books above it. Books. Obviously Thad Conway could read and write. For some odd reason, that pleased her very much.

Caroline was grateful that Thad had given her the water. She had a sudden thirst and drained the glass. These strange spices, she decided, should be taken in small doses until she was more accustomed to them. She felt Thad watching her and knew without looking that he was laughing at her.

When Rosita began to clear the table, Caroline insisted on helping her.

"There has been much excitement about your arrival," the young woman said as she washed the dishes and Caroline dried them. "The people of the town have long awaited a teacher."

"And it feels as if I've been waiting a lifetime for an opportunity like this."

"Then you are happy here in Hope? You do not, as the townspeople feared, find it too small for your taste?"

"It feels just right."

From his position at the fireplace Thad heard Caroline's words and was warmed by them.

"Do you live here on the ranch?" Caroline asked.

"Oh, no. Manuel and I have our own ranch, just over that rise. Actually, the land belonged to Señor Conway. When we had saved enough money, he sold us a piece of his own land. With the money we earn from Señor Conway, we are able to add to our herd and enlarge our holdings." Her smile grew dreamy. "We are planning to make this land our home for generations to come."

"That's what I find so wonderful about this part of the country," Caroline said softly. "There's so much land, so much space. Even a person from the humblest of beginnings has a chance for a better life."

Thad heard the layers of pain and hope in her tone and grinned. Damned if she wasn't falling under the spell of the land already.

When the dishes were put away, Rosita went in search of her husband, who had already hitched their wagon for the ride back to their ranch.

"Good night, Señorita Adams."

"Good night, Rosita. Thank you for the lovely supper."

"It was nice having another woman at the table." With a smile she bid good-night to Thad and hurried out to the wagon. Minutes later Rosita and Manuel were on their way home.

Thad turned from the doorway. Caroline was standing in front of the fire, deep in thought, her arms wrapped tightly around herself. Despite the heat of the fire, she shivered.

"All right." Thad's eyes narrowed at the movement, but he remained where he was. He'd seen the nerves in her when she'd first arrived. Though she was calmer now, the fear was still there, just below the surface.

He had no intention of offering her the comfort of his arms again tonight. He knew where that would lead. He'd merely hear her out and send her on her way. Clean. Simple. That was the way he intended it.

"What brought you all the way out here, Teacher?"

She couldn't meet his eyes. Instead she continued staring into the fire as she said calmly, "I'd like you to show me how to use a gun."

It took Thad a full minute to recover from the shock. Her strange request was the last thing he'd expected.

"A gun." He indicated a pair of rocking chairs on either side of the fireplace. "I think you'd better sit down and tell me what this is all about."

While he sat, she continued to stand. She was clearly too agitated to sit calmly and talk.

"I've decided that you were right. I think I ought to have a gun in my cabin. And if I'm to have a gun, I ought to know how to use it."

He watched as she clasped and unclasped her hands. Agitated, yes. And afraid. But of what?

"Did something happen today?"

"It was the first day of school. I've been very busy."

She still hadn't met his gaze. She stared at the flames, then began to pace.

He struggled to keep the impatience from his voice. "I mean, did something happen at your cabin today? Did someone bother you? Threaten you?"

She whirled. "Why are you asking these questions? You were the one who suggested I keep a gun. Have you changed your mind?"

"No. But I'm puzzled as to why you were so against it last night and so eager for a gun today."

"You convinced me. Isn't that enough?"

He kept his tone level. "No, Teacher. There's something you haven't told me."

Exasperated, she turned away. "I can see I've come to the wrong man for help. I just thought since you know so much about guns..."

"Whoa. Just a minute, Teacher." He moved with the swiftness of a panther and caught her roughly by the arm as she started toward the door. He could feel the tension pulsing through her. "I just wanted to know what brought about this change of heart. But I didn't say I wouldn't help you."

He saw the light that came into her eyes. "You'll show me how to handle a gun?"

He stared down at her, his own eyes narrowed in thought. "I'm probably going to regret this. But I guess I'll be the teacher's teacher."

"Can we start now?"

He shook his head firmly. "Now I'm going to see you safely home. Then I'm going to come back here and fall into bed. I spent at least ten hours in the saddle today, and my body has decided to punish me."

"But I can't wait."

"Looks like you have no choice. I'll come by your cabin tomorrow, after your students have gone. I'll bring along a gun I think you can handle. Now come on," he said, leading her outside. "Let's get you home."

"You don't have to go with me. I know the way."

"Stop giving orders, Teacher." He helped her into the wagon, then headed toward the barn. Minutes later he emerged with his horse saddled and ready.

On the way back, Caroline found herself looking out over the hills and wondering if anyone was out there watching. She shivered and was grateful that Thad had insisted on accompanying her.

When they reached the cabin, he unhitched her horse and turned it into the small enclosure. While he worked he noticed that she remained outside with him.

Something was clearly bothering her. She was afraid to go inside her own place.

He walked to the door of her cabin. "How about a cup of coffee before I head back?"

"Yes. Of course." He saw the brief smile that tugged at her lips and knew he'd made the right choice. She was definitely afraid to be alone.

Inside, he saw her glance around before walking to the fireplace. Tossing a log on the hot coals, she filled a blackened coffeepot with water from a pitcher and placed it over the fire.

While she worked, Thad took a few moments to glance around the neat cabin. He thought it odd that the bed covers had been pulled down. The glint of metal in the middle of the bed had him moving closer. As he drew near he caught sight of the knife. Picking it up, he turned it over and over in his hand, examining the ornate handle, the finely honed blade.

Somehow it didn't suit the woman who was busy filling two cups with steaming coffee. But then, she was a woman of mystery. So many things about her seemed contradictory.

She was carrying the cups to the table when he asked softly, "Yours?"

She turned her head, then spilled the coffee as she hastily set the cups down. A savage oath escaped her lips before she seemed to catch herself and bite her lip. Again, for that one brief moment, he'd glimpsed a side of her she rarely displayed.

"You burned yourself."

"No."

She pulled her hand away when he tried to inspect it. He glanced at the knife, then back at her.

"That settles it." He sat down at the table, picked up one of the cups and began calmly drinking.

"Settles what?" She couldn't seem to tear her gaze from the knife that glittered dully in his hand. Seeing the direction of her gaze, he set it down on the table.

"Something's wrong." He'd already decided the knife couldn't be hers. She'd arrived here without a weapon. Except, he thought grimly, for the club she'd used for her protection that first night. There would have been no need for a club if she'd had possession of a knife like this. "And I'm not leaving here until I have an explanation."

"You can't stay here." She seemed genuinely shocked.

"And why not? There's a big empty room on the other side of that door."

"It's a schoolroom. The children will be arriving in the morning."

"If you're worried about your precious reputation, don't bother. I won't soil it. By morning I'll be gone. But for now," he said, draining his cup, "I'm going to sleep." As he yanked open the door he said gruffly, "Leave the door ajar. And, Teacher—" he picked up the rug from the hearth and spread it on the cold floor of the schoolroom "—see that that outer door is firmly latched."

She watched as he calmly lay down on the schoolroom floor and pulled his hat low over his face. She remembered the first time she'd met him. He had fallen asleep in the middle of a storm with only a saddle for a pillow.

She banked the fire. As he'd ordered, she left the door between the two rooms ajar and latched the outer door. And then, with a final glimpse at the knife on the table, she quickly undressed and climbed into bed.

Though she would never admit it to him, she was grateful for his presence. At least for tonight she would be able to sleep without fear.

Tomorrow would be soon enough to worry about the rest of her life.

Chapter Ten

Thad leaned a hip against the window of the schoolroom and watched the first faint red light of dawn bleed into the horizon. Out of habit he checked his pistol before thrusting it into his holster.

Moving softly, he crossed the floor and pushed open the door separating the schoolroom from Caroline's private room. He walked to the side of the bed and stared at the sleeping figure.

She was curled on her side with one hand tucked up beneath her pillow. Her hair spilled forward, covering her cheek and eye.

She appeared incredibly young. And dangerously tempting.

He lingered a moment longer, enjoying the vision. Then he turned away.

As he passed the table, he saw the glint of the knife. With a frown he remembered that she had given him no explanation last night.

He jammed his hat on his head and let himself out, closing the door softly behind him. She could have a reprieve for the day to concentrate on her students. But later he'd be back. And this time, he'd get some answers.

* * *

"Why do we blink, Miss Adams?"

"It is an involuntary action, Lisbeth. Like breathing. On the other hand, Jack," Caroline said pointedly, "staring out the window is a voluntary action, and one that signals your disinterest in what is being discussed here in school."

Several of the students began laughing as Jack's fair head swiveled to face the teacher.

"Sorry, Miss Adams. I saw a man outside. He was too far away to make out. I thought he might be coming here, but all of a sudden he turned and went over that rise. I'm pretty sure he saw me watching him."

Caroline's heart started racing, but she was determined to keep her fear hidden from her students.

"All right, boys and girls. It's time to do our sums."

There was a collective groan from the children and Caroline gave them an encouraging smile. "As soon as we've finished, we'll stop for lunch. Frank," she called, "if a rancher sold your father a dozen cows and four of them died, what would you have?"

"A gunfight," the little boy said in a serious tone. "My pa would go gunning for anyone who sold him sick cows."

The classroom erupted into gales of laughter. Minutes later, still chuckling, Caroline said, "I think we'll take our lunch break now and finish doing our sums later."

Her announcement was greeted with cheers as the children scurried to a corner of the room to retrieve saddlebags and baskets filled with food. Afterward the entire schoolroom emptied as the laughing, shouting boys and girls, accompanied by their teacher, scampered outside to play.

Watching the children chasing one another in a game of tag or swinging from the sturdy limbs of a tree, Caroline shaded her eyes and stared off into the distance.

Her mind was troubled, her heart heavy. She knew the stranger Jack had spotted. And she knew why he'd come. Was he even now somewhere nearby, watching her? She shivered despite the warmth of the sun.

Caroline waved as the last wagonload of students left for the day. As soon as she was alone she hurried to the door between the classroom and her private quarters. She opened the door and peered inside cautiously.

Nothing seemed amiss. There was no scattering of ash or flower petals, no sweet scent of pipe tobacco. Upon checking, she found the door still firmly latched.

Still, the fact that he hadn't entered her cabin gave her no relief. Finding the door latched, he could have easily left without being seen. She had the uneasy feeling that he'd wanted her to know that he'd been here. That was why he'd allowed young Jack to spot him.

He was toying with her.

She'd once watched a cat torment a wounded bird. The bird, its wing broken, its flesh torn, was allowed to take several halting steps before the cat swiped with its paw, dragging the bird close. After inflicting a little more pain, the cat allowed the bird a few more feeble attempts at freedom before, growing weary of the game, it dealt the final blow.

Caroline's hands curled into fists. She was not a helpless bird. There were ways to fight a predator.

"Ready for your first lesson, Teacher?"

With a gasp, she spun around.

Thad Conway was leaning casually against the school-room door. He saw the flash of fear in her eyes before she composed herself.

"Sorry." He straightened but made no move toward her. "I didn't mean to frighten you."

"You didn't frighten me. You merely startled me. Haven't you ever heard of knocking?"

"I did knock. On the schoolroom door." He motioned over his shoulder. "But I guess your mind was somewhere else."

"Did you bring a gun?" She chose to ignore the question in his eyes.

He opened his hand to reveal a small pistol. "This is a Remington. It has a little more range than a derringer, but it's still small enough that you can carry it in a pocket of your dress."

She took the gun from his hand and balanced it in her palm, weighing the small piece of metal. It was lighter than she'd expected. And still warm from Thad's touch.

"Will you teach me how to shoot it now?"

"Not yet." When she looked up in surprise he said, "That's the last thing you'll learn. First you have to learn how to load it."

Taking a handful of bullets from a small pouch, he set them on the table and showed her how to load and unload the gun. Then he handed it over and watched as she did the same, fumbling several times with the bullets.

"Not bad," he said with a trace of admiration. "You're a quick study, Teacher. But there's more to it than that. Practice loading and unloading with your eyes closed or in the dark."

He saw the question in her eyes and said firmly, "Remember, gunfights don't always happen in daylight. And your opponent won't call a truce while you take time to load more bullets. You have to be able to do these things in a matter of moments, while your life hangs in the balance. You won't have the luxury of making a mistake twice."

She swallowed, and he realized he was finally getting through to her.

"Now let's see if you can learn to shoot it."

He led her outside and set several small stones on a flat rock. Returning to where she stood, he took up a position behind her and brought his arms around her.

They both felt the sudden, jolting shock. And both struggled to remain calm.

Holding the pistol at eye level, he brought his lips to her ear. He realized he was enjoying himself. Though she was probably uncomfortable being held like this, she would have to endure it if she wanted to learn what only he could teach her.

With his lips close to her ear he felt her little shiver as he murmured, "Use the barrel of the gun as a sight." He felt her tremble and brought his lips even closer until they were brushing her ear. "When the target is dead center, gently squeeze the trigger while keeping the gun level."

Caroline struggled to concentrate on the words. But it was difficult when Thad was standing so close and his warm breath was whispering over her skin.

He kept his hands over hers as he lightly squeezed her finger on the trigger. The gunshot echoed in her ears as the first small rock shattered, scattering fragments into the air.

"I hit it!" she cried excitedly.

As she turned her head, his lips brushed her cheek. She saw the way his eyes narrowed slightly as he corrected, "We hit it. Now it's your turn."

She took careful aim, then closed her eyes and fired. Fifty feet from the target the bullet embedded itself in the dirt, sending up a spray of sand.

"I missed," she complained.

"How could you hit anything with your eyes closed?"

"My eyes weren't closed."

"They were."

"Well, I was confused. You're standing too close."

At her admission, he grinned and took a step back. He watched as she took aim again. This time as she squeezed the trigger, she kept her gaze on the target. One of the stones shattered.

"I hit it! Of course," she admitted sheepishly, "it wasn't the one I was aiming at. But at least I hit something."

"Still not good enough, Teacher."

She cast him a withering look and aimed again. This time she hit the target she was aiming at and gave a little squeal of delight. "You see," she called. "I'm getting better each time."

"You have a long way to go," he said. "Remember that these stones aren't firing back. If they were, you'd already be dead."

The smile was wiped from her lips as she took aim again.

Thad stood back and studied her. It seemed unbelievable that the woman in the modest gray gown who had just dismissed a school full of children could be calmly standing here learning how to shoot a gun.

The breeze caught a strand of her hair and sent it dancing across one cheek. She brushed it aside and lifted the gun, taking careful aim. As she squeezed the trigger he heard her little laugh of triumph.

"I hit it."

"Now do it again. And keep on doing it until you can hit it every time."

He saw the look of determination in her eyes. And then he noticed something else. She had removed her spectacles. Odd, he thought. Wouldn't she need them to see the target?

His eyes narrowed. Could it be that the lady didn't need those spectacles at all?

But why would a beautiful woman do such a thing? They could be a disguise to make her appear more scholarly. They would also hide a pair of beautiful eyes. Now that was an interesting thought, and one that intrigued him. It wasn't the first time he'd suspected as much. But why would she want to hide her beauty? Unless... Why would Caroline Adams be afraid of men?

He studied the too large gown that cleverly disguised a lush body and noted her attempts to tame a mass of gypsy hair. He thought back to the times he'd touched her. In every instance she had initially pulled back in alarm. His gaze became more piercing.

"I hit the target three times in a row!" she called, her voice high with excitement.

"Still not good enough." He saw her frown before she returned her attention to the task at hand.

"I'm going to do it." She flashed him a bright smile. "Before long I'll be able to hit the target every time."

His voice lowered. "Remember something, Caroline."

At the tone of his voice she lowered the gun and turned to him. The look in his eyes was stern. "Hitting a target is one thing. If you aim that gun at a man, you have to be prepared to take his life." He thought of the terrible lesson he'd learned when he was just a boy. "That's an awesome responsibility. And once done, it can never be undone."

Her smile faded. She nodded solemnly. "I'll remember."

For a moment he thought she'd changed her mind. But then he saw the way she stiffened her spine.

"There are some," she said just as solemnly, "who deserve to be shot."

With teeth clenched she aimed at the target and fired four times in a row. All four stones shattered on impact.

"One more thing," Thad said softly. "Don't expect this gun to suddenly keep you safe from any and all harm. Your best defense is still here." He touched a finger to his temple. "Your mind. When you feel threatened, keep your wits about you. That, and not your gun, is what will keep you from being hurt."

She checked the gun, loaded the empty chamber and placed it in her pocket. "I'll use my wits if I can. But if I have to, I won't be afraid to use my gun." She offered her hand. "Thank you. For the gun and the lessons."

He looked at the small hand and braced himself before accepting it. As always, he felt the current that seemed to pulse between them at the slightest touch. "Don't be so quick to thank me. You haven't heard what payment I'll demand."

She patted the pistol resting in the pocket of her gown and gave him a smile that sent his heart spiraling out of control.

"Better be careful, Texan." She laughed, low and deep. "If the price is too high, I might make you answer to my gun."

With a bemused expression Thad muttered, "See what happens when you wear a gun? You start to think you can push people around. Well, if we're going to duel," he said, walking to his horse, "we'd better do it on full stomachs."

"What are you doing?"

He removed several linen-wrapped articles from his saddlebags, then opened the door to her cabin and waited for her to enter.

At her arched brow he followed her inside and explained, "I'm going to feed you. Rosita outdid herself today and made enough to feed half your students."

Though she was surprised, Caroline had to admit to herself that she was delighted. While she set the table, Thad unwrapped the pottery dishes to reveal a spicy venison stew and a loaf of bread still warm from the oven.

"These dishes look like they've traveled a long way." Thad picked up one of Caroline's precious chipped cups and examined the delicate morning glory design.

"They were my mother's," Caroline said softly. "And before that, her mother's."

There was a wistfulness in her words that had him watching her closely.

"Did you know your grandmother?"

She shook her head. When he tried to get her to talk about her childhood, she became strangely silent.

"Tell me about your life here in Texas," she urged.

Thad smiled, thinking how deftly she had managed to turn the tables once again. But the truth was, he needed little persuasion to tell her about his childhood. It seemed the most natural thing in the world to talk to her.

"I suppose to some it was hard. But it was a fine time to be young and carefree. Despite all the hardships, I wouldn't trade it for anything."

Caroline thought how handsome he was when his eyes crinkled in a face bronzed by the sun.

"I could ride a horse before I could walk," he said softly. "And Jessie made sure I could read and write. Not that I took to it," he said with a laugh. "Book learning was for Dan. He couldn't get enough of it. But I loved the land and the freedom and the horses. I guess the horses have always been my downfall. I'd go clear to California for a horse with good bloodlines."

While he regaled her with stories of his childhood adventures, Caroline savored the food, eating until she was satisfied.

Relaxed, replete, she was caught completely off guard when Thad said calmly, "Now, tell me about this man."

"Man?" Her hand holding the cup paused in midair.

"The man who has you learning to use a gun."

"I don't know..." She set the cup down with a clatter and refused to look at him.

When she started to stand, he got to his feet and caught her roughly by the shoulder. His voice lowered. "You know who I mean, Teacher. The man who's made you so afraid to be a woman."

"How dare...? I am not afraid..."

"Aren't you?" He dragged her close and saw the way her eyes widened with sudden fear.

She tried to cover her fear with a display of anger, but her voice trembled slightly. "Take your hands off me."

"That was a good try, Teacher." His words were low, gruff. "But what you've commanded is impossible. You see, every time I get too close to you, I seem to lose control." Dragging her roughly against him, he covered her mouth with his.

For a moment she brought her hands to his chest to brace herself. But as the kiss deepened, she could do nothing more than hold on.

Would it always be like this when he touched her? Would her mind always empty and her blood heat? She had made a promise to herself. A promise to hold all men at arm's length, to make her way in life alone. But every time this man was near, she forgot everything except the pleasure of the moment.

He lingered over the kiss, drawing out all the wild, sweet flavors that were unlike anything he'd ever sampled. She made him yearn to lie with her beneath a full moon on a hot Texas night. She made him think about bartering all his freedoms for one night in her arms. She made him wish...

He lifted his head and studied her lips, still swollen from his kiss. "When are you going to trust me enough to tell me what's going on?"

For long minutes she clung to him and thought about telling him everything. It would be so wonderful to have someone else to help her bear the burden she'd been carrying alone for so long. But as she surfaced, her mind slowly cleared.

How could she possibly confide in this man? Or in anyone? Pushing free of his arms, she took a step back, and then another.

He watched as Caroline fled across the room to pace in front of the fireplace. "Don't ask me. I can't tell you."

It wasn't much of an admission, but at least she had stopped denying that there was anything to tell.

"I could help, if you'd be willing to trust me."

Trust. He didn't understand what he was asking of her. She refused to look at him as she shook her head and turned to stare into the flames.

His voice was low and edged with steel. "Good night, Teacher. I hope that pistol keeps you warm tonight."

He tore open the door and strode into the darkness. Climbing into the saddle, he gave a last look at the door of the cabin.

As his horse's hooves ate up the miles, he pondered again what it was about that damnably independent little woman that had him so bewitched. He'd never before spent so much time with someone who made him so comfortable and uncomfortable at the same time. Like the finest leather saddle, he thought. With a burr under it. One he couldn't seem to dislodge.

Chapter Eleven

For Caroline, the days passed in a blur of work. She was grateful that every waking moment was filled with demanding chores. The hard work kept her from worrying about the danger that lurked just beyond the door of her cabin. Each day there had been a new clue to remind her that the predator was still circling his prey.

But why? Why was he toying with her like this?

The answer came swiftly. To torment her. To make her so fearful that when he finally showed himself she would be too terrified to resist him.

His tactics were thorough, the result predictable. She was terrified. But she would never give in to his demands.

Caroline guided the horse over the rolling fields, past a few small outbuildings, until she pulled up in front of a small, neat wooden house. Taking a book and slate from the rig, she walked to the front door and knocked.

Cora Meadows, wiping her hands on her apron, opened the door and stared in surprise. "Miss Adams. I never expected to see you out here."

"And why not? Didn't you say you had a son?"

"Well, yes, of course. But Ben's—he's crippled. He can't leave his bed."

"He still has a mind, doesn't he?"

The woman seemed taken aback before she nodded.

"Good. Then I'll bring the reading and writing to him."

A small wiry man, his arms corded with muscles, came in from the fields and stared at their visitor in surprise.

"Ab," Cora said, "the new teacher, Miss Adams, came out here to meet our Ben. Miss Adams, this is my husband, Abner."

The man removed his hat and nodded a stiff-lipped greeting.

Caroline followed Cora down a narrow hallway. In a small room in the back of the house, overlooking the fields, lay a boy of about ten. Copper hair and a dusting of freckles across his nose made him look the picture of health. But his eyes were sad and unsmiling.

"Ben, this is the new teacher, Miss Caroline Adams."

"Hello, Ben." Smiling brightly, Caroline offered her hand.

With an effort the boy extended his hand, all the while studying her closely.

"Can you read, Ben?"

"Some."

"How about writing?"

He shrugged. "A little. But my hands won't always do what I want."

Caroline had noticed his weak grip. She would have to determine whether he could grasp the chalk.

Opening a beginner's book, she handed it to him, saying, "Do you think you could read a few pages to me?"

The boy glanced at his mother, then, seeing her nod of approval, accepted the book. In slow, halting words he struggled through two pages before Caroline thanked him.

"I'll leave you two alone," Cora said, backing from the room.

As she headed down the hall she heard Caroline say, "Now, Ben, let's try to do a few of our sums on the slate."

When Cora returned a half hour later, Caroline was reading a story. Though Ben's look was still grave, he followed every word with rapt attention. Cora halted in the doorway and watched for several minutes before turning away.

It was nearly two hours later when Caroline stood. "I have to leave now. If you'd like, Ben, I could come by once a week and check your progress. During the week your mother could help you with your lessons. Would you like that?"

He seemed surprised by her offer. And though he didn't smile, there was a light of enthusiasm in his eyes. "I guess so."

Caroline handed him the slate and the book. He accepted her gifts as reverently as if they were gold.

"Remember, Ben, once you've mastered the words, you can travel all over the world in the pages of a book." She saw the faraway look that came into his eyes. "Goodbye, Ben. I'll be back next week."

In the kitchen she accepted a cup of coffee from Cora and explained the lessons for the week. Then, taking her leave, she hurried to the rig, eager to return to her cabin before dark.

As she drove away, Cora turned to her taciturn husband and said, "I tell you, Ab, he was hanging on to every word she spoke."

"It won't help him walk."

Cora studied her husband, seeing beneath the guarded look the pain he suffered for his only son. "No. But I haven't seen Ben this alert since the accident. If nothing else, she took him away from his loneliness for a few hours."

That night Caroline awakened from a sound sleep to an eerie bright light flashing against the window. Sitting up, she listened to a strange crackling sound and breathed in the scent of burning wood.

Fire. She jumped from her bed and raced from her room to the schoolroom. Finding nothing, she ran to the window. A fire blazed in the middle of the school yard.

She stormed outside in her nightgown and stared at the flames leaping toward the night sky from a pile of kindling.

A man's deep voice called from the cover of the surrounding woods. "Take a good look at my power. That could just as easily have been your cabin set ablaze while you slept. Take heed."

His oddly high-pitched laughter scraped over nerves already stretched to the breaking point as she raced inside and latched the door. On trembling legs she shoved the table and chairs against the door, then climbed into her bed, shivering beneath the covers.

She lay there, dry-eyed and terrified. She was helpless against this predator. Her fingers curled around the gun, cold and menacing beneath her pillow. What good would a gun do against this sort of man? She had been a fool to think that she could keep him away by the simple threat of force.

The fire was, she knew, another grim reminder that she was still being stalked. Each threat would become more violent until he finally showed his hand.

In the morning Caroline shoveled sand over the ashes to discourage any questions from curious students. But as she spent the day with the children, she found her mind drifting and had to force herself to concentrate on the lessons.

It was nearly two weeks before the predator struck again. As Caroline lay sleeping, a single gunshot was fired through the open window. The bullet landed just inches above her head, sending splinters of wood flying as it embedded in the wall.

She bolted from her bed and cowered, trembling violently, in a corner of the room. As her eyes adjusted to the darkness, she saw the shadow of a man outside the curtained window.

"You are such an easy target," came his muffled voice. "Remember this. If I had wanted you dead, you would already be lying in your own blood."

Caroline bit her lip to keep from crying out. She would not give him the satisfaction of seeing how he affected her.

In the silence that followed, she heard his laughter, high and shrill. It was the most purely evil sound she had ever heard.

"Anytime you're ready, pretty lady, I'll call a halt to this game."

Caroline hugged her arms around herself. Her nerves were at the breaking point. She knew what he wanted of her. It was far worse than fire or gunshots or even death.

As she sat trembling in the darkness, she found herself thinking about Thad, who had not returned since the night he'd brought her the gun.

If only she could confide in him. He was a gunfighter. He'd find a way to keep her safe. But, she reminded herself, it wasn't his fight. And it wasn't fair to bring anyone else into her trouble. Especially now that she knew the depth of this man's determination. Though he didn't intend to kill her, he would have no hesitation about killing anyone who stood in the way of his schemes.

She remained huddled in the corner of the room, cold, terrified, until morning light streaked the sky. Then she forced herself to her feet and stumbled to the window. Her stalker was gone. He was so sure of himself he hadn't even bothered to erase his tracks from the sand.

Caroline carried two buckets of water from the river, one to be used by the children during school hours, the other for her own use. Since the weather had grown hot, she no longer had the chore of adding logs to the fireplace to heat the schoolroom.

As always, the hours spent with the children seemed to fly by. During those hours when she was their teacher, Caroline's troubles were forgotten. And this day, quite by accident, she discovered a new power within herself. With gentle persuasion, she could even heal some of the wounds among the townspeople.

It started innocently enough with a spelling bee, which was won by Runs With The Wind. While the other children congratulated him, the runner-up, ten-year-old Emma Waverly, complained, "I don't think it's right to give the trophy to an Indian."

At once, five children rushed to Runs With The Wind's defense. While Lisbeth and Frank and Danny and Kate stood beside their brother and cousin, Jack took it upon himself to grab the offender by the back of her neck and demand an apology.

"Just a moment," Caroline said sharply. "This is still my class, and I'll handle this. All of you," she said sternly, "sit down."

As the children took their places, she searched her mind for an answer that would satisfy everyone. Softly she said, "Emma, would you lift my table, please."

Emma looked startled, but she obediently stood and walked to the teacher's desk. For several minutes the big, rawboned girl leaned her weight into the table, then turned and said apologetically, "Sorry, Miss Adams. It's too heavy."

"And you, Jack?" she asked. "Do you think you and Emma together could lift the table?"

Though they managed to lift it, they couldn't move it.

"Now," Caroline said gently, "Runs With The Wind, would you give them a hand?"

Still glaring at the girl who had hurled an insult at him, he walked to the other side of the table. Grunting, the three managed to lift and carry the heavy table.

"Where do you want it?" Emma asked.

"Back where it was," Caroline said.

Puzzled, the children set the table down, then stood, waiting for her explanation.

"Alone, Emma, you could never have moved that desk. Even with Jack's help you couldn't do it. But when the two of you worked alongside Runs With The Wind, you could move it anywhere. Isn't that right?"

The girl nodded.

"You'll find that to be true of life, as well. Working with others, you can often accomplish twice as much as when you try to carry the burden alone."

"But why should we have to work with Indians?" Emma asked. "My uncle was killed by his kind."

"And my father was killed by white soldiers," Runs With The Wind stated firmly. "But my *tía*... my aunt," he said by way of explanation, "is married to the finest man I know. Dan Conway, my foster father, is a white man. I love him as much as I revere the memory of my father, Two Moons, great chief of the Comanche."

When Emma opened her mouth to speak, Caroline said, "Return to your desks."

As the children took their seats she added, "It is true that Runs With The Wind is a Comanche, the son of a chief who was killed by white soldiers. And you, Emma, had to see your aunt grieve over the death of your uncle at the hands of Indians. All of you are proud of your heritage, as you should be. But I do not concern myself with your backgrounds. I am far more concerned with what you make of your own lives. And in this schoolroom, your journey must begin with accepting that we all have the right to be different. And while we are different, we can still work together."

The children had gone very quiet.

"The spelling bee was a fair test of your ability. Runs With The Wind won it fairly. If any of you would like to have his trophy, you will have to win the next contest. Until then, he will take the trophy home for safekeeping." Caroline's gaze roamed each student, pausing for long moments on Emma. "Is that understood?"

They nodded.

"Emma, do you have anything to say?" the teacher prodded.

The girl twisted in her chair and extended her hand to the young Comanche. "Sorry," she muttered.

Runs With The Wind accepted her handshake.

Opening a book, Caroline said, "I think it's time to read the next chapter of our story. Lisbeth, would you like to begin?"

The little girl stepped to the front of the room and took the book from her teacher's hands. Soon the students were smiling and nodding, lost in the wonder of the adventure story.

When the children left for the day, Caroline cleaned the schoolroom and prepared for the next day's classes.

That completed, she washed her meager supply of clothing and hung it to dry, then tended the small garden she had planted beside the river. After hours spent at her desk, the hard, physical labor challenged her.

With a hoe she dug at the weeds that encroached on her tender plants. To a child of the city, born among the sprawling shacks, this verdant land was like a soothing balm. Seeing the tiny shoots break free of the soil was like the miracle of birth. A miracle that brought her rich, simple pleasure.

Now, as she tended a row of plants in her garden, she looked up in alarm at the thunder of dozens of horses' hooves heading her way. With a quick, nervous gesture she reached a hand into the pocket of her gown. Each day she'd honed her skill with the little gun. Each night, alone in her cabin, she had loaded and unloaded the chamber in the dark until she was confident she could do it with ease. Still, aiming the pistol at a man and snuffing out his life seemed an impossible act for her.

The horses topped a ridge and came racing toward her. For a moment her heartbeat matched the pounding of hooves. Then she caught sight of a thatch of white hair on the stocky figure in the lead.

"Sheriff Horn." She felt a rush of weak relief.

"'Evening, Miss Adams." He doffed his hat. "Seen a pair of riders heading north?"

"No." For a moment her heart stopped. Had they somehow discovered her predator and the cruel tricks he'd been playing on her? Could the sheriff be hot on his trail?

"Fox broke out of jail. Had an accomplice. Someone came up behind the deputy and knocked him cold. When he woke up he found himself locked in Fox's cell. Fellow at the mercantile saw Fox and a stranger riding like the devil himself was after them. Last anyone saw, they were headed this way."

Seeing the look of fear that came into her eyes, he soothed, "Don't you worry now, ma'am. Those two won't be bothering you. They're too smart to stay in these parts. They'll probably get halfway to California before they even slow down."

The sheriff touched a hand to his hat. "We'll say goodnight now, ma'am. Got to stay on the trail while it's still warm."

The men turned their horses and thundered up the hill.

Caroline's fingers, wet and slippery, were still wrapped around the pistol in her pocket. Gardening had lost its appeal; she had a sudden need to return to the safety of her cabin. She was almost there when a lone horse crested the ridge and headed directly toward her.

Dropping the hoe, she began to run. A deep voice called out to her, but with the wind whistling past her as she ran and the heaving of her labored breath, she couldn't make out the words. She knew only that the solitary rider was almost upon her.

There were perhaps a hundred yards left to run. With her lungs crying out for air, she pushed herself to the limit and struggled to reach the cabin. The hem of her skirt tangled beneath her feet, sending her flying. With a cry of fear she tumbled, landing facedown in the dirt. As she fell, she saw the horse's hooves alongside her and was convinced that she would be trampled.

Work-hardened hands grasped her shoulders, dragging her roughly to her feet. She was twisted around. And found herself looking into puzzled blue eyes.

"Thad." His name came out in a choked cry. For a minute her fingers tightened on the front of his shirt. She wanted to hug him. Then she stiffened and tried to push away. She wanted to strangle him for causing her such fright.

"Didn't you hear me call your name?" He studied her heaving breasts, her look of confusion. No matter how much she denied it, she'd been absolutely terrified.

"I . . . no." She wiped her hands along her skirt and looked around for the fallen hoe. It must be back by the river. She felt completely disoriented. "Why are you here?"

"Can't a neighbor stop by for a friendly visit?"

She eyed him suspiciously. "What are you up to?"

"Don't you remember? I promised to make a latch for the cellar door." He removed some tools from a saddlebag and walked to the side of the cabin. While he bent to his task he asked casually, "I take it you've heard that Fox escaped jail?"

Her gaze was arrested by the taut muscles of his shoulders as he worked. The thought of those arms, so strong, so inviting, caused her throat to go dry. "The sheriff and his men passed by here a while ago. And I have to admit, the news did cause me some concern."

"I just passed them, too, and heard the news. I guess it's a good thing I picked tonight to lend a hand. Maybe I'll just stay awhile and keep you company. I figure since

Fox was the man who attacked you on your arrival in Hope, I'll stay and see he doesn't make a habit of it.'' He kept his tone level, but she sensed the steel beneath the softly spoken words.

Relief flooded through her, though she tried not to show it. "Have you had supper yet?"

He shook his head. "I was hoping you'd invite me to stay."

She laughed. "Why don't you come inside when you're finished and I'll fix supper for both of us."

"Thanks, Teacher." He gave her a heart-stopping grin. "I'd like that."

A short time later Thad turned his horse into the enclosure and walked into the cabin. The first thing he noticed was Caroline kneeling beside a small pen, made out of four logs, next to the fireplace. Inside the pen were six baby chicks, who kept up a constant chorus of high-pitched peeping.

"Taken up chicken raising, Teacher?"

Caroline looked up, still petting one of the little yellow balls of fluff. "Runs With The Wind brought them this morning. He said Dan was given them in payment for some surgery he did and Morning Light thought I might like them." She set the chick down with the others. "Aren't they sweet?"

"You won't be saying that in a few days," he said dryly. "When your cabin smells like a barnyard."

"Oh, they'll be outside by then. I just thought they needed a couple of nights beside the fire before I turn them out into the yard."

"You'll probably make pets of the lot of them," he commented. "And when it comes time to chop off their heads, you'll say you'd rather go hungry."

"I will not," she protested. But he could see the way she glanced fearfully at the chicks, as though she'd already become their protector. "Wouldn't they be more valuable laying eggs instead of being stew in a pot?"

"For a while. Until they grow too old to lay." A smile lurked in his eyes. "Of course, by then you'll have given them all names and you won't want old Suzie to become Sunday supper."

"I was wondering…" She cleared her throat. "Do you think the coyotes will venture into my yard?"

"Coyotes consider baby chicks a delicacy."

He saw the stricken look on her face and nearly choked with laughter. "I suppose tomorrow I could build a small shed for them."

Her eyes widened with pleasure. "Would you? Oh, Thad, that would be wonderful."

He leaned back in the hard chair and stretched out his legs, crossing them at the ankle. As she carried food to the table, he wondered what the hell was happening to him. He had enough work to do on his own ranch without wasting an entire day building a chicken coop. Still, he thought, stealing a glance at her happy face, the reward was worth the effort.

He inhaled deeply. A hunk of venison roasted over the fire. The fragrance of biscuits perfumed the tiny room, along with the aroma of strong coffee bubbling over the fire. To make the meal more festive, Caroline brought out the jar of peach preserves that Cora Meadows had presented her at their first meeting.

There was something about this little cabin that reminded him of his childhood.

Rolling up his sleeves, Thad washed his hands and face in the basin she indicated and accepted a small towel embroidered with pink morning glories.

"Your handiwork?" he asked.

She nodded, feeling oddly pleased that he took notice of something so simple. "I made the stitch to match the design on my mother's china."

"You have all kind of talents, don't you, Teacher?"

At her flush of pleasure he handed the cloth back to her and took a seat at the table. When his plate was filled he tasted the venison and looked up.

"Did young Jack give this to you?"

She nodded. "When he brought it to school, I asked him to tell all the children about his hunt. You should have seen his face, Thad. He was so proud. And later, when I asked him to write about it, he filled his slate with a story about his grand adventure." Her eyes grew dreamy. "I think I finally managed to reach him. For the first time Jack felt as if he had contributed something worthwhile to the class. They all loved his story. Now that I've found the key, I don't think I'll have any problem with him. Suddenly he seems eager to learn all that I can teach him." She chuckled, thinking about the blond, blue-eyed boy who reminded her so much of his uncle. "He's even eager to master sums, now that I've explained that such skills will help decide how many cattle should be in a single grazing area or how many logs it will take to fill a wagon. Once he realized that knowledge will help with ranch chores, he stopped fighting me."

Thad studied the way her eyes glowed. "It means a lot to you to teach the children, doesn't it?"

She said softly, "I know what it is to be hungry to learn, to want with all your heart to be able to form the letters and read the words."

"Did your mother teach you?" Thad asked.

Lying didn't come easily to her. But if she couldn't lie, at least she could evade. "I had to go away to learn."

"That's when you went to that school..." He thought a moment. "Miss Tully's School for Ladies."

Too many questions. She wanted to change the subject, but she felt compelled to reply, so she said simply, "I proved to be an apt student." Avoiding his eyes, she handed him the biscuits. "Tell me what you think of these. I asked your sister, Jessie, to tell me how she'd made hers last Sunday."

She was doing it again. Every time he tried to get her to talk about herself, she managed to change the subject. He shrugged and decided to let her have her way. For now.

As he tried a biscuit with peach preserves, a slow smile touched his lips. "Now this is heaven. I haven't tasted biscuits like this since I was a kid in our sod shack."

Thad leaned back, sipping hot coffee and watching the young woman as she crossed the room to toss another log on the fire. He hadn't seen her in days. He'd told himself it was because of the many chores around his ranch. But the truth was, he had been deliberately avoiding her. He'd needed to prove to himself that he could walk away from her. If he wasn't careful he'd wind up wanting to protect her all the time. And that could lead to all kinds of complications.

"The chicks are settling down to sleep." She filled his cup, keeping her voice low.

"You don't have to whisper, Teacher. They could sleep through a Texas norther."

She crossed the room and studied the tiny chicks, huddled together as much for comfort as for warmth. "Will they sleep through the night?"

"Yep." He drained his cup and walked to her side. "But they'll be awake at dawn. And I promise you, you will be, too."

Bending, she picked up one chick that had been nudged away from the flock. Running a finger along his downy back, she pressed him to her cheek before setting him down in the midst of the others.

"I think you're right." Her gaze was tender. "They're probably all going to become pets."

She stood a moment, deep in thought. Then, crossing to him, she reached into her pocket and handed him the pistol, along with the pouch of bullets. "You may as well take this back, Thad. I'll never be able to use it."

"Why not?"

"I couldn't even shoot at coyotes if they attacked my chicks. How could I ever aim it at a man?"

His eyes narrowed. "What brought all this on?"

"I suppose it's been growing in my mind for some time. But several things happened to seal my decision. First of all, you should know that I'm trying to teach my students that we can all live together in harmony. I don't see how I can say one thing and live another. And tonight, even though I had no idea it was you coming up behind me on your horse, I never thought to use the gun." She trembled, remembering. "It convinced me that I'll have to find a way to survive without it. But I want you to know I'm grateful for all your patience in teaching me how to handle it."

An unexpected anger surged inside him. "I can see that your life has been too sheltered, Teacher. Do you have any idea of the dangers lurking here in the real world?"

Sheltered? Did he have any idea? At his words, Caroline was shocked into silence. It was the perfect opportunity to confide in him. Instead, she let the moment pass.

Thad felt a wave of frustration. How the hell could he protect her when she wouldn't even try to protect herself?

He didn't like the way she looked, all soft and tender. There was too much temptation here. Turning, he picked up his hat and headed toward the door. His tone turned suddenly gruff.

"It's time I got back to my ranch."

Chapter Twelve

Caroline awoke to the shrill peeping of the baby chicks. As she bounded across the floor to check on her tiny charges, she realized that her sleep had not been disturbed once during the night. There had been no fire, no gunshots, no ominous footsteps.

Could it be that her tormentor had left town? Maybe, a small voice inside her mind whispered, he really had been the one who had helped Fox escape jail, and the two of them had been forced to flee together. But why? What connection could he have with the outlaws who had attacked her stage?

She thought back to that fateful day. The gunmen hadn't seemed surprised to find a lone woman aboard. And they had chosen not to kill her.

Now Fox was gone. And so was her tormentor.

She picked up a chick and danced around the room in her nightshift. Oh, if only it could be true. Her happiness would be complete.

She suddenly felt like working. Like celebrating with a frenzy of cleaning.

She gazed out the window at the clear, cloudless sky. Because it was Saturday, there were no classes for the next two days. That would give her time to clean out the cellar and begin preparing space for the bounty of her garden. On a wonderful day like this, her enthusiasm was boundless.

She hurriedly dressed. Hiking her skirts up around her ankles, she picked up a lantern and headed for the cellar. An hour later, at the sound of a horse and wagon approaching, she crawled out from the underground room, her hands and face, as well as her gown, soiled and dirty.

Thad had already climbed down from the wagon and was busy unloading lumber. He looked up as she approached and endured the usual jolt at the sight of her. Her hair had pulled loose from its knot and tumbled wildly around her shoulders. A long white apron, streaked with dirt, called attention to her tiny waist. This morning she was a street urchin in a woman's body.

He deliberately kept his tone light. "'Morning, Teacher. How'd your pets sleep?"

"Like babies. But you were right. They woke me at dawn. And you were right about something else," she added with a shy smile. "My cabin is beginning to smell like a barnyard."

"We ought to have those chicks moved into their own place before the day is over."

He glanced up to see that her gaze was fixed on the rocking chair in the back of his wagon. When she shot him a questioning glance he said casually, "I had two of them. Thought you might have a use for one."

"A rocking chair?" Her face was wreathed in smiles. "Oh, Thad, thank you."

He carried it inside the cabin and placed it in front of the fireplace. When he stepped back, studying it, he realized it looked right there. And when he saw the light in Caroline's eyes, he realized she looked right, too. Everything about this woman and her tiny cabin were just right.

He glanced at the dirty smudge on her cheek. Without thinking he touched a finger to the spot. "Looks like you started your chores already." At the first touch he felt the strong sexual pull and cursed himself for his foolishness.

She felt the tug, as well, and was startled by it. For a moment she was unable to move.

He pulled his hand away and let it drop to his side.

She took a step back, reminding herself to be more careful in his presence.

Swallowing, she glanced down at her smudged hands and clothing. "I may be dirty, but the cellar is clean." Nodding toward the wagon outside, she asked, "Can I give you a hand?"

The last thing he needed was her standing near, distracting him. "Don't let me keep you from your chores, Teacher."

As she followed him outside and walked toward the cellar, his gaze followed her until she disappeared beneath the cabin. Then he picked up a hammer and began work on the shed.

Caroline stood in the bright sunshine, draping the heavy muslin sheet over the clothesline. The breeze caught and lifted her hair, sending it dipping low over one eye. Pausing to brush it aside, she turned and found Thad staring at her. Even from so great a distance she felt the intensity of his look.

In the blink of an eye he bent to his work.

He had removed his shirt and tossed it carelessly over the branch of a tree. His muscles bunched and moved as he set another board into place and began to pound nails.

Sweat glistened darkly on his skin. She experienced an odd little shiver along her spine.

Picking up an empty bucket, Caroline headed to the river. A few minutes later she returned and handed him a dipper of cool water.

He turned to her, sweat dripping from his forehead. Without thinking, she lifted the hem of her long apron and blotted his face. The intimacy of her action caught them both by surprise.

He gave her a quick smile before draining the dipper. Wiping the back of his hand across his mouth, he handed it back to her. They stood, quietly admiring his work.

"That's a sturdy-looking shed."

"It ought to keep your pets safe from coyotes."

"That's a comfort."

He gave her another smile and she felt her heart stop. No man had ever affected her the way this man did. She was achingly aware of him. So much so that she had to look away for fear of revealing her feelings.

"I'd...better see about fixing you some food." She left the pail of water and crossed the yard to the cabin.

When she disappeared inside, Thad went back to his work. But only part of his mind was on the shed he was building. The other part seemed to return again and again to the shy, complex Caroline Adams.

When Caroline called Thad for the noonday meal, he walked down to the river and plunged his face and arms into the cool water. Splashing it over his naked chest, he hurriedly washed before pulling on his shirt and tucking it into his pants. When he entered the cabin, he was combing his fingers through his wet hair.

"Something smells wonderful." He took a chair.

"I made a stew of the venison that was left." She ladled steaming food into two bowls and carried them to the table.

Setting them down, she sliced through a loaf of hot, crusty bread. They ate in companionable silence until their hunger was satisfied.

When he leaned back he said, "That was as fine a meal as I've had in a long time, Teacher."

She felt herself blushing. To avoid his disturbing gaze she wrapped a towel around the handle of the blackened coffeepot and lifted it from the fire. "Then you must have been starving. I'm a very plain cook."

He studied her as she paused beside him to fill his cup with coffee. "Believe me, ma'am, there's nothing plain about you."

The color on her cheeks deepened. She turned away quickly and busied herself at the fireplace.

He drained his cup and scraped back his chair. "I'd better get back to my work. Thanks again for the food."

She watched as he strolled to the shed. Stripping off his shirt, he tossed it aside. Then he bent once more to his hammer and nails.

By late afternoon the shed was completed and the chicks had been introduced to their new home. While Caroline scattered grain, Thad made a nest of straw in the corner.

"They'll use the roosts," he said, pointing to the shelf that ran the length of the shed, "when they're a little bigger. But for now they'll just huddle together here in the corner."

"Will they know enough to come in each night?"

The worried look on her face had him smiling gently. "Don't worry, Teacher. They'll learn. All you have to do is latch the door each night and your lucky pets will be safe from predators.''

If only life could always be so simple, she thought. Just latch the door and hold the world at bay.

He tugged on a lock of her hair. ''Where did you go to just then?''

She looked up into his worried eyes and gave a quick smile. ''I was thinking how lucky I am that coyotes don't know how to unlatch doors.'' A little breathlessly she held out her hand. ''Thank you, Thad. It seems I've been saying that a lot lately. But I truly mean it. For the chair, for the shed, for all the kind things you've done for me. Will you stay for supper?''

He looked down at their joined hands and continued holding hers a moment longer than necessary. Then, releasing it, he shook his head reluctantly. ''I have a skittish mare back at my ranch that needs tending.''

He climbed to the wagon seat and picked up the reins. ''My sister-in-law asked me to invite you to her place tomorrow for Sunday supper. Morning Light said the whole family will be there.'' His smile widened. ''Think you can stand another gathering of all the noisy Conways?''

She lifted a hand to shade the sun from her eyes. ''I think it sounds wonderful.''

''Then I'll stop by for you on my way.''

She nodded and watched until his wagon was out of sight.

Sunday service was more crowded than usual. Walking up the aisle, Caroline nodded and smiled at all the familiar faces that turned to acknowledge her. How much easier it was, she thought, now that these people had names to go with the faces. Someday, if she was very lucky, she might even be able to call them friends.

Knowing her position in the community, Caroline had taken great pains with her appearance. Despite the heat of the day she wore the brown dress buttoned to her throat and a shawl draped modestly around her shoulders. The matching brown bonnet was pinned on top of her tightly knotted hair. Though her feet were roasting inside heavy boots, she endured. She was determined to ignore the pinch of her spectacles across the bridge of her nose. Whatever the cost, she would be regarded by everyone who saw her as a proper lady.

Cora and Abner Meadows took a seat near the back of the church. Caroline wondered idly if Ben was all alone back on the ranch or if they had a ranch hand who stayed with the boy.

Belva Spears, looking thin and frail enough to blow away in a good wind, sat all alone in a pew. As the other families began filing into church, Belva watched without expression until, suddenly, she seemed to sit up straighter, her gaze locked on a stocky figure moving toward her.

Caroline watched as Sheriff Horn took a seat beside Belva. His thatch of white hair had been slicked back and still bore traces of water. His clothes, though faded and worn, were clean and neatly pressed.

Both Belva and the sheriff stared straight ahead. Both seemed stiff and uncomfortable. But when the organist played the first notes of the opening hymn, Belva opened the songbook and moved closer to share it with the man beside her. She and the sheriff, keeping their gazes firmly on the printed page, moved their mouths woodenly. The sheriff's neck had turned very red.

Reverend Symes's voice was urgent, almost pleading, as he reminded the congregation about the wily devil who walks the world in the form of temptation.

"The devil coaxes us to lie," he whispered, eyes bright with zeal, "and one lie leads to more and more until the truth is buried. Once we begin to lie and cheat, we put aside all the things we were taught at our mother's knee."

To cover the guilt she felt at the preacher's words, Caroline concentrated on the devil. The devil, she decided, was a ruthless man with all the power that wealth can command. The devil was a cruel tormentor who had vowed to follow her to the ends of the earth until she gave in to his evil demands. She prayed her own personal devil had gone for good.

As the preacher's voice droned on, Caroline found her thoughts drifting. Why did Thad never come to Sunday services with his family? In fact, why did he shun Hope and its people?

She glanced at Sheriff Horn. What was it he'd said on the day she and Thad had first ridden into town? She'd been too distracted to pay much attention; she strained to recall the words.

"The only time we ever see you is when we need you or you need us. And you haven't needed us in all the years I've been here."

Obviously, then, they'd needed him. She wondered what Thad had been called upon to do for the people of Hope. Even though most of the people seemed to consider him the next thing to an outlaw, they gave him a great deal of respect. Like a man much feared. And yet from all that Caroline had seen, he was a kind, considerate man who wanted nothing more than to be left alone.

Did he ever need anyone? She couldn't imagine it. He was the strongest, most self-sufficient man she'd ever met.

She was startled when the preacher called out in ringing tones, "There is nothing so terrible as a lie. For once told, it must be repeated again and again. Remember, my good people—" he stretched both hands out and lifted them toward heaven "—the truth shall set you free."

With that, the congregation got to its feet and began another hymn. Caroline, her cheeks burning, leafed through the pages until she located the words and joined in the singing.

Later, as they filed from the church, Caroline found herself walking beside Sara Waverly and her two children.

"Wasn't that a beautiful sermon?" Sara whispered.

"Why...I..." Just then Caroline's hand was caught in the firm grasp of Reverend Symes.

"Good morning, Miss Adams."

"Good morning, Reverend." Seeing Cora's face in the crowd, Caroline suddenly decided to play matchmaker herself. "You know Sara Waverly?"

"Of course." He nodded, offering his hand.

"Sara and I were just discussing your beautiful sermon." Caroline turned to see Sara's cheeks suffused with color.

"Were you?" Reverend Symes turned soulful eyes on Caroline, and she had the distinct impression that he could read her mind. If he could, he knew that she hadn't heard a word of his sermon.

"The truth shall set you free," Sara repeated. "That is a beautiful testament." Her cheeks reddened. "I especially liked the part about learning at your mother's knee," she added a little breathlessly. "Reverend Symes, these are my children, Ethan and Emma."

As if in benediction, the reverend placed his hand on each young head, then dropped his hands lightly to their shoulders. The children, surprised by his gentle touch, shifted from one foot to the other, staring up at their mother.

"Since the death of my husband, I've had to be both mother and father to them. James believed in the stick and the belt, and I fear that I'm not nearly strict enough with my children," Sara said, lowering her eyes.

Caroline shuddered to think that Sara might become even tougher with her children. They were already so cowed they could hardly move without her permission.

"And each night," Sara continued, "knowing we're all alone, I pray that I've taught them the proper lessons to prepare them for life."

"You're never really alone," Reverend Symes said softly.

"Oh, I know. Without that knowledge, I swear I wouldn't be able to make it through a single day."

"Perhaps I should prepare another sermon on the power of love."

Caroline glanced at the young mother and then at the preacher. Sara was hanging on his every word. The children, standing between them, seemed to visibly relax as they glanced from their mother to the preacher and then back again.

Caroline edged away. With a backward glance, she realized they never even missed her.

As she climbed to the seat of her rig, Morning Light called, "Did Thad remember to invite you for supper today, Miss Adams?"

"Yes. I'd be pleased to come."

"Then we will look for you this afternoon."

Caroline nodded and flicked the reins, mentally planning which biscuits she intended to bake.

"You're late, Uncle Thad," Lisbeth scolded. "I was afraid you weren't coming."

"And miss doing this?" Thad caught the little girl and tossed her high in the air, causing her to squeal in delight.

Caroline watched their play with a smile of pure pleasure. She'd never seen a man who was so in tune with what children liked. Amazing, considering Thad had no children of his own.

"Where's your father, Little Bit?" He lifted his niece to his shoulders before helping Caroline from the wagon.

"He and Uncle Dan are in the barn with the boys." The little girl wrinkled her nose slightly at the mention of boys. "They're looking over Uncle Dan's new bull."

"Then I guess that's where I'm headed. Want to come with me?"

"And look at that ugly old bull again? No thanks. I'd rather stay here and help with supper."

"And how about you, ma'am?" he asked, grinning at Caroline. "Want to look at an ugly old bull, or would you rather help with supper?"

"I'm going with Lisbeth," Caroline said with a laugh. "But I think the ugly old bull will suit you just fine."

His niece was giggling uncontrollably as Thad settled her on the ground and strolled away.

Taking Caroline's hand, Lisbeth led her up the steps and called, "Miss Adams is here!"

Jessie and Morning Light hurried from the kitchen to greet their guest. After an exchange of pleasantries they settled into a comfortable routine, with Caroline and the girls setting the table while Jessie and her sister-in-law finished up in the kitchen.

Afterward, while they waited for the men to return from the barn, Morning Light gave Caroline a tour of the fascinating house she shared with the doctor and their children.

The cool interior reflected two cultures, with sturdy tables and chairs and colorful handwoven rugs. The walls were hung with tapestries painstakingly depicting the history of the Comanche people.

"For Runs With The Wind, Danny and Kate," Morning Light said simply. "So they will know their heritage."

"That's beautiful. Maybe one day they can use it in class to teach the children something of the history of your people."

Pleased with the idea, Morning Light said, "Runs With The Wind told me about the words he exchanged with Emma Waverly. I wish to thank you for what you said on his behalf."

Caroline seemed embarrassed by her words. "I didn't do anything special."

"But you did, Miss Adams," came a voice from behind her.

Caroline turned to find Dan standing in the doorway. Behind him were Cole and Thad and the boys, Jack, Frank and Danny.

Walking closer, Dan gave her a probing look. "It was very brave of you to suggest that, despite the differences in cultures, all people can succeed by working together. It's not something most people want to hear."

Caroline felt her cheeks grow hot, knowing that all eyes were on her.

Dan continued, "A few parents may be offended by your words. The wounds between the whites and the Comanche are still very raw."

"I suppose so. But Reverend Symes said it best today during his sermon. The truth shall set you free. They needed to hear the truth. There was a time," Caroline said softly, "when this land was divided by the cruelest of wars, and even those wounds are healing."

"She's right." Thad ruffled his nephew's hair and studied the light that came into Caroline's eyes whenever she started sounding like a teacher. "And the truth will set us all free. But right now, could we eat?"

They broke into gales of laughter as they trooped into the large dining room and sat down to a wonderful meal of venison and pork, with early garden potatoes and vegetables and dark rich gravy spooned over hot biscuits. For dessert they were treated to peach preserve cobbler sweetened with thick cream.

"Are you excited about next week, Miss Adams?" Lisbeth asked.

Caroline looked puzzled.

"The town social," the little girl explained. "Didn't anyone tell you?"

"It's a party," Jessie broke in, seeing Caroline's confusion. "The town holds one every year to celebrate summer. For two days the ranch chores are forgotten. Folks from miles around come to town and spend the night in their wagons or even under the stars. There will be fiddlers and dancing and..."

"Games and contests for the children..." Lisbeth added.

"And swimming in the river," Jack said excitedly.

Jessie smiled at her husband. "Saturday night there's a potluck supper and dancing. And Sunday all the women pack baskets of food and the men bid on them."

"Bid?" Caroline saw the intimate glances exchanged by Jessie and Cole. Though they'd been married for years, it was obviously some sort of courtship ritual they still enjoyed.

"A man has to pay to share a lady's basket," Dan explained. "The money goes to the church."

"Doesn't that sound exciting?" Lisbeth asked.

"Yes. Yes it does." Caroline found herself getting caught up in the enthusiasm. She'd never been to a social. She wouldn't even know how to act. But it did sound like fun.

"Are you going, Uncle Thad?" Lisbeth asked.

Thad looked distinctly disinterested. "You know I never bother with such things, Little Bit."

"But it would be more fun if you came."

He gave a negligent stretch of his shoulders. "I'm busy these days with a very expensive mare who's going to give me the most beautiful foal ever born in Texas. In fact," he said, scraping back his chair, "I'd better be getting back. I don't like leaving her alone for too long."

Caroline helped the women with the dishes, then followed Thad to the wagon. On the ride back to her cabin she lifted her head to watch the clouds scudding across a full moon. Somehow, the thought of the town social didn't seem nearly as exciting as it had when she had first heard it mentioned.

"You're awfully quiet tonight." Thad's deep voice roused her from her thoughts. "Worried about your chicks?"

She shook her head. "They're safe in the shed you built."

"Something on your mind?"

"Just pleasantly tired."

"Will you be going to the town social?" His voice sounded deeper as the darkness closed in around them.

"I suppose I should. It would be expected of the new teacher."

"Ever been to one before?"

"No." She turned her head slightly. "You?"

"No. I don't have time for such nonsense." He cleared his throat. "Still, it might be fun seeing my nieces and nephews running races and swimming."

The wagon drew to a halt in front of her cabin. As she made a move to climb down, Thad's hand on her sleeve stopped her.

"Hell, why not admit the truth and be set free?" he said with a chuckle. "Maybe I'd find out I like sharing a basket lunch with a pretty woman."

Her heart seemed to fly to her throat and lodge there.

He climbed from the wagon and raised his hands to assist her. But as she started to step down he suddenly caught her in his arms.

"Dammit, woman," he muttered thickly against her cheek, "you don't weigh as much as a sack of flour."

For long moments she was held, her feet not touching the ground. She could feel the tension humming through him. Then, almost roughly, he set her on her feet and climbed back into the wagon. With a crack of the whip he was gone.

Chapter Thirteen

"Remember, I'd like you older children to assist the younger ones, please."

In single file Caroline led the children from the schoolroom to the big farm wagon that Thad Conway had agreed to loan her for the day. What she hadn't known was that he would insist upon driving it. She'd expected to see Manuel.

It was always a shock when she saw Thad. His shoulders were so wide they stretched the rough fabric of his shirt tautly. The callused hands holding the reins were so big and work-roughened. His arms, covered by fine golden hair, were bronzed by the sun. And his eyes, hard, ice blue chips, always seemed to see more than he admitted.

"'Morning, ma'am." He touched the tip of his wide-brimmed hat.

"Good morning. I didn't want to take you away from your chores. I know how busy you are with that mare."

"No trouble."

He watched as she herded her young charges into the back of the wagon.

"Hey, Uncle Thad," young Jack called in surprise. "Are you going with us?"

"Looks like."

Lisbeth crawled up to the front seat and planted a kiss on her uncle's cheek before sitting down beside him. "How come you're here?" she asked.

"Your teacher needed a wagon, and mine was available."

"I'm glad." The little girl wrapped her arms around his arm and looked up at him adoringly.

When everyone was settled in the hay, Caroline sat cross-legged in their midst. Thad flicked the reins and they started off across the hills. While they rolled along, Caroline asked the children to name every plant, tree, bird and animal they saw.

The varieties seemed infinite. The hills were carpeted with bluebonnets and Indian paintbrushes, while the more rocky crags were cloaked in dark green juniper. Deer leaped across a meandering stream, and flocks of doves took flight with a flutter of wings as the wagon approached. Prairie dogs stood on hind legs to watch as they came near, then disappeared into their tunnels to escape the danger.

Over his shoulder Thad glanced at the young woman who had the ability to transmit her own curiosity about everything around her to the children. She managed to direct their attention to all the ordinary things about their lives that they had begun to take for granted. Through her eyes, such mundane things became extraordinary.

"Mountain lion." Thad pulled the wagon to a halt so the children could see the sleek creature moving along a jagged rocky shelf high above them.

Caroline lifted her head, shading the sun from her eyes. On her face was an expression of pure pleasure.

"What good is a mountain lion?" Ethan Waverly asked. "Pa used to say all it does is kill cattle."

"But it also kills other predators, like wolves and coyotes," Caroline pointed out. "And its coat can keep us from freezing in the winter. I'd say the mountain lion, no matter how dangerous, can be our friend."

"Maybe some things should exist just because they're beautiful." Thad wasn't looking at the cat. His gaze was arrested by the young woman surrounded by her students.

Seeing the direction of her uncle's gaze, Lisbeth caught the flush on her teacher's cheeks and was puzzled by it.

A short time later the wagon pulled up in front of the neat little house owned by Cora and Ab Meadows. The children, eager for their new adventure, tumbled out of the wagon.

Cora Meadows, looking slightly flustered, met them at the door to her house.

"Is Ben ready?" Caroline asked.

"He's been ready since sunup." Cora glanced at the crowd of children gathering around the porch and became even more flustered. "I don't think he slept a wink last night."

Neither had Caroline, but she wouldn't admit it.

While the children watched, Ab Meadows carried his young son out the door and set him on a blanket spread beneath a giant oak. Cora brought several plump pillows and placed them under the boy so that he was almost in a sitting position.

"Are you sure you want to do this?" Ab whispered. "There's still time to send them away."

"No, Pa. I'm fine. Really."

For a minute the older man continued to kneel, his hand on his son's shoulder as if to protect him from this invasion of curious outsiders. Then, getting to his feet, he dusted the knees of his worn pants and walked a short

distance away, head down, shoulders sagging. Nervously Cora followed her husband.

At first the children seemed wary of their friend who
could no longer walk. They held back, afraid to look at
him, afraid to come too close.

"Hello, Ben," Caroline called in her most cheerful
tone. "Did you do the sums I gave you?"

"Yes, ma'am." Ben proudly held out his slate.

While she looked it over, Caroline said casually, "You
may all take your seats in a semicircle around Ben."

From his position in the wagon Thad watched in puzzled silence. No one had told him what this was about.
But now, seeing the scene unfolding before him, he realized what Caroline was up to.

The fear experienced by Ben's parents was palpable.
And the discomfort of the children was obvious. They
fidgeted, and many of the younger ones clung tightly to
the hands of older brothers or sisters. They didn't know
what they were afraid of; they knew only that this boy
was somehow different from the boy they had once
known.

Seeing his uncle watching him, young Jack shuffled
over and stiffly extended his hand to the boy who had
once been his riding and fishing partner. "Hey, Ben.
How're you doing?"

"Okay, I guess." Ben caught Jack's outstretched hand,
pumping it up and down in his nervousness.

Jack knelt in the grass next to Ben. Shrugging his
shoulders for emphasis, he said, "I didn't know if ... I
mean, I thought you might not want to see me, since we
were friends and all."

"We're still friends." Ben squinted up. "Aren't we?"

"Yeah." Jack smiled and Ben's lips curved upward.

Slowly, uneasily, the other children followed Jack's lead, calling greetings as they sat or knelt on either side of Ben.

Caroline watched as the children eyed the boy, some staring boldly, others looking away whenever he caught their curious glances. When she'd learned that most of them had never come to see him since his fall, she'd realized that they all needed to learn how to deal with his infirmity. It wasn't cruelty, she had assured Cora, that kept them away from their old friend; it was ignorance.

"They have to be taught that Ben is the same as he was before," she'd told Cora. "That even though he can't walk, he still has a fine mind, and a need for friends."

But even though Ben had been excited by the prospect of seeing his old classmates, Cora hadn't been convinced. Nor had her husband, Ab.

Caroline's heart went out to them. They had been as wounded by Ben's accident as the boy had. Now they feared seeing him hurt again. She prayed she hadn't made a terrible mistake.

Caroline handed Ben his slate. "They're all correct. You've earned another perfect mark in my book."

Cora and Ab, standing to one side, saw the look of pride in their son's eyes. Wearing identical frowns of concern, they turned away. Cora made her way back to the house, while her husband came to stand beside Thad's wagon.

"Didn't know you were coming," Ab said almost apologetically.

"I didn't know it myself." Thad stepped down. "Did I hear you have a new foal?"

Ab nodded absently. It was plain that his mind was still on his son and the children who were eyeing him with distrust.

"Why don't we have a look at it?" Thad offered.

Ab swallowed and pulled his gaze away. "Sure thing. Come on." He'd never taken the time to know the gunman called The Texan. But since he was here with a wagonload of children, Ab guessed he'd show Thad Conway some courtesy. Besides, rumor had it that he had the finest herd of mustangs in Texas.

The morning seemed to drag by as the children read or did their sums in small groups. Those assigned to Ben's group were urged to gather around him while Caroline explained simple division. She noticed that the children were being careful not to get too close to Ben or to touch him. And she realized that they weren't so much afraid of him as they were afraid of hurting him.

They thought he was fragile, she realized. They were treating him like a sick child and not like their old friend and classmate.

The sun was directly overhead now, and the children took refuge beneath the low-hanging branches of the oak, drawing into an ever tightening circle around Ben.

When Caroline announced that it was time for lunch, the children opened their baskets and saddlebags and spread the food on the grass, talking, laughing, sharing.

At Caroline's urging, Cora had prepared a basket for Ben, even though she had wanted to have Ab bring him inside for lunch.

"He'll be tired after the long morning outside," Cora had argued. "Ben isn't used to the fresh air anymore."

"But it will be a good tired," Caroline said simply. "You said he often wakes in the night with bad dreams. Maybe after a day outside he'll sleep better."

In the end she had prevailed and Cora had packed the basket with Ben's favorite foods.

Seeing the horses grazing on a nearby hill, Emma Waverly asked without thinking, "Which one were you riding when you took your fall, Ben?"

In the shocked silence that followed, Ben pointed. "That one. The big black with the four white stockings."

Realizing that this was the perfect opening, Caroline guided the children into an easy discussion about accidents, and this led Emma to say, "Why don't you tell us about your accident, Ben?"

"I was on old Blackie." He polished off the last of his apple and tossed the core aside. A flock of birds descended, adding their chorus to the background. "I was coming home from the creek with a couple of fish for supper. I remember thinking that Pa would be happy, 'cause Ma had killed our old rooster the night before and Pa said he was too tough to eat. There was a storm coming up, and I was in a hurry to make it home before it hit." His voice lowered, half-dreamy, as he slipped into the memory. "We were coming up the ridge just beyond that one." He pointed and the children turned to stare at the high, rocky ridge looming in the distance. "There was a big crack of thunder and I dug my heels into old Blackie's sides and let out a holler. And then the rain came pelting down, and when we got to the gap in the stone, I just gave him his head, expecting him to take the jump like he always did. But I guess with the rain and all . . ." His voice trailed off.

Caroline glanced around. The children had grown strangely silent.

"I don't remember hitting the ground," Ben said more softly. "I just remember old Blackie stumbling, and me sailing through the air. When I woke up, he was gone, and I figured he'd run off. It was pouring rain and I was soaking wet. I remember looking around for my fish, and when I saw them, I started to get up. But I couldn't. And I thought, well, I guess I'll crawl over. But I couldn't.'' His tone sounded incredulous, as though he still couldn't believe what had happened. He shrugged. ''I just couldn't move.''

''How did you get home?'' Ethan Waverly asked.

''I just laid there, shivering, for hours. It was dark, and I figured my folks would be worried sick about me.''

Caroline could see that the children were caught up in the story, imagining what they would do in such a cir-cumstance.

''Did you cry?'' Lisbeth asked.

Ben shrugged, unwilling to talk about crying in front of his friends. Especially in front of girls. ''There was too much rain falling to know if I was crying. Besides, I was more worried about my pa and ma.''

''How did they find you?'' Jack asked.

''Pa said when Blackie came home without me he knew something was wrong. So he loaded his rifle and came looking for me. When he fired it, I heard it over the sound of the storm. I started hollering and didn't stop until he finally found me.''

''When did you find out you couldn't walk?'' one of the bigger boys asked.

Ben, growing bolder during his narrative, answered with a matter-of-fact ''The next day. I guess I slept a long time. When I woke up, Doc Conway was in the kitchen with my folks.'' Ben glanced toward Runs With The Wind and young Kate and Danny, wondering if their fa-ther had told them much about the accident. But they seemed as curious as the others. He continued, ''I tried to get up and I couldn't. I couldn't feel my legs at all. For a minute I thought maybe he'd cut them off, and I let out a holler. By the time they all came running in, I had the bed covers off and saw that my legs were still there. But I couldn't feel 'em at all.''

Caroline turned to Runs With The Wind, who accompanied Dan on most of his rounds. "Can you tell us what Dr. Conway found?"

"He said it was an injury to the spine. And he thought," the boy said carefully, "that because Ben feels no pain, the injury is more serious than if he could feel pain."

Suddenly growing bolder, the children asked to see Ben's legs and even to touch them.

Unselfconsciously the children gathered around.

When they asked him to explain how his legs felt, he grew thoughtful before giving them an answer. "They just feel like they aren't there."

"Do they hurt?" tenderhearted Lisbeth asked.

He shook his head. "I just can't feel them at all."

"How do you get around your house?" Ethan Waverly asked.

"My pa has to carry me. Mostly I just lie in bed, 'cause Pa's so busy with all the farm chores. Without me to help, he has to do even more than before."

Caroline was surprised to note that even now Ben was more concerned with his parents than with his own suffering. For one so young, he was remarkably generous. Once again she became aware of the pain his infirmity had caused his loving parents.

Even the youngest children seemed to have lost their fear when they were finally allowed to ask all the questions that came to mind, and to stare at Ben's lifeless legs and even touch them.

When their curiosity was satisfied, Caroline said, "I think it's time to put away our lunch baskets and get back to our studies."

While the older students worked on their sums, Caroline helped the beginning readers, who clustered around her in a small group. As she worked with them, she glanced over at the group of boys and girls seated around Ben. No longer did they shun him. They had completely taken over the blanket, with Ben in the middle.

Jack had apparently appointed himself protector, seeing that no one got too close. Lisbeth held the slate while Ben wrote with chalk. When his hand got tired, Lisbeth passed the slate to someone else, giving Ben a chance to rest.

When the older students were called on to read aloud, it was obvious that Ben's reading skills had improved so much that he was now better than Emma, who until now had been considered the best reader in the class. As a reward for his efforts, Caroline handed Ben the treasured book of adventure stories.

"At the end of every day, the student who has shown the most effort is permitted to read a chapter to the class," Caroline explained. "I think we would all agree, Ben, that today that privilege is yours."

While the children settled back to listen, Ben began to read.

Seeing the rapt faces of the children, Cora stepped outside to investigate. Abner and Thad, strolling from the barn, joined her. The parents were overwhelmed to see the way the students had responded to their son. The boys and girls lay in a cozy circle around Ben, some with eyes closed, others staring at the clouds that dusted the sky. Young Jack's hand rested casually on Ben's shoulder. Lisbeth turned the pages while Ben read.

Ab and Cora were stunned to hear their son's voice washing over the crowd of children, taking them to a land none of them would ever see.

Cora turned to her husband, and he could see the glitter of tears on her cheeks. Touching a big, work-worn hand to her face, he wiped away her tears and awkwardly drew her to his chest. They stood together, feeling their hearts alternately breaking and mending. The shining look in their son's eyes was something they had thought lost forever. Now, seeing it, hearing his voice strong and clear, they began to feel the first faint stirrings of hope.

They seemed completely unaware of Thad, standing in silence to one side, his eyes narrowed in concentration.

"Thank you, Ben," Caroline said when the chapter was finished.

"That was good reading, Ben." Jack clapped a hand on his friend's shoulder.

"I have a lot of time to read now that I can't do farm chores."

"Maybe I'll come by next week and we can work on our reading together."

"I'd like that," Ben said softly.

"So would I," Jack said with a laugh. "You're so much better'n me, my grades are bound to improve."

"All right, children," Caroline called. "It's time to get to the wagon."

Their departure was not at all like their arrival. It was obvious that the children had become so comfortable around Ben that they were reluctant to leave. They punched his shoulder or slapped his hand as they bid goodbye. And Ben, no longer self-conscious about his infirmity, laughed and shouted to each of them.

The older children helped the younger ones into the wagon while Caroline walked to where Cora and Abner stood together.

"Thank you for allowing us to come," Caroline said.

"I'm glad now that I let you talk me into it," Cora admitted. "But I was afraid."

"You had a right to be worried." Caroline gave her a bright smile. "The truth is, I was worried, too. But I think now..." She glanced toward Ben, still lying on the blanket, his face wreathed in smiles. "I think it's going to be all right."

Abner looked at this young woman and thought how angry he'd been when his wife had first told him of her plans. The thought of the children coming to ridicule and taunt his son, to flaunt their ability to run and play, had been like a knife to his heart. But now, seeing the look in his son's eyes, his heart was nearly overflowing with a mixture of relief and joy.

His eyes were still haunted; his lips still tight and pinched with the pain he had carried all these long months alone. But his handshake was firm as he caught Caroline's hand in his and said, "You come back now, hear?"

"I will, Mr. Meadows. We all will, if you'll have us. As long as the weather allows, I'd like to bring the class often."

He nodded, then turned to where his son lay beneath the tree. Ben's eyes were bright with excitement as his father lifted him and carried him to the front porch.

The children waved and shouted until the wagon disappeared below a ridge. Cora stood, the blanket folded over her arms, waving until they were out of sight. Ab stood beside her, holding his son. When they went inside, he carried his son to his bed and found he had to swallow several times before he managed to get by the lump that had formed in his throat.

When the wagon rolled to a stop at the schoolhouse, the children scrambled down and headed for their own horses or wagons to continue the journey to their homes.

"Goodbye, Miss Adams," they called.

"Goodbye."

When the last child had gone, Caroline turned to Thad.

"Thank you for the use of your wagon. I know how busy you must be at your own ranch."

"I was glad to do it."

He studied the way she looked, hair teased by the wind, eyes still shining from the excitement of the day. Did she have any idea of the miracle that had just occurred?

As he picked up the reins he fixed her with a probing look and added, "You're an amazing woman, Caroline Adams. The people of Hope have no idea how lucky they are to have you teaching their children."

Before she could react, he was gone in a cloud of dust.

Chapter Fourteen

Saturday, the first day of the town social, dawned bright and clear. By noon the sun shimmered in an ice blue sky unblemished by a single cloud.

Caroline spent the morning in a frenzy of cooking and baking. Besides Sunday's picnic lunch, Jessie had explained to Caroline that each woman was expected to supply a dish for the Saturday evening potluck supper, which would be followed by dancing until, as Jessie explained, "the fiddlers stopped fiddling or the jug went dry."

While the last of young Jack's generous gift of venison roasted over the fire, along with several plump fish from the river, Caroline dug precious potatoes and picked tender young vegetables from her garden. At the table she rolled out pie dough, cutting it into fancy strips and fluting the edges carefully over tart cherry filling. The wonderful aroma filled the tiny cabin.

Caroline had carefully washed and ironed both her dresses. She would wear the brown one today and save the dove gray with the white collar and cuffs for tomorrow's church services and the picnic. She detested the thought of trying to dance in her old brown boots, but she had no choice. They were all she had.

Scattering grain on the floor of the shed for the chicks, she latched the door. She was taking no chances on coyotes coming upon them before she returned.

She carefully placed the blackened pots of roasted meat, fish and vegetables in the back of the wagon, then returned for the cherry pies. When everything was loaded, she climbed to the seat of the wagon and flicked the reins. The horse took off at a gentle clip.

When Caroline reached the town of Hope, she was surprised by the number of horses and wagons littering the street. Everywhere she looked, people clustered around, calling out greetings. Children and dogs scampered about, chasing each other among the wagons.

The festive atmosphere was contagious. For two glorious days, the ranch chores could be forgotten, the tough business of survival could be put aside.

She guided her horse and rig the length of the congested street to the church. Inside, the men had set up long planks to hold the array of food being brought by the women.

In a corner of the church Reverend Symes was having a whispered discussion with Sara Waverly. They looked up when they caught sight of Caroline.

"Ah, Miss Adams. Perhaps here is our solution, Mrs. Waverly." Waving Caroline over, the preacher explained, "It seems we have a problem with some of our girls. I think a young lady like yourself is the perfect one to handle the situation."

"What did they do, Reverend?"

Sara, looking as if she'd eaten something sour, replied, "They found the boys swimming in the creek and decided to join them."

"Oh dear. And do you mean they don't know how to swim?" Caroline turned away, ready to rush to the rescue. "We must go help them at once."

"That is not what I mean."

Sara's stern words had her turning back. "Are they fighting?"

"Of course not."

Caroline was clearly puzzled. "If they're not drowning and not fighting, what's wrong?"

"You see nothing wrong with girls and boys swimming together?"

"Well..." Caroline thought back to her own childhood. There'd been no time to be carefree, but she had managed to slip away to the river sometimes, just to escape the tedium. But always she'd been alone, not by choice but by circumstance.

Mistaking her silence, Sara said sternly, "I realize, Miss Adams, that you are as shocked and disgusted as I, but far too much of a lady to show it."

Shocked? Disgusted? Caroline covered her confusion with another question. "Is Emma one of the girls swimming?"

"The reverend assures me he saw her there just minutes ago."

"Do you object to Emma swimming?"

The preacher fixed his gaze upon the young widow as she replied, "Well, no. I've always let my daughter go with her brother. But, of course, he's much younger." Sara glanced at the man beside her. "My late husband used to tell me that boys often...remove their clothes before diving in."

"Oh." Caroline wanted to laugh, but the look on the the young widow's face stopped her. As for Reverend Symes, his own good sense appeared to be waging war against the widow's persuasiveness, and good sense was losing.

"I'll go to the creek right now and...resolve this." Caroline hoped her calm, reasonable tone would reassure both Sara and Reverend Symes.

"Thank you, Miss Adams," the preacher said with a sigh of relief.

"I think a lecture on the proper behavior of young ladies would be in order," Sara called after her.

"I think you're right." Caroline hurried away before the laughter that was bubbling up inside happened to spill over and ruin her image.

She had no difficulty finding the children. The sounds of their laughter could be heard long before she broke through the tangle of brush and came upon them at the creek.

As she watched, young Jack caught hold of a thick vine and went swinging high over the water, twirling in dizzying circles. He had discarded his shirt and boots and wore only his britches. With a shriek of laughter he let go and dropped like a stone. Seconds later he broke the surface, spitting a mouthful of water like a fountain to the cheers of the children.

For long minutes Caroline hid behind a curtain of leaves, reluctant to spoil their pleasure. They were having so much fun. The kind of fun that only innocent children could enjoy.

Sitting down on a rock, she waited, drawing out the moment when she would have to keep her promise to the preacher and Sara. She would have waited even longer, but when she saw Sheriff Horn heading toward her from one direction and Belva Spears from another, she decided it was time to make her presence known.

"So this is where you've all gone to." She made a great deal of noise as she pushed aside the bushes and stepped into the clearing beside the creek. "Doesn't this look like fun. Are you all having a good time?"

"Miss Adams, look," Ethan Waverly said, slipping below the water and coming up on the other side of his sister. "I can hold my breath under water."

"That's very good, Ethan."

Caroline was pleased to see the boy playing with the others. Usually Ethan, cowed by his mother's strict rules, was shy and withdrawn around the other children.

"Emma," Caroline called gently, "I told your mother I would come and find you and the other girls."

"Do I have to go back to the church now?" The girl began wading toward shore, and Caroline was relieved to see that she still wore her dress. The wet skirt clung to her legs, dripping water as she walked.

"I thought maybe you girls would like to come with me. And leave the boys here to swim alone."

"Where are we going?" Emma called.

"It's a secret."

"I love secrets." With no further coaxing, Lisbeth hurried from the creek with her cousin Kate following.

"Good afternoon, Miss Adams, children," Sheriff Horn and Belva called in unison. Each seemed not at all surprised to see the other, and Caroline wondered if they'd arranged to meet away from the prying eyes of the town.

"Miss Adams is taking us to a secret place," Lisbeth said conspiratorially.

"That sounds like fun. Just don't go too far," Belva cautioned. "The children's races will be starting in a little while."

Caroline and the girls set off in one direction, while Sheriff Horn and Belva Spears returned to town.

As soon as they were alone, the boys stripped off their wet clothes and hung them on tree branches to dry. With hoots of laughter at their freedom, they dived back into the water, splashing and screaming.

Caroline led the girls along the banks of the creek until they were out of sight of the others.

"I wish we could swim some more," Emma complained loudly. "It isn't fair. The boys have all the fun and we have to go back to the church and help with the food."

"They don't really need us at the church yet." Caroline slowed her walking, and the girls looked up at her.

"You mean we could swim some more?" Lisbeth asked.

"I don't see why not. How about right here?"

"You mean this is the secret?"

Caroline nodded. Though she hadn't planned it, allowing the girls a little more fun in the water seemed perfectly natural.

"The secret is that the boys sometimes like to shed their clothes while they swim. And they can't do it with us around. But—" with a conspiratorial smile, Caroline drew the girls close "—there's no reason why you can't have the same fun."

With giggles and shrieks the girls stepped out of their dresses, tossing them quickly over the branches of low-hanging brush. Wearing only their shifts, they raced into the water. With a laugh Caroline stepped onto a large boulder and watched as the girls frolicked and splashed.

"Who wants to race?" she suddenly challenged.

"I do. I do." All three girls took up the challenge.

"To that submerged rock out there," Caroline called. "On the count of three."

They were off and racing, their hands sending up a spray of water as they cut through the creek's smooth surface.

Emma reached the rock first and climbed on top, proclaiming herself the winner. When Lisbeth reached her she helped her up. By the time little Kate got there, the two girls helped her onto the flat rock, where they joined hands and danced and twirled around and around until, dizzy, they slid back into the water and headed for shore. There they sat, the water lapping over their legs, catching their breath for the next race.

"Isn't that much more fun than trying to swim with those heavy skirts?" Caroline asked.

The three girls nodded, enchanted by the fact that a grown-up would understand them and spend so much time with them. Especially one in a position of authority. Their hearts swelled with affection for their teacher.

"My ma used to swim with us," Emma said softly.

Caroline glanced over. The girl's eyes had suddenly gone sad as they focused on the rock in the middle of the creek. "But since Pa died, she hardly ever laughs. I like the Reverend Symes's laugh," she declared suddenly. "And I like the way his eyes crinkle at the corners when he laughs."

It occurred to Caroline that the preacher spent a good deal of time around Sara Waverly and her children lately. He was a man with a great deal of love in his heart. And they were a family in need of such love.

"What does your mother think about the reverend's laughter?" Caroline asked softly.

Emma shrugged. "I don't think she's taken the time to notice. Ma says there's no time for anything anymore. Especially no time to have fun with us."

"Your mother probably needs your help, Emma. It would be hard to be mother and father to two children. I'll bet there are times when she's afraid for all of you."

"Do grown-ups get afraid?" The child turned to study her teacher.

"Of course. Everyone's afraid at some time in their lives."

"Not my Uncle Thad," Lisbeth said proudly. "My ma says he's the most fearless man she's ever known."

"But that's different," Emma said matter-of-factly. "He's a gunfighter."

"He is not."

"Is, too. My ma told me."

Lisbeth stood up indignantly. "You take that back."

Emma jumped up to face her. "Everybody knows he's killed hundreds of men."

"Emma," Caroline gently chided her, "I think that's only a silly rumor."

"Maybe," the girl replied, "but everybody knows he killed a man when he was only seven."

Stunned by the words, Caroline went very still. Were there no secrets in this small town? She glanced at Lisbeth, whose face had turned pale.

Lisbeth lowered her head and said softly, "My ma said he didn't have any choice. She said he saved her life."

In the shocked silence that followed, Caroline scrambled down from the rock and splashed through the shallows to Lisbeth's side. Drawing her arms around the little girl, she held her for a moment.

"Has your mother ever talked about it?"

Lisbeth shook her head. "All I know is most of the people around here think my uncle is a gunfighter. And I guess—" she sniffed and wiped her tears with the back of her hand "—maybe he is. But I don't care. I love him."

"I know," Caroline whispered against the little girl's temple. "And you keep right on loving him."

Lisbeth lifted her gaze to her teacher's and said with all the wisdom and innocence of a child, "You understand, don't you, Miss Adams? You know why I love Uncle Thad?"

Caroline swallowed, refusing to meet the girl's eyes. But in her heart she knew. And struggled to deny it.

The stillness was shattered by the sounds of whistling and shouting.

Emma's head came up. "That's the boys heading back to town. That means the races are starting. We'd better get dressed."

"Will you come and watch us race, Miss Adams?" Kate asked.

"Of course I will. I wouldn't miss it. How about you, Lisbeth?"

The little girl swallowed back her tears. "I guess I wouldn't miss it, either."

"Good girl."

The three children hurriedly pulled on their dresses, which were nearly dry.

"Go ahead," Caroline called. "I'll be right behind you."

She watched as the girls took off at a run. Giving a last glance around the creek, she started to walk away, then, almost against her will, she was drawn back.

It was so hot. The water looked so tempting. And all the while that the girls had been swimming, she had wanted to join them.

She wondered what Harvey Hattinger's rule would be for such an occasion. She supposed a teacher ought to be ever vigilant about preserving her image. But right now she yearned to be rid of these heavy boots and skirts and feel cool water against her warm, sticky skin.

Furtively she glanced around. The place was completely isolated. The brush was so thick it was impossible to see or be seen. An impish smile touched her lips. "Only for a minute," she whispered to herself.

She removed her heavy boots and wiggled her toes. Oh, it was heavenly to be rid of them. Carefully stepping out of her gown, she hung it on the branch of a tree, taking pains to see that it didn't snag. She removed her petticoats and carefully folded them atop a sun-warmed rock.

Wearing only a modest chemise, she started toward the water. Catching sight of herself in the clear surface, she burst into gales of laughter. Her hat was still perched atop her head. Removing the pins, she slipped it from her hair and set it on top of her folded petticoats.

Then she stepped into the water. It was marvelously cool against her skin. With a shiver she waded deeper, then deeper still, until the water lapped against her breasts.

She really shouldn't get her hair wet, she thought. But giving in to yet another temptation, she dipped beneath the waves and came up sputtering.

With slow, lazy strokes she navigated the creek, occasionally rolling over onto her back and closing her eyes against the noonday sun.

Several pins had pulled loose from her hair. Removing the rest, she shook her head, allowing her hair to fall free of the neat knot and fan out on the water like a dark veil.

She lifted her face to the sun and gave a deep sigh of pleasure. This was probably the most foolish thing she had done since her arrival, but she wasn't sorry. She felt more alive than she had in years.

Still smiling, she swam toward shore, then stopped abruptly.

Thad was standing beside the boulder. In his hand was one of her petticoats. On his lips was a teasing smile.

"Well, Teacher, I'd heard that I would find the town social very entertaining, but I had no idea you would be the entertainment."

She felt her cheeks growing pink. "How long have you been hiding there?"

"Hiding?" He set aside the petticoat and took a step closer to the water, standing with feet apart, hands on hips. It was a stance she was very familiar with. "I've made no attempt to hide myself. I was on my way to town, Teacher, when I just happened upon you."

She glowered at him. "Here in a dense thicket?"

"The brush offers shade from the sweltering sun."

"Do you always travel so close to the water's edge?"

"It's a hot day." His smile grew. "I was thinking about taking a swim. And I knew this spot would be secluded enough to shield me from the prying eyes of others. How could I know that someone else would discover my secret place?"

She was beginning to tire of treading water. Moving closer to shore, she was relieved when her feet touched bottom. "Well, now that I'm here first, I hope you'll have the decency to leave."

"Leave? Why should I leave? This creek's big enough for both of us." He unbuckled his gun belt and began to unbutton his shirt.

Caroline was horrified. "What are you doing?"

"What does it look like, Teacher? I'm preparing to join you for a swim."

"But . . . you can't."

Enjoying her discomfort, he stifled the urge to laugh. "I don't see how you can stop me."

Her tone became pleading. "Thad, if anyone from town should come upon us, my reputation would be ruined."

"Ah." He dropped his shirt on a rock beside her folded gown. "You're probably right, Teacher. Maybe you'd better step out of the creek and get yourself dressed."

"I will." As she took a step closer, she saw the way his gaze fastened on the water lapping at her breasts. Heat stained her cheeks. "Turn around and give me time to cover myself."

He leaned a hip against the sun-warmed rock and crossed his arms over his naked chest. "And if I won't?"

She blinked. "But you must. I—I can't parade around in my wet chemise."

"Why not? I can't think of a lovelier sight, unless, of course, you'd like to remove it and parade around as nature intended."

Her voice chilled. "I don't find this amusing, Thad Conway. Now turn away and let me get out of here."

"How can I refuse such a command?"

She could see his shoulders shaking with laughter as he turned around.

Stepping quickly from the water, she shimmied into her petticoats and was just reaching for her gown when he turned. His smile faded as he studied her. On his face was a look that made her heart stop.

His hand closed over hers holding the gown. Taking it from her he tossed it aside. "Do you have any idea how lovely you are? It's a shame to hide all this beauty under such a plain cover."

"Don't, Thad." Her voice was little more than a frightened whisper.

"Tell me how to stop, Teacher." He lifted both hands to her hair and buried his fingers in the wet tangles. "Every time I'm near you I want to touch you like this."

She closed her eyes, steeling herself against the pleasure that rippled through her at his simple touch.

Framing her face with his hands, he allowed his gaze to roam her lips, her cheeks, her eyes, as if memorizing every line, every curve. "I've walked away so many times when I've really wanted to stay. I've turned away rather than touch you. Because I knew," he muttered thickly against her temple, "that if I ever started, I'd never be able to stop."

His arms came around her, pulling her roughly against him. She could feel the tension pulsing through him as his hands stroked her back.

Somewhere in a distant part of her mind she heard the warning, but it was already too late. Her hands slid along his arms, across his shoulders, seduced by the warmth of his naked flesh.

"I want you, Caroline. I want you as I've never wanted anyone or anything in my life."

She waited, feeling her breath catch in her throat as he lowered his face to hers. His lips covered hers in a searing kiss.

As he took the kiss deeper, she felt her bones soften and melt. Something deep within her soul seemed to flicker to life, then begin to flame.

He wanted her. The thought thrilled her even while it frightened her. If the truth be told, she wanted him, too. Desperately.

His hands were no longer gentle as he dragged her closer and savaged her mouth with kisses. His breath was coming faster now, and she felt it hot against her cheek.

"Sweet Jesus, Caroline." His words were muffled against her throat. "How I want you."

Arching herself in his arms, she shivered as he ran hot kisses across her shoulder and buried his lips in the hollow of her neck.

He'd never known such need. A hard, driving need that threatened to shatter the last of his control.

"Stay with me here," he muttered, "and let me love you. It's what you want, too, Caroline. You know it is."

How could she allow herself to listen to the soft words, the whispered promises? Unless she found the strength to resist, she would be lost.

Pushing free of his arms she drew in deep drafts of air to steady her breathing. Her voice was strained as she whispered, "Wanting is not the same as needing. I don't need you in my life, Thad Conway. And you don't need me."

With as much control as she could manage, she turned away from him and pulled her dress over her head, then smoothed it over her hips. With quick, deft movements she twisted her wet hair into a neat knot and secured her hat with pins.

When she turned back, he was standing very still, watching her through narrowed eyes.

"God in heaven, Caroline, what's been done to you?" There had been terror in her eyes. Stark terror.

He waited for her response, but she said nothing.

A gunshot exploded the summer stillness, causing both of them to lift their heads.

Seeing the way her eyes widened, Thad said soothingly, "It's only the start of the races."

When she turned away he said, "Don't run away again, Caroline. Tell me what's wrong."

Evading his look, she muttered, "I promised the children I'd watch their races."

Pushing through the brush, she nearly ran in her eagerness to escape his probing look.

He took a long time to roll a cigarette and strike a match across the rock. As he drew the smoke into his lungs, he considered all that he'd said to her and her strange reaction to his words.

When he pulled on his shirt he realized that his hands were none too steady. The taste of her was still on his lips. And the wanting was stronger than ever. But she'd been right about one thing, he thought angrily. He didn't need her. He'd be damned if he'd need anyone.

From behind a cover of thick brush, where he'd watched and listened, the stranger closed his hands around his rifle. An evil smile curled his lips. He could drop Thad Conway where he stood. But he had a better fate in store for The Texan. A much better fate. Let the fool fall in love. He'd never have her. Not when he learned the truth about Caroline Adams.

Chapter Fifteen

Thoroughly flustered and shaken, Caroline smoothed down her skirts and patted her wet hair, praying no one would call attention to her state of dishevelment.

Pushing free of the brush and vines that snagged at her skirts, she scanned the crowd and had no trouble locating the children's races. Almost everyone, it seemed, had a child competing for blue ribbons and prizes. Parents and friends clustered around as the sheriff announced the rules for the next race.

"It's the three-legged race. Two boys, two girls or a boy and a girl."

As the children lined up in pairs, Jessie and Sara Waverly began tying bandannas around the contestants' legs.

Caroline watched as Emma and her brother, Ethan, stood beside Jack and Runs With The Wind. Eight-year-old Lisbeth and her cousin Kate were busy good-naturedly taunting Frank and his cousin Danny.

Suddenly a wagon rolled up and everyone turned to see who was arriving so late. The children let out a cheer when they spotted Ben Meadows lying in the back of the wagon, cushioned on a layer of quilts. Ab Meadows lifted a chair from the wagon and placed his son in it, then began pushing the chair closer.

"A chair with wheels," Sheriff Horn called out. "Ab, where'd you come up with something so clever?"

As the children gathered happily around their friend, his mother said, "Thad Conway made it."

"The Texan?" came an incredulous voice from the crowd.

Cora nodded. "Can you imagine? He brought it over this morning."

"I'm not surprised," Jessie said in answer to the murmurs from the crowd. "My brother makes beautiful furniture. He made my dining room table and chairs and several pieces in my home."

"He ought to make coffins," came another voice. "He's filled enough of 'em."

Ignoring the jeers, Ben flashed a brilliant smile. "Now I don't have to lie in bed all day. Pa says I can go just about anywhere I please." Spotting his teacher, he called, "Look, Miss Adams. Pa says he might even be able to bring me to school sometimes."

"That's wonderful, Ben." She walked over to admire his gift. In the boy's eyes was a bright light of happiness that seemed to touch all his features with radiance.

At a sudden thought she turned to the sheriff. "Maybe Ben could be the judge for the children's races."

"Why, I think that's a fine idea." Sheriff Horn turned to the boy. "How about it, Ben? Want to be the judge this year?"

"Yes, sir." Ben shot a grin at his father and mother. "I'd like that."

"Come on, then." Sheriff Horn led the way while Ab Meadows pushed his son's chair to the finish line. Cora walked proudly beside them.

Turning to the crowd of contestants, the sheriff shouted, "You know the rules. You can walk, run or crawl. First team over the finish line wins blue ribbons. And two of Belva Spears's peach tarts." He patted his ample stomach. "I can attest that they're the finest in all of Texas." He added with a chuckle, "Had to taste a couple, just to make sure."

He pointed his pistol to the sky and called, "Ready. Get set." With a loud report, the gunshot signaled the start of the race.

With one leg free and one leg tied to their partner, the children started off hopping and within a few steps were hopelessly tangled around each other. As quickly as they managed to stand, they would fall again, often tripping two or more of the other contestants as they landed in a tangle of arms and legs.

Parents and friends stood on the sidelines shouting out words of encouragement, all the while laughing at the scene of confusion.

Caroline looked around at all the happy, smiling faces and wondered when she'd ever felt so content. This town, these people, made her forget all the evil in the world. Maybe, just maybe, she had found her own little piece of heaven right here in Hope, Texas.

On the fringe of the crowd she caught sight of Thad, standing alone. Their gazes met and held. And like every other time, she felt his touch, as intimate as a caress. She shivered and turned away, breaking contact.

Ben shouted encouragement to his friends. Lisbeth, catching sight of her beloved uncle, broke into a wide smile and wrapped her arm around her cousin's shoulder. Suddenly finding their rhythm, Lisbeth and Kate made a final dash toward the finish line, racing past the boys, who stumbled and fell.

"Looks like we have our winners," the sheriff called. "What do you think, Ben?"

The little boy nodded and declared them the victors.

Lisbeth looked as if she would burst with happiness as the sheriff presented her with a blue ribbon as well as one for Kate. When the two girls received their peach tarts, they made a great show of eating them in front of the boys, who watched jealously from the sidelines.

Then Lisbeth flung herself into her uncle's arms and hugged him fiercely.

"What was that for, Little Bit?"

She grabbed hold of his ears and kissed him before being released. "Just for being here, Uncle Thad."

When she walked away, she could be heard saying to Emma, "Did you see what my uncle made for Ben? I guess he's just about the best furniture maker in Texas."

"You've just made another conquest," Caroline said softly, coming up to stand beside him.

"That's nice." He turned to her and stared into her eyes. "But it's not the one I'd hoped for."

She knew she was blushing, which only made her blush all the more. "Did you enjoy your swim?"

"I decided it wouldn't be any fun alone. In fact, Teacher—" his voice lowered intimately "—most of the things I'd like to do can only be done with you."

She felt the rush of heat. "I think I'd better get over to the church and help with the food." As she started away she paused and turned back to him. "Will you be staying for the dance?"

"It's tempting." He studied the way the sunlight turned the ends of her hair to blue-black silk that would put a raven's wings to shame. "But I've been away from my ranch chores too long."

Feeling a sting of disappointment, she turned away quickly. Spotting Ben seated proudly in his new chair, surrounded by his friends, she suddenly turned back again. "That was a fine thing you did for Ben Meadows."

With a swish of skirts she was gone.

It was a happy, laughing crowd that surged through the doors of the church.

The long wooden planks groaned under the weight of platters of chicken, pheasant, quail, whole roasted pigs and pots of stewed rabbit. There were breads, biscuits, rolls, all lovingly baked and proudly displayed. On a second plank, at the opposite side of the room, were cakes, pies, tarts and cookies, all being zealously watched over by an army of women to see that hungry little boys didn't sneak any of the treasures before they ate a proper supper.

Caroline joined the ranks of the women ladling out the food and seized the opportunity to chat with the parents of her students. She was amazed that such a small, sleepy little town could produce so many strangers. Some of the ranchers had traveled many hours to join the festivities. And many of their children had never read a book or met a teacher before.

When everyone had been served, the women filled their own plates and joined their families. Some sat inside the church, taking advantage of the wooden pews. But most chose to sit in the grass or on blankets spread beneath the shade of giant oaks.

After such an enormous meal, some of the fathers and their children drifted off to sleep while the women sat around in small groups of four or five, fanning themselves and catching up on all the news of the past year. For some of the more isolated ranchers and their families, this was the only contact with the people from town.

As the sun slowly made its arc to the western sky, torches and lanterns were lit around the tents and wagons. The scent of wood smoke filled the air as children played tag around the camp fires that punctuated the gathering darkness.

A fiddler plucked the strings of his violin, then started in with a rousing song. Minutes later he was joined by a mouth organ and then a guitar. Men and women got to their feet and began to clap their hands. Soon, not only the grown-ups but the children were dancing to the happy, toe-tapping music.

Caroline joined the crowd that formed a circle around the dancers. Clapping her hands in time to the rhythm, she waved to Cole and Jessie as they circled past.

"Having fun?" Jessie called.

"Oh, yes." Caroline barely had time to get the words out before she was grabbed by Sheriff Horn and spun into the mass of twirling couples.

She wasn't sure what to do, but she soon discovered that all she needed to do was to hold on. The stocky sheriff had no sense of rhythm, but he kept her moving in the same direction as the other couples, and once in a while he twirled her in circles until her head was spinning.

As abruptly as they started, Caroline was returned to the sidelines, where she struggled to catch her breath.

"Thank you, Miss Adams. That was mighty fine dancing."

Mopping his brow, Sheriff Horn paused only long enough to catch sight of Belva Spears dancing with Reverend Symes. Moments later he tapped the reverend on the shoulder and spun away with Belva in his arms.

Caroline watched as the preacher scanned the crowd, then walked resolutely toward Sara Waverly and her family. A few minutes later, as the widow and the reverend began to dance, Caroline caught the look of happiness on the faces of Emma and Ethan.

"Miss Adams?"

Caroline turned to find Manuel and Rosita standing beside her. From their flushed faces, she could tell they had been dancing.

"Hello," she called. "Are you having fun?"

They both nodded.

"Rosita says she is too tired to dance again." Manuel bowed slightly to Caroline. "Would you like to dance?"

"Why, I'd be honored."

Placing her hand on his shoulder, she allowed him to take her other hand and slowly lead her through the steps of the dance.

"You have not done this before?"

She shook her head.

"Do they not dance in the East?"

She shrugged self-consciously. "Oh, they dance, the same as here, I suppose. But I never had time."

Because Manuel was not much taller than her, their gazes met directly. "Are you glad you came to Hope, Miss Adams?"

"I'm very glad, Manuel. I like it here very much."

"Rosita and I have heard good things about you. The people are happy to have such a fine teacher for their children."

"Not nearly as happy as I am to be teaching them. It's like wishing on a star and suddenly having your wish come true."

He nodded gravely. "I understand about such things. Since I first came here, I wanted the chance to own a piece of my own land. And thanks to Señor Conway, I now have my wish."

The words were barely out of his mouth when he looked up and broke into a wide smile. Dropping her hands, he gave a little bow and walked away, leaving her alone amid the twirling couples.

Puzzled, Caroline turned. Thad stood directly behind her.

For the space of a heartbeat she forgot about the torches and the music and the people that moved and laughed and talked all around her.

"You came back."

He nodded. "I tried not to. I thought, if I stayed busy with enough chores, I could forget about the dance."

He opened his arms and she stepped close, placing her hand in his. She no longer worried about moving her feet to the music. It seemed the most natural thing in the world to fit herself into his embrace, her body moving in rhythm with his.

"But then," he murmured against her temple, "I thought about you here, in the arms of all these men, and I couldn't go on working."

He gave a wry laugh. "I couldn't even do simple chores like pounding nails." He held up his hand and she could see the dark bruises. "I hit my thumb with the hammer. That's when I knew I had to give in and admit defeat. I needed to be here, holding you, leading you through the dance."

She gave a deep sigh of contentment as he drew her close against his chest. Her hand, resting along his shoulder, brushed the pale hair at his collar, sending strange sensations rippling through her.

"I suppose this must seem tame after the dances at that fancy school you attended."

He felt her stiffen before she admitted shyly, "I've never been to a dance before."

"Then I hope your first dance is special."

"It is," she murmured contentedly.

Her hand lay in his large, work-roughened palm, held as gently as if it were a fragile flower. His other hand rested at her back, his fingers splayed along her spine. She could feel each one pressing against her flesh, leaving its imprint forever on her soul. She closed her eyes, swaying with him to the music. She would know him even in the dark. For such a big man, his touch was exceedingly gentle.

"Where do you go when you get all quiet like this?" he murmured.

"I haven't gone anywhere." She lifted her head and her lips grazed his cheek. "There isn't anywhere I'd rather be than right here, dancing with you." She fell silent for a moment longer before adding, "I just wanted to hold on to the moment before it ended."

"What makes you think it will end?"

"The good times always do. It's the bad times that seem endless. The bad times—" her voice lowered to the merest whisper "—seem to go on forever."

Without thinking, he drew her closer, as if to offer his strength. "It doesn't have to be that way, Caroline."

"No, it doesn't." She forced a smile to her lips and met his steady gaze.

The fiddler drained his jug and announced the last dance. Instead of another toe-tapping song, the violin soared and dipped with the sad, haunting strains of a song about a home far away and a love left behind. The mouth organ picked up the notes, followed by the guitar.

Couples drifted off to their tents or wagons. Torches flickered and died. Candles were snuffed. As the song ended, only the light from the stars illuminated the few couples who were still dancing.

Thad and Caroline paused beside the trunk of an ancient oak. It seemed the most natural thing in the world to keep their arms around each other. And as she lifted her smiling face to him, he couldn't resist the chance to brush his lips over hers.

This kiss was different from all the other times. She felt the change even as she returned his kiss. There was a gentleness. From a man who had never been gentle with her before.

She felt the change inside herself, as well. The answering softness, as though he'd tapped some new well deep inside her. The need for tenderness. The wanting. The needing. Always before, she'd been able to ignore her needs. She felt for the moment as if all her defenses had been lowered.

He stepped back a pace and touched a hand lightly to her cheek. "You're tired."

She nodded. "I've been up cooking and baking since dawn."

"Are you going back to your cabin tonight?"

"No. Sara Waverly invited me to spend the night here in town at her place."

He felt a momentary stab of disappointment. The thought of accompanying her back to her cabin had tantalized him. Still, this was infinitely safer. For both of them.

"Come on." Catching her hand, he led her through the darkness. "I'll see you to her door."

When they reached Sara's house, the preacher was just taking his leave. He called out a greeting and hurried on toward the church.

As Sara waited in the doorway, Caroline whispered, "Will I see you tomorrow?"

Thad shook his head. "I doubt I can spare any more time. I already told Manuel and Rosita to take the day off."

"Well then." She was achingly aware of his hand resting at her elbow. "Thank you for walking me to Sara's home."

"I wouldn't have missed it." He knew that Sara Waverly was watching, but he couldn't resist the temptation to touch her one last time. Brushing the backs of his fingers across her cheek, he added, "Or the chance to hold you while we danced."

"Miss Adams." They both looked up as the sheriff emerged from the darkness.

Touching a hand to his hat, he said gruffly, "I wanted you to know that my deputy found Fox an hour ago. Actually," he added before Caroline could speak, "I should say, Fox's body."

"He's dead?" She held her breath.

"Yep. And the strange thing is, he was hardly out of town before he was shot. Almost as if whoever helped him escape only did it to get rid of him."

Thad's head came up sharply. "And the other man? The one who helped him escape? Has there been any sign of him?"

The sheriff shook his head. "Not a trace. Odd thing, though, that a man would break him out of jail just to kill him." He turned to drop a hand on Caroline's arm. "Don't you worry, Miss Adams. The man would be a fool to stay around these parts. I have a hunch he's a hundred miles from here by now, if he knows what's good for him."

Despite the heat of the night, Caroline felt a small shiver along her spine. She was grateful that she was spending the night in town rather than alone in her cabin.

"Thank you, Sheriff Horn." Her voice trembled only slightly, but it was enough for Thad to notice.

As the sheriff hurried toward his office, Thad waited until Caroline disappeared inside Sara's house.

He stood for long minutes, deep in thought. The sheriff had found it strange that the man who had freed Fox had killed him so quickly. It wasn't strange at all. To Thad it made perfect sense. Especially if the man didn't want anyone around who could identify him.

It all went back to the attack on the stage. The stage bearing Caroline Adams to town.

Chapter Sixteen

Thad mucked the stalls and forked fresh hay, then hauled buckets of water from the creek. Lifting the hat from his head, he wiped an arm across his brow and glanced at the sky. The sun was a hazy amber globe in the heavens. A gentle breeze rustled the leaves and bent the grass. A good day for a picnic. The thought crossed his mind, and just as quickly he brushed it aside.

He should be grateful for the hard, physical labor, but the truth was, even hard work couldn't keep him from thinking about Caroline. As much as he disliked going to town, he wanted to see her. No, he corrected, needed to see her. It was a need bordering on obsession.

Even working with his prized mare brought him no joy. He led her into a corral and latched the gate, then leaned against it and watched as she broke into an easy trot. She would give him a perfect foal. In fact, many foals to add to his herd.

Why, then, did it suddenly seem so meaningless? What would it matter if he bred the finest bloodline in Texas? He glanced around the rolling hills, the sturdy outbuildings, the graceful ranch house. What would any of this matter if he didn't have someone to share it with? Someone? *Caroline.*

He experienced a quick flare of anger. He'd never met anyone he couldn't walk away from. Until Caroline. He'd never fought a battle he couldn't win. Until Caroline.

He had spent a sleepless night wondering and worrying. Who wanted to harm her? And why? What was she running from? And when was she going to trust him enough to confide in him?

He slammed a fist against the corral and whirled away. He had a better use for all this pent-up anger. There was timber to be cut. And, by God, he'd cut it all before this day was over.

Caroline walked beside Sara and her two children. Her hands grasped the handle of the basket she had prepared for the picnic. There were pale smudges beneath her eyes, the only clue that she had spent a night tossing and turning. And worrying.

The fact that Fox had been found dead had not reassured her. In fact, it had increased her fears. Despite the sunny day and the friendly faces all around her, Caroline couldn't shake the feeling of impending doom.

"Wasn't it nice to see the church so full this morning?" Sara asked.

Caroline pushed aside her morbid thoughts. "Reverend Symes was in rare form. I liked what he said about building bridges instead of cursing the swollen streams."

Sara gave a deep sigh. "He makes life sound so simple. I think, when he's been here long enough, he'll understand just how difficult life can be, especially in Texas."

"What makes you think it's any harder here than somewhere else?" Caroline asked.

"Just take a look around you." Sara's pursed her mouth in distaste. "Belva Spears loses a husband to a gunman. Cora Meadows is forced to watch a son lie paralyzed. And look at my own children. They lost their father before they had time to know him.''

''Those same bad things happen everywhere, Sara. Life in the city is no better.''

''Maybe.'' The look in her eyes said she didn't believe a word of it.

''Sara?'' Caroline paused, wondering how to ask the question that had bothered her for so long. ''Do you know why Thad Conway shuns the people of Hope?''

Sara shot her a surprised look. ''I thought by now you would have heard.'' When Caroline shook her head, the woman cast a glance around at the tranquil scene. ''You wouldn't know it to look at this little town,'' she said, ''but there was once a bloody battle fought here. There was a gang of gunmen known as the Colby Gang that left a trail of killings across Texas. When the sheriff heard they were headed this way, he warned the citizens, and they formed a committee to ride out to Thad's ranch and ask him to help. He was, after all, the best gunman in these parts.'' She shielded the sun from her eyes and stared into the distance a moment, remembering. ''Thad agreed to stand with the men of Hope, but by the time the Colby Gang got here, most of the men had gone home to their families and refused to leave them unprotected to come to town and fight. So in the end, Thad Conway and the sheriff and a few of the men ended up facing up to the gang by themselves.''

''What happened?''

Sara frowned. ''It was a bloodbath. A dozen gunmen lay in the street dead. Every one of the men who'd fought had a wound of one kind or another. Thad's wounds were the worst. For a while, Doc thought he'd lose him.''

"But why would the town shun him if he nearly gave his life to save them?"

Sara paused, deep in thought, then turned to Caroline. "I suppose part of it was because he made some of the men of the town feel ashamed for not standing with him. And, too, we all saw just how savage a gunfight is. We gave him a job to do and he did it. Too well. The way Thad Conway stood and fought made everyone a little more afraid of him. And we've always been afraid that his reputation with a gun would bring more gunfighters to town, looking to be the one to kill The Texan. I'm sure that day will come. It's just his fate."

"But that's so unfair," Caroline cried.

"Maybe." Sara shrugged. "But that's the way we feel."

Caroline looked shocked. "You don't mean that."

Sara's lips tightened. "I was raised to believe that everyone has to accept whatever lot is theirs in life. Standing up to every fast gun in Texas is Thad Conway's. Being left alone to raise two children is mine."

"Not necessarily."

Caroline was aware of Sara's sharp-eyed look.

"And what does that mean?"

Caroline shrugged. "Thad could put aside his guns and concentrate on the horses he loves. And you, Sara. You could always marry again. If you're lucky enough to find a man who loves you and your children."

Beside them, Emma, who had been listening, brightened. "Reverend Symes doesn't have a wife."

Before Sara could respond, her daughter added, "There's something about Reverend Symes that makes me feel good. I like his laugh. And I like his eyes, Mama. They're just about the kindest eyes I've ever seen."

"He said he's going to teach me how to drive his horse and rig," Ethan piped up.

"Ethan Waverly, you're too young to handle the reins."

"I'm not a baby, Mama. At least Reverend Symes doesn't think so."

Sara shot a glance at her young son. "That's exactly what you used to say to your father whenever you thought I was holding you back from something you wanted to do." For a moment she clamped her mouth shut. But the little frown line on her forehead grew deeper as she murmured, "Funny. Your pa always agreed with you. He used to say, 'Stop being a mother hen, Sara, and let the boy make a few mistakes along the way.' But now, now that I know what it's like to lose someone I love, I just can't seem to let go of you. Of either of you."

For a moment her eyes grew misty. Then, squaring her shoulders, she said curtly, "You two run along and play now. Caroline and I have work to do before the picnic starts."

As the children joined their friends, she stood for long minutes staring after them. Then she tightened her grip on her basket and caught up with Caroline.

Men stood off to one side of the church, tossing horseshoes. With each clang of the post, a cheer would go up from the onlookers.

The older boys had returned to the pond for a final day of swimming. The younger children raced around in frantic games of tag, knowing that this was their last chance to be together. Tomorrow they would return to the routine of ranch chores and lessons.

A cluster of women sat in the middle of a shady patch of grass, finishing up the binding on a quilt. While they worked they exchanged recipes, child-rearing tips and even remedies for infections, broken bones and tooth-aches.

When Caroline and Sara joined them, Belva fixed Caroline with a penetrating look. "Did I see you dancing with Thad Conway last night?"

Caroline felt the heat begin at the base of her neck. She glanced up to see Morning Light and Jessie watching her. "Yes. I also danced with Sheriff Horn and Manuel Alvarez."

It was apparent that the others didn't count. Among these curious women, the only one that caused any interest was Thad Conway.

"I believe that's the first time I've ever seen your brother in town for one of our socials," Belva said to Jessie.

Jessie merely smiled and said nothing. But Caroline could feel the curious stares of the others.

At the tolling of the church bells, they all looked up.

"Looks like we'll have to stop." Belva began rolling her thread and the others followed suit. When the quilt was folded, they stood and made their way to the grassy knoll beside the church, where the bidding on the women's baskets would take place.

"How will the men know whose basket they're bidding on?" Caroline asked Jessie.

"They aren't supposed to know. It's supposed to be a surprise." Jessie laughed. "But if a woman's wise, she lets her man know which one is hers. Or else she'll find herself eating supper with someone else's man."

"Has that happened?"

Jessie and her sister-in-law, Morning Light, shared a laugh. "It happened last year. Becky Carver's basket looked just like Sara Waverly's. But the men quickly straightened things out, and everyone went home happy."

"What happens to those who don't have a man to do the bidding?"

"Don't worry," Jessie soothed. "Sheriff Horn sees to it that every woman's basket is bought." Her eyes twinkled with laughter. "I happen to know a certain someone has already made plans for yours."

"Who is it?"

"You'll just have to wait and see." Jessie thought about the dollar young Jack clutched in his hand. If no one else bid on his teacher's basket, the prize would be his.

"Shh. The sheriff is about to begin," Morning Light cautioned.

They gathered around to watch the fun.

The first basket offered for bidding was a pretty thing, pale yellow in color with red and yellow ribbons tied around the handle.

Sheriff Horn, clearly enjoying his job, lifted the cover to display the contents. "We have a whole roasted chicken," he said, "and buttermilk biscuits. And will you look at these." He held aloft a pair of blueberry pies, causing a roar of approval from the men in the crowd.

"Who'll start the bidding?"

"One dollar" came a boy's high-pitched shout.

Everyone turned to see Ben, seated in his wheeled chair, holding up a dollar.

"One whole dollar," Sheriff Horn called. "That's a lot of money, son. Do I hear more?"

"Two dollars," called Ab Meadows, standing behind Ben's chair.

The boy and his father shared a secret smile, while Cora Meadows giggled.

"Two dollars." The sheriff made it sound like a hundred before he called out, "Do I hear more?"

In the silence that followed, Sheriff Horn announced, "Going once, going twice, sold to Ab Meadows for two dollars. Will the lady who made this basket come forward to claim it?"

Cora Meadows blushed like a schoolgirl as she made her way to the front of the crowd. Her husband, clutching the basket, walked to her side. The two joined their son and watched as the bidding on the rest of the baskets continued.

Some of the women poked their husbands in the ribs when their baskets came up for bidding. The men dutifully held their money aloft and claimed the proper basket.

A few of the young, unmarried women had several men bidding on their baskets. Though the bidding never got too heated, it caused a stir of excitement among the crowd.

"Now here's a pretty little thing," Sheriff Horn said, holding Belva's basket aloft. As he opened the lid he said, "Cold slices of beef and sourdough bread. Mmm." His eyes glazed. "And a whole mess of cherry tarts. And could this be...?" He sniffed at a flask and rolled his eyes heavenward. "Elderberry wine. I think I may have to bid on this basket myself, folks." He cleared his throat and stole a glance at Belva Spears, whose cheeks had gone as red as the ribbon on her dress.

"I bid three dollars, and I dare anyone to offer more."

In the laughter that followed, he shouted as quickly as he could without pausing for breath, "Going, going, gone. Would the lady who made up this fine basket please stand up?"

Belva made her way through the crowd to stand beside him.

Handing her the basket, he said, "If you'll find a shady spot, I'll be there to share this food as soon as I've disposed of the rest of the baskets."

She stepped back to the applause of the crowd.

Caroline watched as Reverend Symes bid two dollars on Sara Waverly's basket and threw in a dollar more to have Emma and Ethan join him. The children beamed with pride as their mother stood to claim the basket, and the four of them, looking very much like a family, stood restlessly in the crowd, eager to enjoy the bounty of Sara's kitchen.

Sheriff Horn held up a basket woven with bright ribbons. As he lifted the lid, Rosita blushed, and it was clear that she had prepared a very special meal for Manuel.

"What do I see here?" the sheriff called loudly. He inhaled the scent of spices and gave a sigh of appreciation. "This smells of heaven or Mexico, but I'm not sure which. I see tortillas, beans, biscuits and..." He held up a little straw doll. "What could this mean?"

Seeing the doll, Manuel looked thunderstruck.

His voice, always deep and formal, climbed several notes higher in excitement. "Does this mean...? Rosita, are you truly...?" He struggled, but no more words would come out.

Her eyes were bright pools of unshed tears. Her voice wavered with emotion. "*Sí.* Yes. It is true."

The handsome young man gave a shout of triumph and lifted his wife high in the air, swinging her around and around until, at her insistence, he lowered her until her feet once more touched the ground.

To the assembled he shouted, "We are having a baby!"

To the cheers of the crowd he swept her into his arms and hurried forward, where he thrust a handful of bills at Sheriff Horn and took Rosita's basket from his hands.

The crowd was still cheering as he carried her away to the banks of the river. The look on her face spoke more than any words.

"Well now," Sheriff Horn said with a laugh, "I don't see how we can top that excitement." He picked up another basket and lifted the lid. "What do we have here?" Rummaging through the contents, he said, "Looks like enough food here to feed most of us. There's a couple of chickens and some proper biscuits. But then there's..." He held up a roll of dough laced with plums, walnuts and dried meat. Breaking off a tiny piece, he chewed, swallowed and gave a wide smile. "I don't know what this is called, but it's just about the tastiest thing ever."

"It is pemmican," Morning Light said. "And of all the Comanche food, it is my husband's favorite."

"I can see why," Sheriff Horn said. "If I hadn't already bid on Belva's basket, I might bid on this myself." Glancing at Dr. Dan Conway, he gave a laugh. "'Course, the doc might decide to leave my next bullet in if I was to do that, so I guess I'll just leave the bidding to him."

As the crowd laughed good-naturedly, Dan said, "I was thinking of bidding two chickens for my wife's basket, but I've decided I'd better stick to dollars. So how about three dollars, Sheriff?"

"Sold," the sheriff called, handing Dan the basket.

Runs With The Wind, Danny and little Kate followed Dan to claim the basket. Minutes later they were joined by Jessie and Cole and their brood, when Cole successfully bid on his wife's basket.

"Will you look at this pretty thing," the sheriff said, holding up a basket adorned with sprigs of wildflowers.

Caroline felt the heat rush to her cheeks and wondered who would bid on her basket.

Peeking inside, Sheriff Horn said, "Well now, someone's going to be lucky enough to taste venison and sour milk biscuits and the finest-looking cherry pie this side of the Rio Grande. It looks like someone went to a lot of trouble to make this. What am I bid?"

"One dollar," young Jack called loudly.

"Teacher's pet, are you?" the sheriff asked with a twinkle in his eyes. "Looks like you have a buyer for your basket, Miss Adams."

The crowd roared and Jack's cheeks darkened to a deeper shade of pink than Caroline's.

"I guess this basket is going once..."

"I hate to bid against my own kin," came a deep voice, "but I think that pretty basket is worth more than a dollar. I'll bid two dollars."

A ripple of excitement ran through the crowd. Caroline spun around to see Thad leaning casually against the trunk of a tree.

At her questioning look he bowed slightly. "After a day of chores, a man can get mighty hungry, especially for venison and cherry pie."

"Well now," Sheriff Horn called, "isn't this interesting?" With a smile in Caroline's direction he said, "I guess our schoolteacher is as good in the kitchen as she is in the classroom."

He turned to young Jack. "Sorry, boy. It looks like your uncle has bought himself a fine supper. Going twice..."

"I bid one hundred dollars," came a man's voice.

The crowd was dumbstruck. Men craned their necks to see who had made such an outrageous bid.

"Did I hear—one hundred dollars?" The sheriff's tone was disbelieving.

"You did."

The crowd parted as a man strode forward. He was taller than most and wore a wide-brimmed black hat and an expensive black jacket that almost covered a pair of dangerous-looking six-shooters at either hip. He reached into a vest pocket and made a great show of withdrawing a handful of bills, which he handed to the sheriff, who immediately counted them.

"It looks like you just bought yourself a supper," the sheriff said, handing him Caroline's basket.

The man turned and the crowd seemed to fall back at the sight of his face. Though he might have once been handsome, with deep-set dark eyes and finely sculpted features, his looks were marred by a jagged, puckered scar that ran from his temple to his jaw. A pipe was clenched tightly in his teeth, emitting a cloud of sweet smoke. His lips split in an imitation of a smile, but there was no warmth in his narrowed eyes as he scanned the crowd.

"Miss Adams," the sheriff called, "you can be mighty proud of the fact that your basket brought the largest contribution ever made to our church. Come on up and claim your basket."

The silence was broken by the sudden buzz of voices as everyone began to look around for the teacher.

"Miss Adams?" Perplexed, Sheriff Horn turned to the edge of the crowd, where Caroline had been last seen.

His gaze fell on young Jack, who seemed as surprised as the others around him.

"Jack, have you seen Miss Adams?"

"She was here a minute ago," the boy called. "But I didn't see her leave."

The sheriff turned to where Thad still leaned against the trunk of a tree. Though he seemed relaxed enough to the casual observer, the lawman knew him well enough to see that he was coiled as tightly as a rattler about to strike.

The sheriff sensed that The Texan had seen more than he let on. But whatever he knew, Thad Conway would keep to himself.

There was only one thing Sheriff Horn knew for certain. And the crowd, unleashing a roar that added to the confusion, had just discovered it, as well. Their new schoolteacher, Caroline Adams, was gone.

Chapter Seventeen

Brambles tore at Caroline's gown and hair as she raced through a thicket. Her breath was coming in shallow gasps, burning her throat, as she forced herself to go on. She had no idea where she was headed. It didn't matter. She knew only that she had to flee this place now or she was lost.

Fool, she berated herself as she plunged deeper into the thicket. Fool. She had never escaped him. Even traveling to the other side of the country hadn't brought her freedom. From the beginning he had known where she was. The attack on the stage was his plan. It had to be. As was Fox's escape. He had done it so that no one was left alive to identify him except her.

And she didn't matter.

He had no need to fear her. By the time he had finished telling the townspeople about her, no one would care what happened to her. Nothing she could say in her defense would matter.

Tears stung her eyes and she blinked them away. She wouldn't cry. She couldn't. She had to keep her wits about her if she intended to evade him.

It was two hundred miles to the nearest railroad. Two hundred miles. And she had no money.

She couldn't return to her cabin. That would be the first place he would look. But if she could stay hidden until tonight, she could use the cover of darkness to begin her journey.

She paused for a moment, struggling to gather her jumbled thoughts. Though she had seemed to be aimlessly running, she had unknowingly chosen a route that led away from town. Just beyond she could hear the swift flow of water, and she knew she was very near the river. That sound would be her guide. As long as she heard it, she would know that she was headed in the right direction. Though the brambles snagged her skirts and slashed her tender flesh, she pushed on, too terrified to stop or even slow down.

Thad stood very still, watching the stranger. The man seemed not the least bit concerned at Caroline's disappearance. In fact, he seemed to be enjoying himself.

He turned and caught Thad's eye. For a long moment the two men studied each other in silence. Then the stranger's lips curved in the slightest hint of a smile.

All around him, the people of the town seemed thrown into a state of chaos. For the moment, electrified by the drama that was unfolding, they buzzed and chirped like a swarm of insects. The women were alternately repelled and fascinated by the stranger's disfigurement. The men were visibly impressed by the cut of his clothes and the wad of bills he had displayed. They seemed unconcerned by the pair of pistols at his hips. To them it indicated that he was determined to protect his wealth. To Thad, it marked the stranger as a seasoned gunfighter.

Sheriff Horn, thrown off balance by the turn of events, made several feeble attempts to restore order to the throng. But the damage had been done. Two days of festivities, ending with such mystery, had sent them into a frenzy of speculation.

"One hundred dollars. Do you think she's his runaway wife?" one of the women muttered, loud enough to be overheard by her neighbors.

"He's old enough to be her father," another huffed.

"Maybe he is." That raised several more eyebrows. "And maybe, after searching the world over, he has found his long-lost daughter here in Hope."

Several of the younger women nearly swooned at the thought that a man would bid one hundred dollars for the schoolteacher's basket.

"But why would she run away from him if she was his wife or daughter?"

"Did you see his face?" Sara Waverly shuddered.

"Did you see his eyes?" Belva Spears interjected. "I'd run away from a man with eyes that cruel."

"She has no place to run except back to the school."

"Look."

At Sara's single word they turned to watch as the stranger pulled himself into the saddle. The crowd had gone deathly silent. The only sound was the clatter of his horse's hooves as he headed out of town, in the direction of the schoolhouse.

"I'll bet he knows where she lives and he's going to get her."

"How romantic."

Through narrowed eyes Thad watched as Sheriff Horn shook his head at a question. His words to a group of concerned townspeople could be clearly overheard.

"I think we should get on with our festivities. Whatever there is between the stranger and Miss Adams is none of our concern. He's obviously a man of wealth.

Maybe he'll even share a bit more of it with the people of Hope.''

While the crowd broke up into small groups to continue their speculation, Thad caught up the reins of his horse and walked slowly between the wagons. At the edge of town he stepped into the woods, still leading his mount.

To Thad's trained eye, Caroline's trail was an easy map to read. Like any novice, she had raced through the thicket, trampling leaves, flattening small brush, even leaving bits of torn fabric fluttering on thorny branches.

It tore at his heart to think of her alone, frightened, lost. He was relieved to see that her trail plunged deeper into the woods. The sanctuary of her cabin or the cool water flowing just beyond the thicket must have been tempting. But she had wisely refrained from taking the easy course, where the stranger would no doubt be waiting.

What did the stranger want with Caroline? He paused, studying the small footprints in the earth. He had seen the way all the color had drained from her face when she'd caught sight of the man. And he had seen the stark terror in her eyes in that moment before she fled.

He clamped his jaw and continued on. This time when he found her, he would have his answers.

Caroline lay shivering beside a rotting log, struggling to sort out the many unfamiliar sounds of the night. Her hair had pulled loose from its neat knot and spilled around her face and shoulders in wild tangles. She had lost one boot when she had heard something in the brush behind her and scrambled up a tree. But though she had waited there for what seemed hours, she had spotted no one.

Her skirt and petticoat hung in tatters. Her arms and legs bled from dozens of cuts made by the barbed brambles.

The sun had long ago gone down, but she was reluctant to leave her hiding place. For the first time in her life, she was frozen with indecision. She knew that once she stepped into an open field or meadow, she would be naked and vulnerable.

He was somewhere out there, stalking her.

She squeezed her eyes tightly shut for a moment, whispering a prayer. "Oh, Mama, why? Why, after all the struggles and all the years and all the tears, has it come down to this?"

She felt the tears—of discouragement, of despair—start to flow. And she remembered Sara Waverly's words. "I was raised to believe that everyone has to accept whatever lot is theirs in life."

"No," Caroline whispered fiercely. The word, spoken aloud, startled her and seemed to give her strength. "No," she said again, louder. "I don't have to accept it." She spat the words from between clenched teeth.

Gathering her courage, she got to her knees and peered into the darkness. It was time. She could hide no longer. Not from him. Not from her past. On trembling legs she stood and began to run.

She was halfway across the meadow when she heard the sound of hoofbeats. Praying it was her thundering heart, she cast a quick glance over her shoulder. Her heart plummeted when she caught sight of the horseman racing toward her.

She continued running even though she knew the horse was gaining on her with every step. Fear clogged her throat, making it nearly impossible to catch her breath.

At last, when the horse was directly beside her, she veered off, but the rider seemed to anticipate her every move.

The horse never broke stride as strong arms scooped her up. She was already raging against her attacker, arms flailing, feet kicking, when she heard a familiar deep voice with an easy Texas drawl say, "Teacher, you sure do like to keep things stirred up, don't you?"

"Thad."

For a moment she could only hold on as she struggled to breathe.

"That's more like it." His arms came around her and he drew her firmly against him.

"Where did you...? How did you find me?" Her breathing was still too ragged to allow her to speak more than a few broken phrases.

In an effort to ease her fears, his lips curved into a smile. He glanced at the night sky, sprinkled with stars. "It seemed like the perfect time to hold a pretty woman in my arms and carry her off to my ranch."

"I can't go to your ranch, Thad."

"Why not? Can you think of a safer place?"

"No place is safe now. He'll find me no matter where I go."

"You let me worry about that."

"No." She pushed far enough away to see his face. "You don't know what sort of man he is. I won't have you dying to protect me."

"It looks like you have no choice, Teacher."

"This isn't your fight, Thad."

His tone was laced with steel. "You're wrong." He nudged his horse into a gallop. "I just made it my fight."

The ranch house was dark and cold. Thad left Caroline standing just inside the door as he made his way unerringly to the fireplace. When he struck a match, she blinked against the sudden light. Within moments the kindling blazed, and soon a cheery fire dispelled the darkness and the cold. But still she stood, her arms hugging herself, shivering.

Thad snatched a blanket from his bed and wrapped it around her, then led her toward a chair pulled in front of the fire.

"Sit here," he ordered.

She was still staring at the flames with haunted eyes when he returned with a bottle of whiskey. He could see the effects of shock setting in. Her eyes were a little too bright, the pupils wide. The flesh of her cheeks was as pale as moon-washed sand.

He filled a tumbler. "Drink," he commanded.

She lifted the glass to her lips and coughed as the fiery liquid burned her throat.

"Finish it." He tilted the glass and held it to her lips until it was empty.

He poured a second glass, but she shook her head in refusal. He stood staring down at her, then lifted the glass and drained it in one long swallow. Setting it on the mantel above the fireplace, he stared down at the small figure hunched into the blanket. His heart contracted at the sight of her. She looked like a broken, wounded bird. Her clothes were torn and muddy. Blood seeped from dozens of cuts and scratches. Her eyes were glazed with pain and fear.

He drew her into his arms and felt her body shake as she gave in to the need to weep. By the time the tears had run their course, the front of his shirt was damp.

With his thumbs he wiped her tears and studied the color that touched her cheeks. The crying had helped a little. But she was still on the verge of exhaustion.

Sweeping her into his arms, he carried her to his bedroom and deposited her on the big feather mattress.

"Now," he said softly, "you're going to sleep."

She clutched at him fiercely and he was surprised at her strength despite her ordeal. "Don't leave me, Thad."

He smoothed the blanket over her, then sat down on the edge of the bed. "Don't worry, Teacher. I'm not going anywhere."

Thad leaned a hip against the sill and drew deeply on a cigarette. Expelling smoke, he stared into the darkness.

On a small bedside table was a basin of water and a towel stained with Caroline's blood. Her torn, muddy clothes lay in a heap on the floor. At first she had tried to fight him when he'd begun to strip and wash her. But at last she'd given in and allowed him to minister to her. Now she lay as still and quiet as death.

She cried out in her sleep and Thad tossed the cigarette into the fire, then hurried to her side.

The mattress sagged as he sat beside her and watched the fierce battle that raged in her mind. If only he could comfort her. But all he could do was wait and watch as she struggled alone with her demons.

In her dream, Caroline traveled back to her troubled childhood.

"Look at you, Caroline." Amanda Adams drew her daughter toward the looking glass and stood behind her. "Whatever am I going to do? You're growing into a beautiful child."

"Beautiful?" Ten-year-old Caroline gave a childish laugh. "Mama, you're the beautiful one." She stared admiringly at her mother's red satin gown, her golden hair piled on top of her head in fancy curls.

Caroline's own dress was faded and dirty and her dark hair hung in limp strands. Her face was smudged, and her bare feet were filthy.

"But he's bound to notice you before long."

Caroline stiffened. Though they never talked about the man who provided the shack they lived in, the fancy dresses for her mother, the carriage that came to take Amanda Adams to his saloon each night, Caroline knew who he was. "What do you mean, Mama?"

Her mother's tone grew clipped and angry. "You mustn't let him see you, Caroline. Not ever."

She gripped her daughter's shoulders and stared at their reflections in the mirror. The mother, small and fair and aristocratic; the daughter, wild and unkempt, with dark hair that had never been cut and skin as pale as fine porcelain.

"You must never let Silas Tate see you. Do you hear me? He'll rob you of your childhood. And your beauty. Promise me, Caroline."

Though she wasn't quite certain of the meaning of the words, the vehemence of her mother's tone conveyed enough fear to have Caroline nod solemnly. "I promise, Mama."

Was it only scant months later that she had stepped from her mother's shack one morning to find herself face-to-face with the man they most feared?

"Well, well. What do we have here?" The man's fingers bruised young Caroline's flesh as she struggled to break free. She nearly gagged on the smell of sweet pipe tobacco that clung to his hair and clothes and breath.

Digging a hand into her hair, he pulled her head back and studied her with a careful eye. Despite the layers of dirt and grime, her youthful beauty was obvious. There were men at his saloon who would pay as much as ten dollars to have such a rare beauty.

Dragging her inside the shack, he stood over the sleeping form in the bed and shouted, "So, Amanda, where have you been hiding this little treasure?"

Caroline saw the way her mother jerked upright in the bed. Then she turned her head in shame as the man dragged her mother from the modest protection of the covers. "You've been holding out on me, Amanda. And you know how I feel about that."

"She's only a baby, Silas."

"She can earn her keep, just like the rest."

"No." Amanda caught her daughter's hand as if to shield her. But Silas shoved her aside and sent her sprawling across the bed.

His words cut like a whip. "Nobody else in this town would help a woman who had a baby without benefit of marriage. But I did, didn't I? I gave you a roof over your head and food in your belly. And I've asked little enough in return."

Caroline watched as her mother stood up to face him without even bothering to drape a shawl over her night-shift. Amanda's body was still young and lush, but her eyes were smudged with pale blue circles and her face in the early morning light showed the effects of too many men, too many sleepless nights.

"You've stolen my dignity, my pride. And I didn't care, as long as I could provide a home for my daughter. But I won't let you have her, too, Silas."

In the blink of an eye, he twisted Amanda's arms behind her and pulled a knife, holding it to her throat.

Caroline leaped to her mother's defense.

"No, Caroline," her mother managed to call.

As the woman cried out, a thin line of blood trickled down the blade of the knife to the handle, where it fell, drop by drop, onto the white shift.

Seeing the terror and pleading in her mother's eyes, Caroline backed away and stood, wide-eyed and silent, cowed into submission.

The man released his hold on her mother.

"That's better. That's just a sample of what you'll both get unless you do as you're told. Now, my fine and fancy lady, you'll do as I say." He bent his lips to Amanda's ear and snarled, "I'll send a dressmaker later today to measure for clothes and shoes for my newest little dove."

His gaze raked the little girl, causing her to hang her head in shame. "See that she has a proper bath." He shoved Amanda aside and strode from the shack.

For long minutes Amanda listened until the sound of his carriage wheels faded. Then she turned to her daughter.

"You can no longer stay here, Caroline. I always knew this day would come. But I'd hoped we would have a few more years together."

"What do you mean?" Caroline watched her mother tear around the shack in a frenzy of activity. "What are you doing, Mama?"

"Bundling up what little we have of value. You'll need it to survive." From a chipped cabinet she removed the china cups and plates and wrapped them in linen towels. From a satin gown hanging against the wall she removed a pearl brooch. "These were my mother's. They're all I have. Sell them if you must. There's a man here in Kansas City. Before my parents died and... all this happened, he and his wife were once kind to me. He was my teacher in Boston, at Miss Tully's School for Ladies. His name is Jonathan Corning."

"I won't go," Caroline shouted. "You can't force me."

Amanda caught her daughter by the shoulders and clutched them painfully. "If you stay here, your life will be a living hell. You'll do as I say. You'll leave. And you must never come back or try in any way to contact me. As of this day you are no longer my daughter. Do you hear?"

"Come with me, Mama," Caroline pleaded. "If this man, Jonathan Corning, was kind to you once, he'll take you in again."

"I can't. Not now. Not after what I've become. Don't you see? No respectable people would offer me haven now. But he'll help you." She spoke more to herself than to Caroline as she added, "Please God, he must."

"I won't go without you, Mama."

Her mother's tone was edged with an anger Caroline had never heard before. "You can no longer stay, Caroline." Her tone softened slightly. "But know this. I'll be content as long as I know that you have made a better life for yourself. Go now," she said, pushing Caroline toward the door.

It was only much later, when Caroline had put miles between herself and the shack and she was prowling the bustling streets of Kansas City, alone and frightened, that she realized she could never return to the shack she'd called home. She would never see her beloved mother's face again. And, worst of all, she had never told her mother that she loved her.

Caroline awoke to the sound of weeping and realized it was her own sobbing she heard. Her lids flicked open and she found Thad seated beside her, his face grave in the firelight.

"Did I . . . speak?"

He nodded. He'd overheard enough of her disjointed ramblings to gather a vague picture of her past. He was fairly sure he knew what her mother had done to survive and why Caroline was so determined to keep herself hidden away.

She had cried out from the depths of her soul. He could only guess at the extent of her torment. But it tore him apart to know that the woman he loved had suffered so.

The woman he loved. The thought filled him with wonder. How was such a thing possible?

He brought his thumbs to her cheeks and wiped away her tears. His touch was so soft, so gentle. It was as if he tried, with one touch, to wipe away all traces of the pain that had burdened her for so long.

"Oh, Thad, hold me. Hold me."

"I'll do more than that," he muttered thickly against her lips. "If you'll let me, Caroline, I'll love you."

Chapter Eighteen

"I've loved you for such a long time, Caroline. But I didn't want to admit it. Not even to myself."

At his words she went very still. Love. How was it possible that now, at the darkest moment of her life, she would find love?

She lifted herself on her elbows and tried to push away from him. "You don't know what you're saying. You don't know me, Thad. My whole life here has been a lie."

He touched a finger to her lips to silence her. "All I need to know is this." He framed her face with his hands and stared deeply into her eyes. "You're the finest woman I've ever met. You're kind to all you meet, and fair with everyone." His voice warmed for a moment. "Not that anything else matters except, ever since I've met you, I'm as churned up as if I'd just stepped on a hornet's nest. The way I see it," he murmured, tracing the outline of her lips with his thumbs, "there's just one cure for it."

For the space of a heartbeat she forgot to breathe as he slowly lowered his face to hers. His fingers skimmed her face, then settled on her shoulders. For that one instant, she felt a flash of the old fear come rushing back. And then just as quickly she dispelled it. He loved her. However reluctantly, he loved her.

His lips were warm and firm and sure as they moved over hers. It occurred to her that every other time he'd kissed her, he'd held something back. But now he poured all the longing, all the need, into this kiss.

He wouldn't be an easy lover or a gentle one. It wasn't in his nature to be either. But it wasn't tenderness she wanted; it was strength. She wanted, for a little while, to forget everything except the mindless pleasure she felt in his arms.

His tongue sought hers, but this time there was no playful teasing. The hands at her shoulders were no longer soft and stroking, but almost bruising in their intensity.

"I've wanted you for so long," he murmured against her mouth.

Even as she felt the first stirrings of passion, she knew a sense of peace, as well. She had always believed that no man would claim her heart. She knew now that she'd been wrong. She'd been waiting all her life for this man, this moment.

She took a deep breath and touched a hand to his cheek, allowing her gaze to roam the fine, strong bones, the sensual mouth. "And I've wanted you, Thad." She touched a hand to the wildly beating pulse at his throat and thrilled with the knowledge that she was the cause of it. "I tried to deny it, but now I realize there's no turning back. I want you to know," she whispered, "that I'm not afraid."

For a moment he couldn't speak. Her admission aroused him to more than mere passion. He was suddenly aware of his own fears and weaknesses, his own vulnerabilities. All his life he'd chosen a lone path, and a lonely one. Now he was opening the door to someone with whom he could share. But that someone could also hurt him more deeply than any bullet.

He was beyond fearing. He had to have her, whatever the risks.

He pressed a kiss to her palm. "I'd never hurt you, Caroline."

"I know that." The knowledge was like a healing balm to her soul. Her life had been a jumble of pain and sorrow. But in this man's arms, she would find only pleasure and peace.

Except for the hiss of flames, the room was silent. The sounds of the night were muted, indistinct. She heard his heart thunder as he lowered his head and traced the fullness of her lower lip with his tongue. It was an achingly sweet gesture. She lay very still on the bed, absorbing the shock waves that pulsed through her. Her lips parted for him, but he chose to hold off the moment when he would claim them. Instead he surprised her by moving his mouth slowly across her face, from her temple, across her closed eyelids, to her cheek.

As he traced the curve of her ear, her contented sigh turned into a low moan of pleasure when he flicked his tongue deep, a prelude of what was to come. Before she could catch her breath he brought his lips to her throat and ran kisses along her shoulder.

With a little gasp she clutched blindly at his waist and her fingers found a gap where his shirt had pulled away. The touch of her fingers on his skin seemed to electrify him.

His mouth covered hers in a kiss that left her breathless.

Heat. He felt the heat pour from her into him and was nearly consumed by it. Lifting his head, he studied her through hooded eyes.

She reached for the buttons of his shirt, and when her fingers fumbled, he helped her until his clothes lay in a forgotten heap on the floor.

Her hands trailed over the corded muscles of his back and arms. She had never known how beautiful a man's body could be. Now she was free to explore, to learn, to study, to fill her inquisitive mind with yet another lesson.

"You're beautiful," she breathed.

She studied his face in the flickering firelight. It looked dark and dangerous, a face of mystery. He was a man who lived by his own rules. A man who sought his own destiny.

"You're trembling, Caroline." *Caroline. Caroline.* Her name was like a beautiful litany in his mind. He would never grow weary of it.

She swallowed, alarmed by the desire that rocked her. Always before, he had avoided her name. Now, hearing it on his lips, spoken in such worshipful tones, she felt beautiful and cherished.

"You're cold."

"No." She could hardly speak, her throat was so constricted. Instead she shook her head before whispering, "It's the . . . wanting."

He felt a sudden thrill at the knowledge that she wanted him. This strong, defiant woman who had fought against such adversity was actually trembling for him.

His hands tangled in her hair as he drew her head back. "Look at me, Caroline."

She met his fiery gaze. In his eyes was a fierce look of desire. "I'm trembling, too," he murmured as his lips covered hers in a hot, hungry kiss.

She melted into him. In his embrace her bones seemed to liquefy and she lay, soft and pliant, as he took the kiss deeper. He accepted her surrender for the moment as he tugged aside the blanket that had become a barrier between them.

He tormented her with hot, nibbling kisses across her face and neck and she lost herself in him.

He smelled of horses and leather and tasted faintly of whiskey and tobacco. The dark, mysterious taste of a man. Her man. Her heart swelled at the thought. Her man.

In the firelight her hair was touched with flame. It flowed, dark and silky, against the paleness of her skin. He remembered the first time he'd seen her skin, untouched by sunlight, as pale as alabaster. Even then he'd wanted to touch it. Now he was free to touch, to taste. To possess.

He studied her eyes, gilded by the light of the fire, gleaming more brightly than a mountain cat's. In their depths he could see himself.

"God in heaven, Caroline, how I've wanted you."

He kissed her with a savageness that took them both by surprise. The kiss was by turns harsh, then gentle. Pleading, then demanding.

She smelled of soap and water and the disinfectant he'd used on her cuts and bruises. A hint of the evergreen forest clung to her. Clean, untouched, he thought. And he, in turn, was being cleansed by her love. She tasted sweet. Sweeter than anything he'd ever tasted. And she was his. His woman. To love, to cherish. To protect.

His lips roamed her throat and the hollow between her neck and shoulder, then dipped lower to capture her breast. Icy needles of pleasure skittered along her spine. But as he nibbled and suckled, first one breast, then the other, her blood quickly heated until it flowed like molten lava.

His hands, his lips, moved over her, drawing out all the hidden pleasures. She lay, steeped in feelings, her body humming with need. Her hands fisted into the bedclothes beneath her and she arched herself. He gave her no time to recover before his lips followed the trail his fingertips had blazed. With his tongue and fingertips he brought her to the first peak.

With the coarse blanket beneath her, his work-roughened fingers arousing her, she experienced pleasure she had never even dreamed of. And still he drove her relentlessly higher and higher.

Shuddering, she struggled for air and arched against him. So this was the dark, mysterious pleasure that men and women had sought from the beginning of time. This was the treasure men killed for.

She touched a hand to his chest and felt the wild thundering of his heart. It gave her a sense of power to know that it was her touch, her taste, that excited him. Drunk with the knowledge, she touched him as he was touching her, and was rewarded with a low moan of pleasure that escaped his lips.

As she grew bolder, he felt a hunger sharper and deeper than anything he'd ever known. Only Caroline could feed it. It was a thirst that only she could quench.

He struggled to bank his needs, determined to draw out the moment. He would make this first time a memory she could carry always in her heart.

Her touch was driving him mad with desire. As he moved over her, he whispered her name and his hand fisted in her hair. The need was so great now that he felt himself whirling toward madness. Desire clawed at his insides, seeking release. And still he waited, relentlessly drawing out every last sensation, every steamy pleasure, until, desperate, she clutched at his shoulders.

Her needs matched his, as did her strength. They came together in a storm of desperation and felt themselves thrown into a raging river of passion.

This was how he had wanted her. No longer cool, controlled, but desperate, demanding. His own control was gone, washed away in a flood of need that left him trembling.

She had known he would not be gentle, but it wasn't tenderness she craved. It was fulfillment.

As they moved together, they whispered incoherent words of love. Each gave and took and gave until, fueled by the madness, they felt as if for one fleeting moment they had died. Still clinging, they raced to the stars and tumbled into a world of exquisite pleasure.

They lay, still joined, their bodies damp and shimmering. Thad's face was buried in her neck. Neither of them had the energy to move.

"Do you know how long I've waited to hold you like this?"

"How long?" she murmured.

"Since I first saw you in that torn gown and ugly hat."

She pushed against him. "My hat was not ugly."

"It was. But then, you knew that. It was part of your plan." He rolled to one side and drew her into the circle of his arms. Grabbing a handful of her hair, he watched as it sifted through his fingers. "And you pinned up all this beautiful hair in an even uglier bun."

She pursed her lips into a pout and sat up. "Was there anything you didn't find ugly?"

He gave her a lazy, heart-stopping smile. "You, Teacher. You took my breath away."

"Did I?" Pleased, she touched a hand to his chest, idly running her fingers through the crisp golden hair.

"Mm-hmm." He lay back, watching her through half-closed eyes. "And I've been breathless ever since."

"When I first saw you," she said, trailing her finger along a thin, raised scar that ran the length of his chest to his side, "I was afraid of you."

"And now?" Did she have any idea what her touch was doing to him? How was it possible that the hunger could begin again so soon?

"Now I'm still afraid. But not of you. It's me." She lowered her lashes for a moment, shielding her gaze from him. He wondered if she knew how seductive that little movement was. "You've made me think about things I never would have dreamed of. And made me want things I'll probably never have."

"Things?" His lips curved into a teasing smile. "I hope one of them is me."

She looked suddenly shy. "Thad?"

She met his eyes, then glanced away quickly. He could see the hint of color that flooded her cheeks. "Are you very tired?"

He was puzzled. "Not very. Why?"

"I thought ..." She moved her hand lower until she heard his little moan of pleasure. "Would it be very wicked of me to want you to love me again?"

He swallowed back the laughter that threatened. She was so serious. "Yes. Very wicked."

"Oh."

She drew her hand away and he caught it firmly in his and placed it back where it had been.

He could no longer contain his laughter. He threw back his head and roared. "Teacher, I can see that you have a whole lot more to learn. So why don't we get on with your lessons."

He pulled her down until her breasts were flattened atop his chest. Her thighs were pressed firmly to his.

"Lesson number one. A gentleman should never refuse a lady's request."

Caroline propped her elbows on his chest and stared down into his eyes. "Never? No matter how tired he is?"

"That's right." He kissed the tip of her nose. "And lesson number two is, a lady should never climb on top of a gentleman if she wants him to sleep. Especially if the lady and gentleman are missing their clothes."

She tried to assume her classroom manner. It wasn't easy. Laughter kept bubbling up, making her eyes dance with mischief. "Is there something I ought to know before we proceed?"

"Woman," he muttered thickly against her throat, "if I didn't know better, I'd swear you had lessons in how to drive a man mad."

"Am I? Driving you mad?" She pressed hot, quick kisses over his chest and stomach. Her hair swirled around him like a dark silken veil.

"Yes." His hand closed in her hair. With a moan he rolled them over until she was lying under him. "But there are still some things I'd like to teach you."

"I'm willing to learn. I think you'll find me a good pupil."

He cut off her words with a slow, leisurely kiss.

Against her lips he muttered, "Now lesson number three..."

With sighs of pleasure they tumbled into a dark river of passion. A place where only lovers can go.

Thad lay with one arm beneath his head. The other curled protectively around Caroline, who snuggled against his chest. He watched her while she slept and marveled again at the love he felt for this little creature.

For most of his life he'd been alone, yet he'd never felt lonely. Now the thought of waking without her beside him caused an unbearable pain around his heart.

She still had not confided in him about the stranger. He wouldn't press her. When the time was right, when her trust in him was solid, she would tell him what he needed to know. This much he already knew—she would never have to face anything alone again.

Her lids fluttered open and he watched as she slowly awakened.

"Is it morning already?"

"Not quite. There's another hour or two before dawn." He touched a hand to her cheek in a gesture of tenderness. "You should sleep awhile longer."

"And miss seeing the sunrise with you?" She surprised him by drawing closer and pressing a kiss to his chest.

He felt desire surface instantly. How could it be that he could want her again? All night they had loved, slept fitfully, then loved again. And each time it was wonderful, and each time different.

They had been rough and tender, greedy and giving, selfish and generous. And this much he knew. He would never have enough of her.

"Do you think you might have something more you'd like to teach me?"

"Why, Miss Adams, I'm surprised at you." He lifted a handful of her hair and kissed her neck. "Is that all you can think about?"

"Is there anything else?"

He lifted his head and thought a minute. "There's food." He ran nibbling kisses along her shoulder. "We didn't eat a thing yesterday."

She shivered. "That's true."

"And there's the fire. It's burned to ashes and the room is cold."

"Is it? I hadn't noticed."

"Then why are you shivering?"

She drew his face close for a slow, lingering kiss. "I always do that when you touch me."

"Like this?" His clever hands began seeking out all the sweet, sensitive places of her body that he had discovered during their long night of lovemaking.

When she gasped he covered her mouth with his in a deep, passionate kiss.

"I guess we'll do without a fire or food," he murmured against her lips.

Their bodies were already heated. And with their love, they fed each other's souls.

Chapter Nineteen

Caroline awoke to see Thad, shirtless and barefoot, tossing a log into the fireplace. For long moments she studied the way he looked in the thin morning sunlight. Pale shaggy hair dusted a wide forehead. A stubble of bronze beard gilded his cheeks and chin. The powerful muscles of his arms and shoulders accentuated a flat stomach and lean hips.

When the flames danced along the log, chasing the chill from the room, he stood and wiped his hands on his pants.

"The bed is cold," she whispered.

Turning, he gave her a smile that wrapped itself around her heart. He crossed the room and the mattress sagged as he sat on the edge of the bed and drew her close. "Someone has to see to the unimportant details like food and warmth."

"Mmm. I can feel the warmth." She snuggled against him. "But where's the food?"

"Rosita is preparing it."

"Rosita." Caroline began to scramble from the bed. "She's already here? She knows I'm here—in your room?"

He hauled her back and wrapped his arms around her, stilling her movements. "Yes and yes."

"But I can't let her see me like . . . Thad, I have to get dressed."

He chuckled. "That's going to be pretty hard to do, Teacher, since you don't have any clothes."

"What happened to my clothes?"

"By the time I got them off you last night, they were rags. I told Rosita to burn them."

"What?" He could see the flush that colored her cheeks. "Now what am I going to do?"

He kissed her lightly to stop the questions. Instantly she wrapped her arms around him and grew soft and pliant in his arms as she returned the kiss.

What was it about this man that he could ease all her fears and silence all her questions? Trust, she thought, with a sigh of satisfaction. She trusted him completely.

When they finally came up for air he brought his mouth to a tangle of hair at her temple. "Rosita sent Manuel back to their ranch for some of her clothes. So until he returns, it looks like you'll just have to stay here in my bed and let me . . . amuse you."

Her fingertips caressed his head, moving in slow, sensuous circles through his hair. He sighed contentedly and drew her closer.

She could remain like this forever, she thought. Just the two of them, hidden away at his ranch, locking out the rest of the world. She had never known such peace, such happiness. Such love.

For no logical reason, she found herself weeping.

Tasting the salt, Thad became alarmed and lifted his head. "Tears?" He touched a finger to the moisture that rolled down her cheeks. "Have I done something to hurt you, love?"

Love. His use of the endearment made her tears flow faster. "No. It's just..." She flushed in embarrassment. "I often heard my mother crying in the night, and I know they weren't happy tears."

"And are these happy tears?" He pressed his lips to the corner of her eye to stem the flow.

She nodded and struggled to compose herself. "In some ways very happy tears. And in some ways sad. I never dreamed that loving could be like this. Somehow I always thought that it was only pleasurable for the man."

She sat very still, loving the feel of him holding her just so, his lips still pressed to the side of her face.

Almost timidly she asked, "Is it always like this?"

"It is if you're with someone you love."

"Then I truly pity my poor mother," she whispered gravely. "She was never with a man who loved her."

"Not even your father?"

"She hardly knew him."

At Thad's questioning look she paused a moment, gathering her thoughts. Then, taking a deep breath, she said, "How much did I reveal when I was having my... bad dream?"

"Enough," he admitted. "You spoke aloud about your mother, having to run away from a man. But you never revealed his name."

He felt her stiffen. Against her temple he muttered, "You don't have to talk about it now."

"Yes." She took in a deep breath. "I do. You have a right to know. His name is Silas Tate. He's a very wealthy, very powerful man who owns a tavern and hotel in Kansas City. When I was ten years old, my mother sent me away to save me from him. You see, she... worked for him."

Thad nodded in understanding.

She looked away, unable to meet his eyes. "After my mother sent me away, I spent three days searching among the shops and crowds in the city until I was able to locate Jonathan Corning, an old friend of my mother's. You can imagine the shock he and his wife must have felt when they saw a ten-year-old girl, hungry, frightened and looking like a filthy beggar. But they were good people. They took me in, cleaned me up, fed me and offered to keep me until I could take care of myself." She smiled despite the painful things she had just admitted. "For Jonathan, who had once taught my mother at Miss Tully's School for Ladies in Boston, the worst sin of all was that I was illiterate. I could neither read nor write. So he undertook to educate me and, to his surprise and mine, discovered that I had a quick mind. I once heard him boast that I was his best student, despite my foul language."

Agitated, she slid from the bed and picked up Thad's heavy shirt. Shrugging into it, she walked to the fireplace and stared into the flames for several minutes before turning to face him.

It gave Thad the strangest sensation to see her in his shirt. She looked so young, with her hair falling in tangles around her shoulders and her long sleek legs so pale against the first slanting rays of morning light. But her youthful beauty hid years of pain.

"I began to dream of being a schoolteacher," she said softly, "and Jonathan encouraged me. Within a year or two, he said, I could even teach at Miss Tully's School for Ladies if I set my mind to it." She smiled dreamily. "It was the greatest compliment anyone could have paid me. But then, one day in the spring when I had thought my past was behind me, I was strolling along the streets of Kansas City and I suddenly felt a man's hand clamp over my mouth. When I twisted around I found myself face-to-face with Silas Tate.''

Thad saw the look of revulsion on her face as she whispered, ''He pulled my head back and ran a hand over my body as though he owned me. And he told me I looked even more beautiful than he'd remembered. And he couldn't wait to show me to all my mother's customers. Then he started dragging me toward his carriage, and I knew that if he succeeded in taking me away, I would never be free of him.''

Thad saw the effort it cost her to retain her composure, but though his heart ached for her, he knew that she needed to tell her story.

''I was fighting him, but he was so much bigger and stronger. He hauled me into his carriage and ordered the driver to start. Then he sat back against the cushions and began to laugh. To laugh.'' She shook her head, as if still unable to believe his cruelty.

''He took a knife from his belt, the same knife he'd held to my mother's throat. And he said, I made your mother pay for disobeying me. And he laughed again as he told me that he'd killed her....'' A tear squeezed from the corner of her eye but she forced herself to go on. ''But, he said, no one would ever care, since she was nothing more than a whore.'' Caroline's voice broke for a moment, but she caught herself and whispered, ''I don't know what happened. Something inside me seemed to snap. I snatched up the knife and slashed his face, then leaped out of the carriage.'' Her voice was stronger now as she added, ''In the confusion, I managed to escape. I knew I was no longer safe in the city. Jonathan had heard about the teaching position here in Hope and suggested that I send my letter and leave town at once.''

''What about the school in Boston?'' Thad asked.

She shook her head. "It was a lie. Jonathan didn't know about it. He wouldn't have approved of using the name of a school I never attended. That was my idea. I was afraid I might not get the job unless I had the proper credentials."

"And Silas Tate?"

Caroline looked at Thad for the first time. Tears glittered in her eyes, but her voice was steady. "I don't know how he found out where I was headed. But he must have known almost from the beginning. And he has played with me like a cat with a mouse. And now he has come to have his revenge."

Thad crossed the room and drew her close against his chest, wishing he could spare her the pain of her memories. "You're not a helpless little girl anymore. You're a bright, educated woman who has a right to defend herself. And there's something else, Caroline. You're not alone anymore. We're in this fight together."

She shook her head. "I knew you'd say that. But I've had plenty of time to think this through. I've already caused my mother's death. I won't have yours on my hands, as well."

She caught a flash of anger in his eyes and was reminded of his ruthlessness when he'd faced her attackers. His voice was low with feeling. "You weren't the cause of your mother's death. And in case you've forgotten—" he made a strained attempt at lightness "—I have a reputation to uphold. Folks around here think I'm the best damned shot in Texas. We can't let them down now, can we?"

"This isn't a joke, Thad. I have no—"

They both looked up at the knock on the door. "What is it?" Thad snapped.

"I have your breakfast, Señor Conway," came Rosita's voice through the closed door. "And clean clothes for Señorita Adams."

"Thanks, Rosita. Just leave them outside the door."

They stood facing each other, listening to the clatter of a tray as it was deposited on the floor. Moments later they heard the soft tread of footsteps retreating. Thad turned away. For the moment, at least, the tension between them dissolved.

"You agree, then," Thad said as he drained a cup of steaming coffee. He took a long, admiring look at Caroline soaping herself in a tub of hot water positioned on a rug in front of the fire. "We'll ride into town and let the sheriff know that Silas Tate is no friend of yours. You'll let him know that you want Tate to leave you alone."

Caroline leaned her head back and closed her eyes. "You make it sound so simple."

"It will be." He wished the day would disappear and night would come upon them again. He'd never be able to coax her back into bed knowing Rosita and Manuel were in the house. But he wanted to. He wanted desperately to love her one more time before they faced the man from her past.

"Once Sheriff Horn knows that this man is here to cause trouble, he'll see that Silas Tate leaves the territory. And if Tate refuses, you'll have the sheriff and the whole town on your side."

"All right. If you say so." As she felt a splash in the water, Caroline's eyes snapped open. "Thad, what are you doing?"

He was kneeling beside the tub, his face so close to hers that his warm breath whispered over her cheek. "I'm washing your hair."

"Mmm." His fingers gently massaged her scalp, and she closed her eyes, letting all the tensions begin to drain away. "You have wonderful hands," she murmured.

"I'm glad you noticed." He continued to massage the soap into her scalp, then commanded, "Close your mouth, Teacher. I'm about to push you under."

He pressed her head underwater and watched the soap float to the surface. When she came up sputtering, he wrapped a towel around her hair and pulled her close for a quick kiss. He touched his lips to the droplets of water that clung to her lashes, murmuring, "You smell like Jessie's roses."

"It's the soap Rosita gave me. She said she mixes it with crushed rose petals."

He drew her closer, pressing his lips to her temple.

"Careful," she warned as the water lapped around the rim of the tub. "If you're not careful, you'll get wet."

He stood suddenly and began slipping out of his clothes.

She looked shocked. "Thad, what are you doing?"

"I'm going to join you, Teacher."

"You can't," she said laughing.

"And why not?"

"Because you wouldn't fit in this little tub with me."

"Want to make a wager on that?"

He stepped into the water and it nearly overflowed.

"See? I told you."

He sat down and pulled her on top of him. Warm, soapy water sloshed onto the floor, soaking the rug. For a minute she was convulsed with laughter. Then, as he drew her head down to his for a long, lazy kiss, the laughter died in her throat.

His hands were already beginning to work their magic. Her body reacted instinctively to his touch.

"How about another lesson, Teacher?"

She wrapped her arms around his neck and said against his lips, "You know I'm always eager to learn."

"You look...beautiful." Beautiful didn't seem nearly eloquent enough, but Thad had never been a man of words.

Barefoot, Caroline stood in front of the looking glass and stared at her reflection. The woman looking back at her was a stranger. She was wearing Rosita's ivory, lace-frosted blouse which fell off her shoulders, and a skirt that fell to her ankles in tiers of vivid scarlet and violet and vibrant yellow. Her black hair fell to below her waist in a jumble of curls.

"We'll have to go to my cabin and pick up a proper dress," she said without turning.

Across the room, Thad had been studying her in silence for long minutes. At her words he seemed jolted out of his reverie.

Crossing the room, he took the hairbrush from her hands and began running it through her tangles. "Are you still afraid to look beautiful, Teacher?"

Despite all that they had shared, she felt herself blushing.

"I've never really thought about it. I suppose, because of my mother's fears for me, I never wanted to be beautiful. But now, looking at your eyes..." She turned and placed her hands on either side of his face. When he gazed down, she saw herself reflected in the blue depths. And for the first time in her life she began to believe that being beautiful was a blessing. He made her feel truly beautiful. And cherished.

"I wish..."

"You wish what, Teacher?"

She moved her hands to his shoulders. "I wish I could always see that look in your eyes."

"You will," he said softly.

"Even years from now?"

"If we live to be a hundred, you'll still see the love I feel for you shining in my eyes." He pressed a kiss to the tip of her nose. "Now sit down."

"Why?"

"Because you can't go into town in bare feet. Manuel made these for you." His hands lingered a moment at her ankles as he slid her feet into soft kid slippers.

"Oh, Thad. I always hated those heavy old boots." She stood and danced around the room, twirling so that the full skirt drifted and billowed around her. "In these clothes I feel . . . I feel so free," she said, laughing.

"You are free." He lifted her and spun her around and around until they were both dizzy.

He lowered her until her feet touched the floor. Still holding her, he bent his head and brushed her lips with his.

A knock at the door had them both looking up sharply.

"Señor Conway." From the other side of the closed door came Rosita's worried voice. "You must come at once."

Thad hurried to open the door. "What is it?"

"Manuel said that many horses are approaching. They are led by the sheriff and—" she looked beyond Thad to where Caroline stood alone "—the stranger who caused Señorita Adams to run away."

Chapter Twenty

"I can't face anyone looking like this," Caroline said in alarm. She cast a quick glance in the mirror and was horrified at her sultry reflection. The townspeople would be shocked to see their new teacher in such a different light.

Hearing the thunder of hoofbeats, Thad said, "Looks like you have no choice. They're already here."

When she held back, Thad led the way to the front porch. Holding the door open, he watched as she stiffened her spine and lifted her head before stepping through the doorway. "Remember, Teacher," he said in a tone meant for her ears only, "the truth shall set you free."

The horses came to an abrupt halt in a cloud of dust. As the dust settled, Caroline could make out the sheriff and Reverend Symes, as well as Sara Waverly, Cora Meadows and Belva Spears. All of them glanced around appreciatively, since it was their first venture onto Thad Conway's property. Until now he had steadfastly kept the townspeople away.

If he was angered by their presence, he gave no indication. He nodded in greeting to everyone, then gave a quick, tight smile to Jessie and Cole and Dan and Morning Light.

Though Caroline was aware of all who were there, her gaze centered on one man, Silas Tate, who rode beside the sheriff.

Despite the presence of so many people, the crowd seemed strangely silent. They remained astride their horses, watching Caroline Adams as she faced the man she had fled.

They couldn't help but notice the change in their teacher. Garbed in brilliant colors, her dark hair soft and loose, she was far different from the prim schoolteacher they had become accustomed to seeing. Many of them seemed disturbed by her appearance. And more than a little shocked.

"Miss Adams." Sheriff Horn cleared his throat and looked extremely uncomfortable. The back of his neck turned red and he pressed a sleeve to the sweat that beaded his forehead.

"Before you say anything, Sheriff Horn," Thad said quietly, "I think you should hear what Caroline has to say."

The crowd waited expectantly. The only sound was an occasional snap of leather or jingle of harness as the horses moved restlessly.

"What is it, Miss Adams?" the sheriff encouraged.

"That man's name is Silas Tate," she said, pointing to the man who sat stone-faced astride his horse. "He killed my mother and has threatened my life."

There were murmurs of shock and disbelief from the others as she added, "I also believe it was he who planned the attack on the stage and who helped Fox escape jail."

"Those are mighty serious charges, Miss Adams." The sheriff glanced at the man beside him, whose face now bore a smug look of confidence. "Can you prove any of them?"

"He admitted to me that he'd killed my mother."

"Were there any witnesses?"

Caroline shook her head. "We were alone."

"When was this, ma'am?"

"When he tried to abduct me from a street in Kansas City."

Sheriff Horn arched a brow. "Kansas City, ma'am? I thought you told us you came from Boston?"

"I . . ." Caroline swallowed and glanced at Thad. She knew now that the truth was her only course of action, even though it seemed buried beneath layers of falsehoods. But was it truly the best course of action? There was no time left to consider the consequences. "I lied."

A ripple of alarm ran through the crowd.

"I wanted desperately to teach children," Caroline said defensively. "And I needed to get out of Kansas City immediately. So I said that I'd been educated at Miss Tully's School for Ladies in Boston."

"And what school did you actually attend, Miss Adams?"

She swallowed again. She could feel Thad's glance but refused to look at him. "I—I didn't attend school. I was taught at home by Jonathan Corning, who had once taught at Miss Tully's School in Boston."

"Jonathan Corning, you say?" The sheriff glanced at Silas Tate, then back at Caroline. "Mr. Tate told us you might say that. He brought along a newspaper clipping about the murder of a Jonathan Corning and his wife. It would seem that your Mr. Corning is conveniently dead and can no longer vouch for you."

Dead. The only man who had ever been kind to her in her childhood. Caroline felt a wrenching loss.

Then, as the sheriff's words sank in, her voice frosted over.

"Conveniently? And what is that supposed to mean, Sheriff?"

The lawman shrugged, looking even more uncomfortable. "Mr. Tate told us that your whole life has been a lie and that he had no doubt that you would lie again to cover your tracks."

Caroline allowed her gaze to scan the crowd of familiar faces. All of them were watching her carefully. And in their eyes she could see the doubt.

All Silas Tate had had to do was plant the seed of distrust.

Desperately she tried again. "What about the attack on the stage? I can't prove that Silas Tate hired the gunmen who attacked the stage. But how else can you explain why they killed the others and spared my life?"

The sheriff sounded truly unhappy as he cleared his throat and said, "Mr. Tate mentioned that himself. He suggested that you might have offered the gunmen—something—in exchange for your life." He looked down at his stubby fingers loosely holding the reins. It pained him to repeat all the things that had been revealed by this stranger, but now it seemed everything Silas Tate had predicted was coming true.

Thad's voice, low and dangerous, caused the sheriff to lift his head sharply.

"You forget, Sheriff, I was there. I saw the way Caroline fought those gunmen. She wasn't making any deals. Even to save her life. And tell me this. Why is it that Luke Cochrane's gang didn't seem surprised to find a lone woman on the stage bound for Hope?"

"Hell, Thad, half the territory knew we had a new schoolteacher arriving on the stage. It was no secret." Sheriff Horn turned to Caroline. "Now, Miss Adams, I want you to know I wish none of this had happened, 'cause we were all happy with the way you were teaching our children. But now that Mr. Tate has told us these . . . things about you, the good people of Hope deserve some answers."

Caroline saw the flicker of a smile on Silas Tate's lips and felt her heart begin to thunder. He hadn't spoken a word. And yet he controlled these people as surely as if they were all attached to strings. Strings he was pulling. The words coming out of the sheriff's mouth were Silas Tate's words. Words that would destroy everything she had begun to build here.

"Mr. Tate has told us some mighty serious things, Miss Adams. He has said publicly that your mother earned her keep by . . ." The sheriff cast a sideways glance at Reverend Symes, then added delicately, "Catering to the base instincts of the men of Kansas City." He shot a pleading look at Thad before saying, "I surely hope you can deny it, Miss Adams."

And the truth shall set you free. Caroline swallowed the bitter gall of defeat. In her case, the truth would ensnare her forever in its ugly slime.

She lifted her head. She would not be shamed by what her mother had done to survive. Caroline had heard her mother crying in the night and had seen the bruises and marks made by men who enjoyed inflicting pain on helpless women. "I cannot deny it, Sheriff Horn."

The crowd gave an audible gasp. Sara Waverly covered her mouth and half turned away, as if offended by the mere sight of Caroline. Cora Meadows and Belva

Spears appeared to be stunned. The others seemed both repelled and fascinated by her admission.

As if by some unspoken agreement, Jessie and Cole, Dan and Morning Light dismounted and moved to stand beside Thad and Caroline. Touched by their support, she turned and gave them a weak nod. But when she tried to smile, her lips trembled and she found herself on the verge of breaking down.

"There is more, Miss Adams," the sheriff said softly. "And I'm afraid it's worse."

Tears glittered in Caroline's eyes as she lifted her head and faced him. Her fists were clenched at her sides. Thad could see that she was losing the battle to control her emotions.

"How can there possibly be anything worse than what I have just been forced to admit, Sheriff?"

"Forgive me, Miss Adams, but Mr. Tate says that from the time you were hardly more than a girl, you…followed in your mother's footsteps."

Thad's gun was out of the holster before anyone had a chance to react. He aimed it at Silas Tate. His words were harsh, clipped, angry. "I know your kind, Tate. All my life I've had to watch scum like you destroy good people's lives with rumors and lies. But you're not going to succeed here in Hope."

Just as quickly Sheriff Tate drew his gun. "Do you want a dozen witnesses to cold-blooded murder? Put the gun away, Texan, or you'll have to shoot me, too."

Caroline put a hand on Thad's arm. In soft, pleading tones she murmured, "Please, Thad. Nothing can be gained by this. I couldn't bear to see you go to jail because of me."

"Jail? Caroline, I'd go to hell and back for you. I'm not going to stand here and let him spread these lies about you."

She could feel the anger pulsing through him. His eyes narrowed on Silas Tate, who continued to sit quietly with a look of supreme confidence on his face.

"Please, Thad. This isn't the way and you know it. If you resort to bloodshed, he'll still win."

She saw the effort it cost Thad to return his gun to the holster. Even then he continued to allow his hand to rest just above the pistol, as though poised to draw if Silas Tate should threaten her.

Everyone seemed to let out a collective sigh of relief, especially Thad's family.

"I'll ask you again, Miss Adams," the sheriff said. "Can you deny what Mr. Tate has said?"

"I do deny it. Silas Tate is lying."

"Then you've never been with a man?"

In the silence that followed, Caroline studied Tate's smug face and knew in that instant that he still had one card left to play.

The flush had crept up Sheriff Horn's neck until his face was now suffused with color. In almost apologetic tones he said, "Mr. Tate told us that he followed you here last night, Miss Adams. And that he knows for a fact that you spent the night. In Thad Conway's bed."

Not a sound broke the silence. The wind stirred in the trees, rustling the leaves. No one noticed. They were staring intently at the young, beautiful creature who had been transformed from a prim, plain, soft-spoken woman into a dazzling beauty. For some, that fact alone was enough to prove the truth of the stranger's claims. Why had she taken such pains to hide her beauty? What other secrets was she hiding?

Thad took a step forward and placed a hand on her shoulder. Further proof to those watching that a bond had been forged between these two. A bond deeper than mere friendship.

Thad's touch couldn't dispel the chill that raced through Caroline, leaving her trembling.

"Since when has that become a crime?" Thad hissed.

"Human nature is human nature," the sheriff said almost sheepishly. "But a teacher's got a calling that sets her above the rest. We need Miss Adams to put our minds at ease. That's all we ask," the sheriff added.

Caroline's gaze fastened on the evil man who had just destroyed everything she had ever valued. With rumor and hints and evil whispers, he had turned something beautiful into something dark and sinister and degrading.

Her voice was low, the tone flat. "You've won, Silas."

"What are you saying, Caroline?" Thad's voice beside her caused her to turn, but only for a moment. She couldn't bear to look at him. It was too painful knowing that the only man she had ever loved was being destroyed along with her. Because of her, the privacy he treasured had been violated. Because of her, his own nieces and nephews would have to withstand even more taunts from their friends.

She no longer minded for herself. She had chosen to lie in order to hide her past. But it wasn't fair to destroy Thad because of his association with her.

Glancing at the sheriff, she said, "I suppose you'll want me to leave town at once?"

He coughed. "I think that would be best. For the children, you understand."

"Yes, of course."

"What the hell are you saying?" Thad looked from Caroline to the sheriff, then back to Caroline again. "You aren't leaving. Where would you go?"

"Someplace where I can make a new start. And the next time, I'll tell the truth about myself before I let anyone take a chance on me."

"And what about Silas Tate?" Thad's eyes narrowed on the man who watched the unfolding scene without emotion.

"He'll have no hold over me as long as I tell the truth. You said it yourself, Thad. The truth will set us free."

"The hell it will. Look at him, Caroline." When she lowered her head he caught her face and forced it up. "Take a good look at him. He's obsessed with revenge. He'll never let you alone."

"Thad Conway," Reverend Symes said softly, "your problem has always been that you've gone looking for reasons to draw that gun. This fine man came all this way just to warn the good people of Hope that their teacher was not what they thought she was. And he has already assured us that he has to hurry back to Kansas City to tend to his business."

"Have you asked this 'fine' man what his business is?" Thad could barely get the words out because of the fury choking him.

"He owns a respectable hotel and tavern." Reverend Symes thought about the large contribution the stranger had made to the church. "And he has invited us all to visit him if we ever get to Kansas City."

Caroline took a deep breath to calm the feeling of quiet despair that had descended upon her.

Turning to the sheriff, she said softly, "Would you mind if I returned to the schoolhouse? Just to pack my trunk?" she added. "I can be on the next stage."

The sheriff nodded. "I'll go there now and pick up your rig. I should be back to collect you in a little while."

Glancing around at the others, he called loudly, "All right, folks. Our business here is concluded."

Silas Tate gave a slight bow of the head before turning his mount. The sheriff and the others followed suit, and within minutes they were gone, leaving only a cloud of dust in their wake. Jessie and Cole, Dan and Morning Light were the only ones who remained.

"The bastard," Thad said through gritted teeth. "He was enjoying it."

He turned to Caroline and saw the way she held herself in such rigid control. If he were to hold her, she would snap.

"I'm not letting you go," he said simply.

"You no longer have a choice, Thad." Through a haze of tears Caroline turned away and fled to Thad's bedroom, leaving him to answer his family's questions.

In the silence of his room she threw herself across his bed and wept as though her heart would break.

"The sheriff is here with the carriage, Caroline."

Jessie's voice roused her from her stupor.

Woodenly she sat up and shoved the heavy hair from her eyes. Her cheeks were still stained with her tears. Her eyes were red-rimmed from crying.

She glanced from Jessie and Cole to Dan and Morning Light, who had all gathered in the doorway. "Where's Thad?"

"The last I saw he was thinking about barring the gate." Jessie paused, wondering how far she dared to intrude on her brother's business. "Caroline, we think we know why you're going. And we want you to know that, although we think it's very noble, we also think you're making a terrible mistake."

It was obvious that they had discussed this in great detail. Caroline brushed past her, but Jessie put out a hand as if to stop the young woman from going.

"Don't, Jessie." Caroline shook her hand away and started toward the door.

"I know my brother very well," Jessie called after her. "And I've never seen him in a rage like this before. He loves you, Caroline. Truly loves you."

"And I care deeply about him, too." Caroline paused with her hand on the door, keeping her back to the others. It would be too painful to speak of love. A love that even now tugged at her, breaking her heart into little pieces. She pulled open the door.

"And that's why you're leaving. Because you think that those of us who love Thad will reject him because of you. But you're wrong. We grew up free, Caroline. Thad and Dan and I broke the law many years ago rather than see our pa hang for a crime he didn't commit. Out here, we never cared what others thought. We never judged a person by what his life was like before he came here. We won't judge you, either."

Caroline turned. Her eyes were dry. There were no tears left. "Thank you, Jessie. That means a lot to me. But I still have to go." She walked through the open doorway.

"Caroline."

At Morning Light's call, she turned back. The young Comanche woman extended her hand. "I want you to know how grateful I am for what you taught my children."

Caroline accepted her hand.

"And I want you to know that I am proud to know you," Morning Light added.

Caroline felt a lump in her throat and tried to swallow it back. "And I'm proud to know you." She turned to include the others. "All of you."

On the porch, Rosita and Manuel stood to one side. They turned as she stepped through the doorway.

From the corner of her eye she saw Thad standing just beyond the carriage. He and the sheriff spoke not a word.

Caroline turned to Rosita. "I'll see that your clothes are returned."

"There is no need, *señorita*." She touched a hand to her flat stomach. "Soon enough I will be unable to wear them anyway. Please wear them and remember me."

"I wish I could be here to see your baby.

Rosita caught her hand. "You should not let them drive you away."

"The choice is my own." She turned to Manuel. "Thank you for the shoes, Manuel. They're the finest I've ever owned."

"You are welcome, *señorita*. I hope you will wear them with pride."

They watched as Caroline made her way to the waiting rig. Before she could climb aboard, Thad caught her by the shoulder.

"Why are you doing this?"

Because I love you, she thought. Because I won't have anyone else hurt because of me. How many have had to die? My mother, Jonathan Corning. Dead because they cared about me.

If she stayed with Thad, she would only bring the trouble to his doorstep. Until now he'd been very adept at keeping the world away. She couldn't bear it if she brought pain and suffering to another person she loved.

The thought of what she was giving up made the night of love they'd shared seem all the sweeter. And all the more poignant, because it was lost to her forever.

But she said none of this. Instead, all she whispered was "Goodbye, Thad."

His grip on her shoulder tightened until his fingers were digging into her flesh. He lowered his voice. "I won't let you go. I can't."

"The decision isn't yours to make."

"This will decide," he said, withdrawing the pistol from his holster. "I'll make them listen to you. They'll have to believe the truth."

"Haven't you learned anything? Even your gun is useless against words." She pushed away from his arms. Though tears threatened, she kept herself under tight control. She would not cry here in front of all these watchful eyes. "They've already heard Silas Tate's version of the truth. That's all they want to hear."

She climbed up beside the sheriff and forced herself to stare straight ahead.

He flicked the reins and the rig jolted forward. As they crested a hill, Caroline turned to drink in the curve of hills, the sturdy outbuildings, the graceful house.

One figure stood alone in the swirling dust.

She felt a shaft of pain around her heart and choked back the cry that sprang to her lips. She watched until they dipped below a ridge and the figure in the distance slipped out of sight.

She closed her eyes against the pain. And only opened them when the rig stopped in front of the small cabin that, for the past few months, had been her home and the source of all her dreams.

Chapter Twenty-One

"There isn't much time to pack, Miss Adams." Sheriff Horn's voice conveyed his sorrow at his unpleasant task. "The stage driver will want to get started before noon."

"It won't take me long, Sheriff."

Not long at all, she thought sadly as she opened the door to the small cabin and stepped inside.

After the heat and dust of the trail, the interior of the cabin seemed cool, serene. Caroline made a slow turn around the room, touching a hand to the crisp white curtains that hung at the windows, stooping to run her fingers over the colorful rag rug in front of the fireplace.

Cora and Belva. The first friends, along with Jessie and Morning Light, to bring her gifts and welcome her to Hope. They had been shocked by her admissions, as she'd known they would be. She didn't blame them.

She removed the curtains and folded them for Cora, then rolled the rug for Belva. Perhaps the women would bring them again when a new teacher arrived. The thought of another teacher taking her place brought a fresh bout of sadness. She ran her fingertips along the smooth wood of the rocker, imagining Thad's hands as they'd shaped and fashioned the chair. The thought of him brought a sharp pain.

Crossing the room, she carefully wrapped her mother's china in the embroidered towels and placed them in her trunk. On top of these she placed her blanket and pillow. Like the dishes, they had once belonged to her grandmother.

She slipped out of Rosita's colorful skirt and blouse and folded them carefully, placing them atop the other items in the trunk. Though she would probably never wear them, it would bring her pleasure to be able to look at them occasionally, to remember a time of magic in a life that had had too few happy memories. But for now, the sight of them made her heart ache.

She slipped on the drab brown gown. Twisting her long hair, she pinned it into a neat knot and secured her hat with pins. A glance in the looking glass had her heart plummeting. For a few brief shining hours she had felt loved and cherished. She'd believed she was beautiful. Now...now she must become again that other person she had tried so hard to be. The one she no longer knew or understood. The liar. The cheat who had come to town pretending to be a fine lady. A lady. She turned away in self-disgust.

Taking a deep breath, she opened the door that led to the classroom.

She stopped to touch each desk, mentally speaking the name of the child who had sat there. She knew them all. Jack, Lisbeth, Frank. Runs With The Wind, Danny and little Kate. Emma and Ethan Waverly. Her heart contracted. She loved them all.

At the front of the classroom she ran a hand lovingly along the top of the table that had served as her desk. A teacher's desk. It was all she'd ever wanted. To teach. To feed hungry minds all the knowledge that she had once craved so desperately in her own starved and lonely childhood.

She swallowed back the tears that threatened to choke her and filled her arms with her precious store of books. Then she resolutely strode from the room and closed the door.

When her trunk was shut and the straps secured, she took a last loving look around. Tears clouded her vision. She'd had such hopes, such dreams. And for a little while she had found heaven. She squared her shoulders and took a deep breath. Now it was time to face the consequences of her actions.

Wrapping her shawl modestly around her shoulders, she opened the door and called to the sheriff, "I'm ready."

He strode inside and lifted her trunk. It was surprisingly light.

"The curtains, rug and chair should be returned," she said. "And I would like you to give away the food in the root cellar to those most in need."

The sheriff nodded as he strapped her trunk to the back of the rig. When he was finished he saw Caroline standing by the shed, kneeling among the chickens, which gathered around her like pets.

She looked up when he approached. "Runs With The Wind gave them to me. You'll see that he gets them back, won't you?"

"Yes, ma'am."

"Thank you."

She scattered grain inside the shed and watched as the chickens scrambled after it. Carefully closing the door against predators, she secured it and turned away.

The sheriff could see the tears that glittered on her lashes. He glanced aside, to give her a chance to compose herself.

"We'd better be leaving, ma'am."

"Yes." She gave a last look around, then climbed up to the seat beside him.

As they drove away, she turned for a final glimpse. To casual observers, she thought, it probably looked like a little shack in the woods, badly in need of repair. But they didn't know. She twisted her hands in her lap and blinked back tears. They didn't know that this had once been a place of great promise. A place where children's futures were forged in the pages of books. A place where one woman had found her whole reason for being.

Thad prowled the empty rooms of his house. He'd sent everyone home. Jessie and Cole, Dan and Morning Light, Manuel and Rosita. He preferred his own company. He needed no chorus of voices, no sympathetic looks.

What he needed was action. What he wanted was to ride into town and challenge Silas Tate to a gunfight. He had no doubt what the outcome would be. There wasn't a man in Texas who could outdraw him.

But even though killing Tate would satisfy his bloodlust, it wouldn't be a solution to Caroline's problems. She would still be guilty in the eyes of the townspeople.

He slammed a fist against the wall. It went against everything he'd ever believed in to stand by and do nothing while the woman he loved was being railroaded.

The sight of the mare loping around her corral caught his attention. Leaning a hip against the windowsill, he paused to watch. The animal's pure bloodlines were obvious to the trained eye. He'd bred her to his finest stallion, a mustang that, until now, had roamed these hills freely since birth.

From another corral the stallion whinnied and the mare stopped and lifted her head. The fire in her eyes was unmistakable. Except for the bars that confined her, she would race to the stallion's side, and despite all the generations of fine breeding, she would gladly follow him to the distant hills, where they would never see a human again.

That was what he wished for Caroline. He wanted to carry her off to his ranch and keep her safe from all the cruel words, the cutting accusations. It didn't matter to him what the others thought. All that mattered was that she be here with him, safe from the Silas Tates of the world.

But, he realized, it would matter to Caroline. Despite what he might want, she had a need for other people and an unquenchable love for children. No matter how much he loved and protected her, it would never be enough. Like the mare, who would never survive life in the wilderness, Caroline would never survive the loneliness and isolation if she had to endure the rumors of her guilt.

He turned away from the window, deep in thought. If he couldn't fight Silas Tate with a gun, he would have to find a way to fight with Tate's own choice of weapon.

"You can wait in my office until the stage arrives, ma'am."

"Thank you, Sheriff."

Caroline felt the stares from the people as their rig rolled through the town. When they pulled up in front of the sheriff's office, she waited until he unlashed her trunk, then followed him inside the jail.

He dropped her trunk on the floor and dusted off a wooden chair. She sat and folded her hands primly, keeping her gaze fixed on a spot on the floor.

At a sharp rap on the door, the sheriff scraped back his chair and crossed the room. Caroline heard the murmur of men's voices before the sheriff called, "Make yourself comfortable, Miss Adams. I'll be gone for a while, but I'll be back before the stage leaves."

Caroline nodded. A moment later she heard the door slam and saw the sheriff walking toward the church.

Caroline looked up as the door opened. Thad strode into the sheriff's office and stood facing her, a look of grim determination on his face.

"Don't try to talk me out of this again, Thad." Caroline turned away and began to pace in anticipation of whatever was to come.

"I won't."

She turned to study him. He seemed so still, so watchful. Squaring his shoulders, he crossed to the sheriff's desk and began to unbuckle his gun belt.

"What are you doing?"

He tossed the belt and pistol down. "Turning in my gun."

"But why?"

"You were right, Caroline. Being quick on the draw isn't the answer anymore. Tate taught me that. Without firing a single shot, he's managed to ruin both our lives."

"I'm so sorry, Thad." Without thinking, Caroline touched a hand to his sleeve. But when she looked up and saw the intense expression in his eyes, she took a step back. "I never wanted you to be hurt. But when I saw all those people invading your land, I realized how selfish I'd been. I hope someday you'll find it in your heart to forgive me."

They both looked up sharply as the door that separated the cells from the sheriff's office burst open and they found themselves face-to-face with Silas Tate. In his hand was a gun.

"Isn't this tender?" His tone was heavy with sarcasm. "Amanda's dirty little brat, Caroline, who now calls herself the very proper Miss Adams. And the hero of Hope, Texas." His gaze slid to the gun lying atop the sheriff's desk. "Unarmed? How noble. Noble and foolish." He laughed as he aimed the gun at Thad. "Think you can reach it in time?"

Thad stood perfectly still. "I wouldn't even try."

"Too bad." Silas gave a satisfied smile as he crossed the room and jammed Thad's pistol into the waistband of his pants. "I'm going to enjoy killing you, Texan."

Caroline felt terror growing in the pit of her stomach. "How did you get in?"

"I removed the grate in the last cell. I had Fox working on it since the first day he was brought in. That's how I managed to break him out of jail without the deputy seeing me. Poor Fox," he added with a laugh, "he thought he was heading toward freedom, but he only made it as far as the grave."

Caroline swallowed the fear that was filling her throat. "The sheriff will be back any minute."

Tate gave a harsh laugh. "The sheriff isn't coming back until the stage arrives."

"How do you know that?"

"I watched him leave and followed him. He's in a town meeting in the church, arranged by the preacher. Practically everyone in town is there. They're probably choosing your successor."

His words caused her unexpected pain. She had given up without a fight and had lost everything. Not only had her lies been uncovered and her job lost, but now even Thad was being forced to pay for her mistakes. And from the hatred that throbbed between these two men, she had no doubt he would pay with his life.

"Come here," Silas ordered.

Caroline felt her heart thundering in her ears as she inched away until she felt the rough boards of the wall against her back.

Tate's hand snaked out, catching her by the wrist. "Where do you think you're going?"

She struggled to free herself but he dragged her closer until she could feel the sting of his breath against her cheek.

"Let her go, Tate."

Silas swung around and brought his pistol to the side of Thad's head, knocking him to the floor. When Thad started to get up, Silas kicked him, sending him sprawling. As Thad came to his knees and shook his head, Silas pressed the gun to Caroline's temple.

"You move, Texan," he warned, "and I'll have to kill your woman."

He gave a satisfied smile as Thad remained on the floor, his eyes hot with fury.

"If you shoot either of us," Caroline cried, "the gunshots will bring the whole town running."

Tate threw back his head and roared. "And who do you think they'll believe? A concerned citizen or a hardened gunman?"

"You forgot about me. I'll tell them the truth," she said.

"You do that, woman. And we'll see who they believe when I tell them you just offered to pleasure me in return for enough money to take you back to Kansas City."

"You filthy animal." She swung her hand in an arc, but he easily caught it and twisted it behind her.

"Now," he rasped against her ear, "you listen, my high-and-mighty lady. Before I'm finished with you, you'll beg me to let you work in one of my shacks."

"Never. I know what it did to my mother before you killed her."

"Do you? Well, did you know that she begged me to spare her miserable life? She even offered to work for nothing if I'd let her live."

At his words, Caroline felt tears spring to her eyes. "You're worse than an animal. I wish I'd killed you with that knife instead of only wounding you."

"You should have," he sneered. "Because you'll never have another chance. I vowed I'd make you pay for what you did to my face if it took me to the ends of the earth." He touched a hand to the jagged scar and his features twisted into a mask of pure malice. "And," he added, "you'll keep on paying until I decide to end your suffering. Like I ended your dear mother's."

"And Jonathan Corning?" Caroline cried. "Did you kill him, too?"

Silas Tate laughed. "The old man swore he didn't know where you were headed. But I knew how to make him talk. I put a knife to his wife's throat and started cutting. He told me everything before I killed them both and burned down their house."

Caroline was blinded momentarily by the tears that spilled from her eyes. How could any man's cruelty against another go unpunished?

She pulled back, and his grasp on her wrist tightened.

"You can force me," she whispered. "But you can't stand over me every minute of the day and make me keep on doing your bidding. No matter what you do to me, short of killing me, I'll escape. And when I do, you'll pay for what you've done."

He laughed again, and the sound sent a chill along her spine. "There's a way to make anyone do anything. Like your cool, elegant mother. And the very cultured Jonathan Corning. They ended up doing what I told them. And look at your hero. Doesn't he look good on his knees?" He twisted her arm painfully. "And you will, too. You'll do exactly as you're told. And you'll start now. The Texan can watch." He pointed the gun at Caroline's temple and said to Thad, "Get up."

Thad got slowly to his feet.

"Walk," Silas ordered. From the sheriff's desk he picked up a ring of keys.

Thad walked to a cell and Silas slammed the door and turned the key. Then he dragged Caroline into the next cell and tossed her down on a narrow cot.

His gaze raked her. "When I saw you that day, a dirty little street urchin with big eyes and long black hair and a body that was just beginning to bloom, I knew I had to have you." He touched a finger to the jagged scar along his cheek. "And when you left your mark on me, I knew that I'd make you pay and pay." He gave a short laugh. "You'll never know how many nights I dreamed of ways to make you pay. I'm going to enjoy every minute of this." He turned to where Thad stood, seething with impotent rage. "I know you'll enjoy every minute of this, too, cowboy."

Tate's hands went to the buttons of his shirt, and then suddenly he froze. Behind him the sheriff's voice said calmly, "Better start with the gun belt, Mr. Tate."

The moment the key twisted in the lock of Thad's cell, freeing him, he pushed his way through the crowd. Silas spun around to find the sheriff and half the town facing him. But it was Thad's fist that bloodied his face and sent him sprawling. Caroline scrambled to her feet and rushed past Silas, falling into Thad's arms with a sob.

"But you were at a town meeting." Silas mopped at the blood with his sleeve and leaned his head back weakly. "I followed you."

"That's what we wanted you to think." Sheriff Horn turned toward Thad, who was watching the color begin to return to Caroline's face. "It was The Texan's idea. He said a bully always has to do a little bragging, if he's given the chance." Sheriff Horn shrugged. "The town has long owed Thad Conway a big favor. It was about time we paid our debt to him." He turned back to Caroline. "So we decided to give him one last chance to prove your innocence. Sorry, Miss Adams. There was no way to warn you."

The sheriff turned to Thad and saw the blood that trickled from the corner of his mouth. "I'm sorry you had to take such a beating."

"I expected it," Thad said dryly. "Although you could have broken in a few minutes earlier."

"We wanted to be sure he'd confessed to everything before we showed our hand."

Removing Silas Tate's gun belt, the sheriff turned the key in the lock. "Thanks for letting me know about that jailbreak. We still hadn't figured out how it was done." He turned to his deputy. "See that the bars in that other cell are secured. Mr. Tate will be our guest until the federal judge arrives for trial."

The sheriff turned to Thad. "I'm real proud of you, Texan. I know it took a lot of courage to face a man like Tate without a gun."

Thad gave a crooked smile and winced at the pain. "It was Caroline who convinced me that it's sometimes more courageous to throw away a gun and face an attacker with your wits."

"In this case it paid off," the sheriff said with admiration.

They all looked up as the stagecoach arrived with a clatter of harness and hooves and drew to a stop in front of the jail. With a sigh the sheriff hurried outside. Caroline could hear his voice raised and a muffled response as if from many voices.

When Sheriff Horn returned to his office he called, "Time to go outside, Miss Adams." His voice was unusually cheerful, and she glanced from him to Thad and then back again.

"What are you up to?"

Thad shrugged. "I guess the only way to find out is to see for ourselves." With his hand beneath her elbow, he escorted her to the door.

She stared around in surprise. A cluster of wagons and people clogged the dusty road. The town was nearly as crowded as it had been for the town social.

The first person Caroline saw was Ben Meadows, being helped into his wheeled chair by his father. At the boy's request, Ab Meadows rolled his son closer.

"Ma said you're leaving," Ben called.

Caroline stopped beside him and knelt down until their eyes were level. "Yes. I have to go away."

"But why, Miss Adams? Don't you like being in Hope anymore?"

"Oh, Ben." She put a hand over his. "I love it here. This is the best town in the world. I guess I'd rather live here in Hope than anywhere I can think of." Her tone lowered. "It's the first real home I've ever had."

"Then why are you leaving us?" Young Jack walked up to join his friend. His troubled eyes, so like Thad's, caused her heart to leap.

Caroline looked up and met his gaze without flinching. "Because I lied, Jack. And the people of this town deserve something better than that."

"What was the lie, Miss Adams?" The high voice belonged to Emma Waverly.

Caroline turned toward her and saw that her arm was around her younger brother, Ethan.

"I never went to a fancy school, Emma. I couldn't even read or write until I was older than you."

"But that's nothing to be ashamed of," Ethan said hotly. "My pa never did learn to read or write. And Ma said he was a man to be proud of."

"Your mother is right, Ethan. The shame, for me, is that I lied. And now I have to make amends."

"Can't you mend here in town with us?" Lisbeth asked tearfully.

"Amends, Lisbeth," Caroline corrected gently. "It means to put right. When people do wrong, it isn't enough to admit their mistake. They also have to do something right to make up for the wrong."

"Then why are you leaving?" Runs With The Wind asked with all the logic of his people. "How can you put something right when you are no longer here with us?"

"You deserve a better teacher," she said simply.

"We've never had a teacher as fine as you," Ben said. "You're the first one who ever bothered to ride all the way out to our ranch and help me read."

"And you're the first one who ever took the time to explain why book learning would help me be a better rancher," Jack said.

"You don't know anything about my background," Caroline protested.

"You once told us," Runs With The Wind said somberly, "that you were not interested in our backgrounds. You said you were far more concerned with what we made of our lives." He shot her a grave look. "Is that not the same for you?"

Caroline could find no words.

"And you taught me that grown-ups can be afraid, too," Emma cried, "and get tired sometimes, and even make mistakes. And ever since then, Ma and I are closer than we've ever been."

"That's right," came a voice behind Caroline. "And you taught me that mothers sometimes forget what it's like to be young, and laugh, and have fun."

Caroline turned to find Sara Waverly standing beside Reverend Symes.

"Please forgive me, Caroline," Sara said softly. "I was so quick to condemn. The sheriff has told us that everything that evil man said about you was a lie."

"Not everything," Caroline admitted. "Much of what he said was the truth."

Sara waved her words aside and lifted her voice so everyone could hear. "I agree with the children. Caroline Adams is the best teacher our town has ever had. And I, for one, would like her to reconsider and stay on."

"I agree." Belva Spears took up a position beside the sheriff. "The town would miss you, Caroline, even though we would understand if you felt you could no longer stay here with us."

"Can you ever forgive us for being so quick to condemn you, Miss Adams?" Reverend Symes asked.

"There's nothing to forgive." Caroline glanced around, seeing for the first time how many of the townspeople had gathered. "I only hope you can forgive me for the lies."

Reverend Symes dropped his arms around Emma's and Ethan's shoulders and drew them close, the way a father might. "I believe my sermon for next Sunday will be 'Let him who is without sin cast the first stone.'"

Caroline glanced around until she located Thad, standing alone, as always. Catching her gaze, he gave her a mysterious look and motioned for her to follow him to the far side of the jail.

"Well, Teacher," he said when they were alone. "What do you say? Think we're enough of a challenge for you?"

"We?"

"The town and me."

It was the first time she'd ever heard Thad Conway link his own name with that of the others. She gave him a timid smile. "More than enough."

"There's just one problem."

"What's that?"

"You're going to have to get married right away."

"Married?"

"Can't have the schoolmarm living in sin, can we?"

She felt her cheeks growing pink and said quickly, "No. Of course not."

"Then it looks like you'll have to marry a man with a bad reputation."

"Is this a proposal?"

He nodded. "Better grab it quick."

Her smile grew. "I guess a bad reputation's not so terrible. Especially since mine isn't very good, either."

"I suppose folks will think we're well matched."

"You'll have to put aside your guns."

"I guess it can be arranged. And you'll have to stop swearing when you lose that temper."

"I don't swear."

"You did say no more lies, didn't you?"

"All right." She blushed again. "I'll give up swearing."

"That could be a problem," he said with a frown.

"Why?"

"We won't have any vices left."

"None?"

He grinned. "Well, maybe one or two. Come here, Teacher."

They both looked up as Lisbeth, who had been spying, clapped her hands in delight. "I knew it. I knew you were sweet on Miss Adams."

"Little Bit," Thad said. "I have something here for you." Reaching into his pocket, he pulled out a coin. "I'll give you a dollar to go join the rest of the crowd."

"A whole dollar? Thanks, Uncle Thad." The little girl skipped away to announce in a voice that could be heard by everyone in the crowd, "Looks like you're going to have a pretty exciting service Sunday, Reverend. I just heard my Uncle Thad ask Miss Adams to marry him. And she said yes. And Uncle Thad just gave me a whole dollar to leave him alone so he can kiss her."

The whole town roared its approval.

Sheriff Horn bent his head and whispered something to Belva, who nodded her head before looking away. Then the sheriff, his neck growing beet red, cleared his throat.

"As long as you're preparing a wedding service, Belva and I thought, maybe... we could make that a double wedding, Reverend."

The crowd raised their voices in another cheer. But moments later the minister tucked Sara Waverly's hand in the crook of his arm and said, "Do you think there's room for three weddings?"

Lisbeth linked arms with Emma and little Kate, and the three girls danced around and around, planning the flowers they would toss as they walked up the aisle ahead of the happy couples.

Behind the jail, Thad heard the cheers from the crowd and drew Caroline close. Pressing his lips to her temple, he murmured, "Looks like Lisbeth has just given away our secret."

As she brought her arms around his waist, he murmured, "I'm not a tender man, Caroline. And the truth is, I'm still not certain I can give up my guns so easily.

When I saw Tate's hands at your throat, it took steel bars to keep me from going in and killing him.''

"But look what you accomplished. I think what you did was the bravest thing I've ever seen."

He drew her even closer until she could feel the thundering of his heart inside her own chest.

"I love you, Caroline," he whispered against her hair. "More than my own life."

She touched a hand to his cheek and felt a thrill at the look in his eyes. A look so tender, so loving, it brought a blur of tears to her own eyes.

"And I love you, my wild Texan. More than I ever dreamed possible."

"Then come back to the ranch with me."

"Now? What about my trunk, and the children, and the townspeople?"

He pulled himself into the saddle and caught her up in his arms. As they raced away from town he said, "This is more excitement than the town of Hope has had in years. Hell, they'll be so busy talking, they won't even miss us for hours."

He glanced at the fading sunlight. "And if we're lucky, Manuel and Rosita will sleep late and we'll have the place to ourselves until noon."

He held her tightly against him and for some strange reason found himself thinking about fences. Maybe he'd build a few, just to keep out predators. And maybe he'd start enlarging the house for the kids they'd be having.

Caroline wrapped her arms around his neck and pressed her lips to his throat.

Oh, Mama, she thought. If only you could have known a love like this.

She felt her heart swell with happiness. She'd had but one dream—to be a teacher. It had never occurred to her that she might be the one who would be taught. Taught all about love by a gunfighter in the dusty town of Hope, Texas. A love that would fill her heart and soul to overflowing. A love that would last an eternity and beyond.

Epilogue

Thad's new piece of furniture, a dining room table, was large enough to accommodate all who had come to supper. On one side sat Jessie and Cole and their offspring, Jack, Lisbeth and Frank. On the other side were Dan and Morning Light, along with Runs With The Wind, Danny and Kate. At one end sat Rosita and Manuel, who took turns cuddling a chubby infant with dark hair and eyes and a smile that would put angels to shame. Thad and Caroline sat side by side at the head of the table.

"When is the christening of little Esteban?" Jessie asked.

"Next month. Just before the town social. My family is coming in from Mexico for the event." Rosita glanced shyly at Caroline. "We would like you and Señor Conway to be the godparents."

Caroline exchanged a long, loving look with Thad before saying, "We'd be honored."

Young Jack, oblivious to the conversation going on around him, polished off a second helping of peach cobbler. "That was just about the best meal I've ever eaten, Aunt Caroline. I may bid on your basket again at this year's town social."

"Find your own girl," Thad said good-naturedly while the others shared a laugh.

Caroline gave Thad's nephew a fond smile that brought a flush to his cheeks. "There's another pitcher of lemonade in the kitchen if you think you could manage, Jack."

The boy, who had grown taller than Caroline, leaped up and returned in seconds with the pitcher.

"How's the foal?" Dan asked his brother.

Thad beamed. "Now that supper's over, why don't we go take a look."

The entire party trooped out to the corral. Lisbeth and Kate sat in the grass taking turns making little Esteban smile while the others, leaning on the rail, watched as the mare and her new foal took the first tentative laps around the circle.

"He's magnificent," Jessie breathed.

Thad watched as the tiny hooves settled into a smooth gait. "I knew this mare would produce the finest horseflesh in Texas."

"It's in the blood," his brother said. "You can always tell good bloodlines."

"And no one is a better judge of that than Señor Conway," Manuel said with respect.

Thad glanced at his wife, then back to the foal, and said with a trace of awe, "Looks like I made a good choice all around." His arm encircled Caroline's waist, drawing her firmly against him. Lowering his voice so the others wouldn't hear, he whispered, "When do you think we should tell them?" He nuzzled her lips. "I want to shout it to the hills."

"And you used to keep everything to yourself." Caroline laughed, a low, intimate sound that would always thrill him. "We'll tell the family in a few weeks, at Sunday supper."

"Tell us what?" Lisbeth looked up from where she was seated, still fondling the baby.

Thad gave a mock moan. "Little Bit, do you have to listen to everything I say to my wife?"

"If you didn't want me to hear," she said logically, "you shouldn't whisper so loud."

"What did you want to tell us?" Jessie chimed in, as eager as her daughter.

"I think it has to do with bloodlines," Dan said with a smile.

"How did you guess?" Caroline turned to Thad's brother and caught the laughter in his eyes.

"I'm a doctor. I'm supposed to know about such things."

"What things?" Lisbeth demanded.

"Oh!" Morning Light caught Caroline's hand and stared into her eyes. "Of course. I should have seen it."

"Seen what?" The children gathered around, hoping for a glimpse of whatever the adults were seeing.

"Oh, Caroline." Jessie hugged her new sister-in-law, then wiped a tear from her eye.

"Mama's crying." Lisbeth was outraged. "Tell me what's wrong, Uncle Thad."

"Nothing's wrong, Little Bit." Thad picked up his niece and swung her around. Setting her back on her feet, he dropped an arm around Caroline's shoulders and said, "We're going to have a baby."

"Is that all?" Jack turned away, amazed at the transformation in his favorite uncle since his wedding. First
Uncle Thad had turned down the sheriff's invitation to
accept his badge and take over the job of sheriff, saying
he'd hung up his guns for good. Then he'd refused an
offer from Don Esteban to travel to Mexico to see his
latest prize mare. And now he was hugging his new wife
and getting all soft and silly about a baby. Next thing he
knew, his uncle would probably become just like his pa,
spending his days on boring ranch chores and his nights
behind closed doors, whispering secrets and chuckling
low and deep in his throat.

"You two look like you're just busting at the seams
with happiness. It should have been a dead giveaway,"
Jessie said with a laugh.

While the men slapped Thad on the back and offered
their congratulations, the women hugged Caroline. As
she accepted the congratulations of the others, she felt
Thad's gaze on her and experienced the sudden rush of
heat. For some unexplained reason, her vision became
clouded.

He caught her by the shoulders. "Tears, Teacher?"

She shook her head and wrapped her arms around her
husband's waist, pressing her face to his chest. "I seem
to cry so easily these days. But they're happy tears."

He gathered her close and she listened to the steady
beating of his heart. Her own heart was overflowing with
love. She was so blessed.

She had come to Texas in search of a dream. But she
had found something far better. Love. Real and lasting
love. And family. She studied these wonderful people
who had become her family. The lonely little girl she had

once been was now forgotten. She was surrounded by love and laughter and people who filled her days, her life.

"Bloodlines," Thad murmured against her temple, and she felt her blood heat at the promise of what was to come. "I always could pick the best."

* * * * *

Author's Note

In my research, I came upon an advertisement for a teacher from the late 1880s. It read: Female to teach. Must be morally upright, churchgoing, unmarried.

This fueled my imagination and became the basis for my heroine, Caroline Adams.

But there was something else playing on the edges of my mind, and I wasn't aware of it until the book was nearly completed. And then I remembered. My mother told me about my grandmother, Clara Kennedy Ryan, who, as a daring young teacher in the 1890s, went dancing in public with the man who would later become my grandfather. Her elderly pastor refused her absolution in confession, saying that a teacher had to adhere to a much stricter code of morals. It was some time before a more understanding priest agreed to allow her to return to the Sacraments of her faith.

Times change; human nature doesn't.

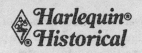

Harlequin® Historical

T E X A S

TEXAS HEART—A young woman is forced to journey west in search of her missing father.

TEXAS HEALER—A doctor returns home to rediscover a ghost from his past, the daughter of a Comanche chief.

And now, TEXAS HERO—A gunfighter teaches the local schoolteacher that not every fight can be won with a gun.
(HH #180, available in July.)

Follow the lives of Jessie Conway and her brothers in this series from popular Harlequin Historical author Ruth Langan.

Harlequin is proud to present our
best authors and their best books.
Always the best for your reading
pleasure!

Throughout 1993, Harlequin will bring you
exciting books by some of the top names in
contemporary romance!

In July
look for
The Ties That Bind by

Shannon wanted him seven days a week....

Dark, compelling, mysterious Garth Sheridan was no
mere boy next door—even if he did rent the cottage
beside Shannon Raine's.

She was intrigued by the hard-nosed exec, but for
Shannon it was all or nothing. Either break the
undeniable bonds between them ... or tear down the
barriers surrounding Garth and discover the truth.

Don't miss THE TIES THAT BIND ...
wherever Harlequin books are sold.

BOB3

Harlequin® Historical

BELLE HAVEN

A colony in New England. A farming village divided by war.
A retreat for New York's elite.

Four books. Four generations. Four indomitable females....

You've met Belle Haven founder Amelia Daniels in THE TAMING OF
AMELIA, Harlequin Historical #159 (February 1993).

Now meet the revolutionary Deanna Marlowe in THE SEDUCTION
OF DEANNA, Harlequin Historical #183 (August 1993).

In early 1994, watch Julia Nash turn New York society upside down
in THE TEMPTING OF JULIA.

And in late 1994, Belle Haven comes of age in a contemporary story
for Silhouette Intimate Moments.

Available wherever Harlequin books are sold.

COMING NEXT MONTH

#183   THE SEDUCTION OF DEANNA—Maura Seger
In the next book in the *Belle Haven* series, Deanna Marlowe is torn between family loyalty and her desire for independence when she discovers passion in the arms of Edward Nash.

#184   KNIGHT'S HONOR—Suzanne Barclay
Sir Alexander Sommerville was determined to restore his family's good name sullied by the treacherous Harcourt clan, yet Lady Jesselynn Harcourt was fast becoming an obstacle to his well-laid plans....

#185   SILENT HEART—Deborah Simmons
In a desperate attempt to survive her country's bloody revolution, Dominique Morineau had been forced to leave the past behind, until a silent stranger threatened to once more draw her into the fray.

#186   AURELIA—Andrea Parnell
Aurelia Kingsley knew Chane Bellamy was her last hope. Only he could help her find her grandfather's infamous treasure. And the handsome sea captain was determined to show her what other riches were within her reach.

AVAILABLE NOW:

#179   GARTERS AND SPURS
DeLoras Scott

#181   THE CYGNET
Marianne Willman

#180   TEXAS HERO
Ruth Langan

#182   SWEET SENSATIONS
Julie Tetel